Praise for *Drowning Lessons:*

"Water flows through these stories, giving Peter Selgin's characters moments of grace from their lives and also propelling them forward, as they try to swim through the problems that face them. *Drowning Lessons* is an extraordinary book; Peter Selgin's writing creates a current that will carry readers farther than they would ever have expected, and leave them on a new shore."
   —Hannah Tinti, author of *The Good Thief*

"A wine-dark blood rushes through the pages of *Drowning Lessons*. Tap a vein and drink deeply and taste the best and the worst kind of love. In these pages you will experience lust, spite, jealousy, fidelity, rose-flavored romance, and doe-eyed affection, sometimes all in the same story. Thank goodness for Peter Selgin, who shares with us the mysteries of the human heart in this electric, revealing collection."
   —Benjamin Percy, author of *Refresh, Refresh*

"Peter Selgin's stories are mordantly funny, at times desperately sad, but always full of hard-earned wisdom and subversive irony. His collection ranges across time and space in a way few other writers have. *Drowning Lessons* is a book that deserves serious attention from all lovers of American short fiction."
   —Jess Row, author of *The Train to Lo Wu*

"A stellar collection deserving recognition. Selgin possesses a mature, complex voice and is able to conceptualize, compose, and perfect stories of brilliant diversity and tone. High emotional intelligence, empathy, courage, and intellectual curiosity fuel this collection, giving it a rare narrative fire beyond the obvious and admirable excellence of craft."
   —Melissa Pritchard, author of *Late Bloomer*

"[Selgin's] ability to sling together desire and suffering in complex and moving ways is singular and memorable."
   —*Booklist*

Winner of the Flannery O'Connor Award for Short Fiction

ALSO BY PETER SELGIN

Drowning Lessons

By Cunning & Craft: Sound
Advice and Practical Wisdom for Fiction Writers

LIFE GOES TO THE MOVIES

life goes to the

6-17-09

movies *a novel* ⅋ PETER SELGIN

to Lea,

with gratitude and

best wishes

db
DZANC
BOOKS

DZANC
BOOKS

1334 Woodbourne Street
Westland, MI 48186
www.dzancbooks.org

Published 2009 by Dzanc Books

Book Design by Claudia Carlson

09 10 11 12 7 6 5 4 3 2 1
First Edition April 2009

ISBN - 13: 978-0-9793123-8-0

Printed in the United States of America

for Paulette

"God's will be done," said Sancho. "I'll believe all your worship says; but straighten yourself a bit in the saddle, for you seem to be leaning over on one side, which must be from the bruises you received in your fall."

This is a love story.
There's no other way to describe it.
I'm taking your advice, Brother Joseph:
I'm writing everything down.

part **ONE**

I

Blacken
the
Space
(Art Film)

"We didn't exactly believe your story,
Mrs. O'Schaughnessy,"
—Humphrey Bogart, *The Maltese Falcon*
THE PERTINENT MOVIE QUOTE WALL

We were blackening pages, all of us, covering them with charcoal, leaving no traces of white showing, turning them as black as Con Edison smoke, as abandoned subway station platforms and third rail rats. As black as the vacuum-packed blackness between stars.

According to Professor Crenshaw there was no such thing as the color white. The air that we breathed was black. What we in our barbaric ignorance thought of as white was in fact an invisible broth of gloomy matter, light turned inside-out, darkness illuminated.

"Do you see this piece of paper?" Crenshaw's P's popped, his crab-eyes bristled. *"This piece of paper is pure, it is pristine, it is virginal! I want you to desecrate it! Rape, plunder, and pillage it with your filthy black charcoal sticks!"*

The figure model, a skinny bored-looking redhead, posed on her carpeted wooden platform, oblivious of the dazzling white tampon string that, in defiance of Professor Crenshaw's theories, dangled from her rusty pubic bush. Professor Crenshaw, meanwhile, waving his blank newsprint sheet like a bullfight-

er's cape, leapt through clouds of charcoal dust, yelling:
"*Blacken the space! Blacken the space!*"

2

That's when I notice him, standing there by the window, smoking a cigarette, blowing smoke out through the cracked case-
ment. I've never seen him before, at least I don't remember
seeing him. He must be a mid-year transfer student, or maybe
he just hasn't been coming to Crenshaw's class. My eyes follow
his as they gaze out across the winter campus, over grimy buildings and grim brownstones, past the blue rusting dinosaur-like
cranes of the Navy Yard (still decked out in Bicentennial bun-
ting), over the frozen East River, at the island of Manhattan, a
gray battleship sunk to its gunwales.

So far I've blackened a dozen newsprint sheets, rubbing fingertips to bone. Talking is prohibited: no sound but the steady
scrape scrape scrape of charcoal on penny paper and the hum of
the electric heater squatting at the nude model's feet. Jimmy
Carter is President, Abe Beame is Mayor. Pay phones cost a
dime. Postage stamps need to be licked. A subway token is still
a brass coin with a Y-shaped hole in the center, and will set you
back fifty cents. New York City is broke, lawless, bohemian, dis-
solute and dangerous.

It's winter, 1977, but in Professor Crenshaw's Rudimentary
Figure Drawing Class it's *always* winter, a black winter of car-
bon snow. Ghost cauliflowers bloom in front of our faces as
we scratch away in scarves, sweaters, coats and jackets, mine a
frayed checkered black and red hunting jacket hot off the half-
price rack at Cheap Jack's Vintage Clothing store, like the one
Marlon Brando wears in *On the Waterfront*. Marlon's my hero,
the latest in a long line of TV and movie heroes stretching back
to second grade when, in emulation of my then-hero Soupy
Sales, on the playground, during recess, having gathered wit-

nesses, I smashed a shaving cream pie in my own face.

"Blacken the space!"

The smoking guy reminds me a bit of Brando, not the flabby-assed Marlon of *Last Tango* or *The Godfather*, but the young Marlon of *Streetcar* and *On the Waterfront*. He's got the same flattened brow and high, bulbous forehead, its skin stretched shiny by whatever lurks whale-like under the bone. His lips are thinner, though, more like Jimmy Cagney's, and he's got a Gary Cooper squint to his eyes. His skin is dark, darker than my Italian skin: swarthy, I guess you could call it. There's something altogether dark about him, what exactly I can't say, but it's darker than this sheet of paper I've just finished covering with charcoal. But of all his parts that forehead is most impressive, so big it seems to charge ahead of the rest of him into the world. The eyes may be Gary Cooper's; the wavy dark hair may be John Garfield. But the forehead...the forehead is absolutely Brando.

"Blacken the space! Blacken the space!"

Done smoking, he smashes his cigarette out against a cracked pane, walks back to his drawing horse and, with his left hand, picks up a charcoal stick. But instead of blackening pages, like we're supposed to, he draws what look to me from across the charcoal-dusty studio like a series of rectangles. Within the rectangular panels the same hand whips up a storm of crosshatchings from which human figures emerge.

Suddenly Professor Crenshaw looms over him. Maybe it's these useless old radiators pinging and hissing up a storm, but I can't hear a word as Crenshaw chews him out—as least I assume Crenshaw is chewing him out, though I can't say for sure, this being a scene *mit oud zound*. But I see Crenshaw's nostrils flaring and his chapped lips pulling back against his teeth and his purple tongue flailing and his crab eyes bristling as flecks of spittle land on that high swarthy forehead.

Having torn the sheet from the smoking student's pad, Crenshaw rips it to pieces, then tosses the bits into the air, where they fall like confetti or snow. The smoking student stands there, expressionless, a soldier being branded. He keeps standing there that way as Crenshaw moves on to terrorize the next student.

After a beat or two he picks up his charcoal stick and starts sketching again, his left arm swinging loose and free, slicing a dozen deft strokes across his pad. Done, he picks up the duffel bag stowed under his drawing horse. With it hoisted on his shoulder and leaving the sketchpad behind he walks out the door.

The rest of us put down our charcoal sticks, and, one by one, step over to see what he's drawn. Our eyes are met not by a picture, but by words:

**SCORSESE
RULES**

3

After class I found him in the snack bar. The snack bar's official name was the Pi Shop, as in the ratio of the circumference of a circle to its diameter, but everyone called it the Pie Shop, as in apple pie. The heat wasn't working down there either. My breath hung clouds in front of my face.

Other students huddled in tight cliques, talking Dada, Duchamp, DeKooning, pissing away their parents' stock portfolios, filling the frigid air with artistic bonhomie and acrid smoke from their tipless Gaelic cigarettes. Not the new guy. He sat alone at a far table, as far away from everyone else as possible. He wore no jacket, just a white shirt with the collar torn off, and a thin black vest, as if his solitude came with its own private heating supply. Between puffs of a Newport he scribbled away in a black hardbound notebook. He was like some foreign country you're afraid to visit because you don't speak the language. I bought two cups of hot chocolate, screwed up my courage and plopped myself down right in front of him.

"My name's Nigel," I said, sitting. "Nigel DePoli. We're in the same drawing class. Or we were, anyway."

I hold out my hand. He keeps on scribbling away in his notebook, ignoring me like I'm not even there. Still not looking up from his scribbling, he says, "Really? Gee, I could have sworn you were Terry Malloy." Flattening his already flat brow, squeezing his nostrils together, he does a perfect Marlon Brando. Chahlie, Chahlie, you was my bruddah, you shoulda looked aftuh me. My cheeks swell with warm fresh blood. Seeing me blush he smiles a sudden smile that eats up the whole bottom part of his face, his teeth glaringly bright compared to his skin and eyes, which are dark gray with bits of paler gray floating around like aluminum shards in them. One of his front teeth, I notice, is a shade darker than the others, a soldier out of step.

"Dwaine Fitzgibbon," he says, shaking my hand. His grip feels warm and friendly. "That's D for Death, W for War, A for Anarchy, I for Insane, N for Nightmare, and E for the End of the World. Pleased to meet you."

(Dwaine, also Dwain or Dwayne or Dewayne or Duane or Duwain or Duwayne or Dwane: an Anglicized form of the Gaelic "Dubhn" or "Dubhan," which can mean "swarthy" or "black" or "little and dark and mysterious.")

4

He wears one of those traditional Irish rings, two silver hands embracing a heart of gold. He asks my name again and I tell him. "Nigel? *DePoli?*" He makes a face like he smells something funny. "How did your parents ever come up with a combination like that?"

"It was my father's idea," I explain. "His invention, I guess you could say. My father"—I've trained myself never to say 'my Papa'—"is an inventor. He invents machines for measuring color, texture and thickness, for quality control purposes, you know, to make sure Batch # such-and-such of Whip 'n' Chill is the same color and consistency as Batch # so-and-so." Dwaine nods. "He's an Anglophile," I continue. "He loves all things English, from Chiver's coarse-cut orange marmalade to under-powered cars with terrible electrical systems. You'd never guess he was born in Italy," I say.

"You're right," he agrees. "I'd never guess."

I don't add that my father is sixty-five years old, or that he pedals a rusty Raleigh three-speed to the post office and back in black socks that come all the way up to his knees and a frayed deerstalker cap. Nor am I inclined to mention that the neighborhood kids all shout, "Hey, Sherlock!" or "Hey, Mr. Magoo!" whenever he passes them by. I'm even less disposed to confess to how much I can't stand my own name, how given a choice I would gladly trade it in for Bob or Joe or Tim or even Fred or Frank—any plain, All-American sounding name, only I don't have a choice. Well, I do, but I won't exercise it out of an irrational fear of hurting my dear old papa's feelings: irrational since dear old papa is so absentminded and egocentric he would probably never notice.

"What about your father?" I change the subject. "What does he do?"

Dwaine blows a smoke ring that swims jellyfish-like up to the ceiling where it obliterates itself. "My father," he says slowly with no inflection at all in his voice, "is a drunken black Irish son of a goddamn bitch." He smiles. "I'll take that hot chocolate now, if it's still up for grabs."

I hand him the hot chocolate. In exchange he offers me a cigarette. I tell him I don't smoke. He nods as if that's very reasonable of me, then smiles again as if being reasonable is, well, ridiculous.

5

He said he was a filmmaker. I was into movies myself. Not making them, but watching them, old black-and-white ones especially. *Best Year of Our Lives, Birdman of Alcatraz, A Night to Remember, The Train.* "I haven't declared my major yet," I volunteered. "Though I was thinking of going into advertising design and production, with maybe a minor in painting or illustration. So what are some of your favorites? Movies, that is?"

But he's not listening. He's too busy framing me with his thumbs. "You've got a good face," he says.

"I do?"

"A touch of DeNiro; a hint of Pacino. Ever acted before?"

"A little," I lie.

"Take off your jacket. Roll up your sleeve."

"What for?"

"I need to see your arm."

"What do you need to see my arm for?"

"Would you mind just rolling up your damn sleeve, please?"

I take off my jacket; I roll up my sleeve.

He looks at my arm.

"What are you doing first thing tomorrow?"

I shrug. "Not much."

"Congratulations, you got the part."

He scribbles something on a corner of his notebook page, tears it off and hands it to me. "Be there at six thirty a.m., sharp."

He shuts his notebook, stands and smiles down at me. I see that front tooth again, the one that doesn't match the others. Seeing me noticing it, he jiggles the odd tooth up and down in his mouth. It makes a thin metallic sound as it rattles against his other teeth. Then he picks up his duffel bag and goes.

▌▌
It's So Good
Don't Even
Try It Once
(Student Film)

▌grew up in two countries, the Europe inside my house in Barnum, Connecticut, and the United States of America outside. Inside were books in foreign languages crammed onto shelves, along with my inventor father's sloppy solid paintings of fountains and statues. Outside were baseball diamonds, woods and white picket fences. Inside was the dust of the Old World (not that my mother failed to keep a clean house; this was the dust of centuries that no amount of Lemon Pledge could annihilate); outside were five and dime stores, hamburger and root-beer stands, and the crumbling ruins of hat factories.

Inside, my parents spoke in clashing foreign tongues, my father's adopted Oxbridge colliding with my mother's salami-thick Milanese. Outside, the neighborhood kids spoke mainly with balls, fists, and spit. I could never get the football to spin like Lenny P., or spit through a gap in my teeth like Sean A., or blow giant pink Bazooka bubbles like Chucky S. I couldn't whistle through my fingers, or get the tilt right on my baseball cap. At being American I was hopelessly inept. That my mother sent me off to school with spaghetti and omelet sandwiches and creases in my jeans didn't help.

America was a foreign country. It scared me. Even the flag scared me. The stripes were snakes and whips; the stars had teeth. The flag wore a huge chip on its broad square shoulder and said, "I dare you." But I didn't dare. I was too meek, too diffident, too European to dare.

Since my father was an atheist we never went to church, so churches scared me, too. So did crosses. So did steeples. So did the words "Lord" and "Savior."

I had nothing to pray to.

2

The next day I got up at six o'clock. Since there was no space left in the dormitories for me, I rented a room in an apartment belonging to a retired church choir conductor. His name was Mortimer Creedle, but I thought of him as Captain Nemo, since he kept an antique church organ in his vestibule and played Mozart requiems to raise the dead.

The apartment had only one bathroom. Captain Nemo had the habit of taking hour-long showers every morning, as if not merely washing himself but trying to expunge from his flesh all of the sins of this fallen world. I kept a Medaglia Coffee can in my room that I used as my "thunder mug." That morning, while Captain Nemo showered, I pissed into it. Then I brushed my teeth over the kitchen sink, and hurried out the door.

3

Truthfully, I'd never acted in a movie before. I'd never done any acting, really, aside from non-speaking parts in a few high school musicals, a Shark in *West Side Story*, a pinstriped spearchucker in *Guys and Dolls*.

The only real acting I'd ever done had been in my head, in front of the bathroom medicine cabinet mirror, pretending to be my favorite movie and TV stars. They were my role models, my pagan surrogate gods. From them I hoped to learn how to be—or at least act like—a real American.

To the medicine cabinet mirror, that's what I'd pray to. I'd pray to make these overstuffed brown eyes of mine paler and squintier, to make my shit-colored curls fairer and straighter, to bleach the olive tinge from my skin and save me from being permanently typecast as the only child of eccentric Italian immigrants born and bred in a crumbling Connecticut former hat factory town. *Nigel DeWop, Nigel DeGuinea, Nigel DeDago* ...

4

It was still dark outside, and cold. Leftover Christmas lights strung on stoops shed cheerful colors that failed to soak up the darkness and gloom. I ran with my gloveless hands in the pockets of my checkered *On the Waterfront* jacket. An icy wind blew in solid gusts from the East River, sucking tears from the corners of my eyes. By the time I got to the address on the slip of paper my ears were frozen.

Dwaine lived over the Chopsticks Express, a Chinese takeout place, one of those lowdown joints with a pair of tables no one ever sits at. As I climbed the stairs the cooking smells grew stronger. I knocked on a door painted so thickly brown it looked like it had been dipped in fudge. The door opened and Dwaine stood there. He looked at his watch.

"You're seven minutes late," he said.

He had me change into my "costume," which consisted of my very own dishwater gray Fruit of the Loom briefs. The apartment was freezing. Goosebumps coated my arms and shoulders. I wondered what I'd gotten myself into. Dwaine took light meter readings off my chin, my ears, my goose-bumped body parts.

5

The movie was titled *It's So Good Don't Even Try it Once*. It was about a heroin addict. (Now I knew why he'd been looking at my veins). I knew nothing at all about drugs. I'd smoked pot three or four times, that's it. Dwaine showed me what to do, then he stood behind the camera and started filming. I'd never felt more nervous. Like a network of invisible wires self-consciousness attached itself to every one of my limbs; every way I tried to move, the wires pulled the other way. I shook all over, and not just from the cold.

"Relax," said Dwaine, handing me a mug of tea. "There's nothing to be nervous about. It's just you and me and this piece of shit Japanese camera." He pointed to the super-8 mounted on its spindly tripod. "Just be yourself. You're made for this part."

Still, at first I found it hard to relax. Being filmed for real felt less like standing in front of the medicine cabinet mirror than like sitting on a doctor's rubber-padded examination table. It took me a while, but I finally managed to calm down and even started to enjoy myself. By the time we got to the part where the character I played fired up his "works," cooking the confectioner's sugar we used as a substitute for the real thing in a bent old spoon over an alcohol lamp, I forgot that the camera was even there.

Between scenes and takes my eyes roamed Dwaine's apartment. There wasn't that much to see. It was the kind of room that poets commit suicide in. A few sticks of furniture, a desk covered with film cans and editing equipment, strips of film dangling from strings strung along the walls, a pile of notebooks stacked under a mayonnaise jar full of pens, a poster for *Taxi Driver* showing a Mohawked Robert DeNiro posing in front of his Checker cab, tacked to the bathroom door. Over the poster, dangling from a leather shoelace snaring a bent nail, was a machete with a long, curved, deeply tarnished blade.

"What's that?" I asked.

"A machete."

"Really? Where did you get it?"

"In Thailand."

"What were you doing in Thailand?"

"Fighting mosquitoes."

"With *that?*"

"It was a gift from some pirates." Dwaine handed me another mug of hot tea. Pirates, I thought, sipping, nodding, like that was a perfectly logical explanation.

One other object caught my eye: five-inches long, black, bullet-shaped, standing upright on the stack of notebooks next to the mayonnaise jar. "Pick it up," said Dwaine.

I did. It was made of rubber.

"I call it The Black Dildo from Hell," Dwaine explained. "It's a rubber bullet, used by police to stun people without killing them. That's the idea, anyway. It so happens that this one passed through a lady's brain. Enough beauty parlor chitchat, babe. Let's get back to work."

6

Dwaine worked from storyboards, black-and-white sketches like panels in a comic strip. Like Alfred Hitchcock he followed them slavishly. We shot through the morning and into the afternoon. I cut three of my classes. Making that movie seemed suddenly much more important than color wheels, the mechanics of typography, and principles of advertising design. Though I liked to draw and was good at it, I didn't have whatever it took to be a real artist. Something was missing. Passion: that was the missing ingredient, the emotion for lack of which I often felt like a ghost haunting myself. That may be why I preferred the old black-and-white movies. I loved the dramatic intensity evoked by the collision of those two non-colors, along with the endless shades of gray existing between them, how through rapidly shifting unequal intensities of light the stories unfolded. But my inner world wasn't black, white, or gray; it was simply colorless, like the bricks that built the hat factories of my hometown—bricks so dull they seemed more gray than red.

By the time I headed home from Dwaine's place dark had

fallen. The streets had an odd glossiness to them. The lights in apartment windows cast a warm, peculiar glow that swung down to kiss the surface of the pavement at my feet. For the first time since moving to New York, I felt as if those streets had something to do with me and I with them. The chilled air hummed with purpose, with passion.

7

Six hours later, after eating and taking a nap, I was back with Dwaine again, on the roof of one of the twin high-rise dormitory buildings, shooting the nightmare sequence to *It's So Good Don't Even Try It Once.* In the sequence I'm pursued by a machete-wielding, gas-masked Mister Softee vendor, who chases me over the edge of the roof and into the arms of an angel who arrives just in time to save my soul. Byron Huffnagel, a graduate film major, played my nemesis, the man in the Mister Softee uniform. Huff, as we called him, weighed something like three hundred pounds. When not in costume he wore three-piece pinstriped banker's suits and perspired heavily. Even in cold weather Huff perspired. He carried a silk handkerchief with which to mop his brow.

"Fitz tells me that you're from Waterbury, Connecticut?" he said between takes on the roof. "That's where they've got all the screw and brass wire factories? The place with the big brick Florentine clock tower, right? I pass through there all the time on the way to visit my uncle in Boston," said Huff.

"Actually," I corrected him, "I come from Barnum, next door."

"Oh, Barnum. Yeah, yeah, I know Barnum. Sure. That's where they got the white elephant, right?" He referred to a sculpted elephant perched over the town square on a tall granite column. Huff wiped his forehead. He had a thick black beard and wore thick Buddy Holly horn rims that accentuated his fat cheeks. His face was like one of those magnetized toys with metal shavings that you manipulate to achieve various distributions of facial hair. His breath smelled like the cages where they kept laboratory snakes and mice in my high school biology department storage room.

"So, what do you think?" He nodded toward Dwaine, who was setting the camera up for my next scene. "Think he's—" Huff twirled a fat finger by his ear.

"Why would I think that?"

"He was in 'Nam. You know that, don't you?"

"Was he?"

"Where do you suppose he got the machete?"

"He told me he got it from some pirates in Thailand."

Huff shook his head. "He was over there, man. Trust me. That look in his eyes, that thousand-yard stare? My cousin Sylvie, he had the same look when he came home. And I'd hate to tell what happened to him." Huff paused, expecting me to ask. When I didn't he told me anyway. "Jumped off a twelve story building. Only no angel caught him. Landed on a convertible MG with the top up. The top broke his fall. Now he's quadriplegic living in a V.A. hospital. Poor guy never did have much luck. Put all his money in Western Union stock. Western Union—can you believe that? Like who the hell sends telegrams anymore? My cousin suffers from BLS, Born Loser Syndrome."

"What's all this got to do with Dwaine?"

"Nothing. I'm just saying—he's a little, you know."

"What?"

Huff shrugged. "Nothing."

The third member of our crew, the one who played the angel who rescued me, was a theater arts major named Veronica Wiggins, but who went by Venus. And though her specialties were costumes and props, Venus acted, too. She made the perfect cloudy angel, since she was an albino. Her hair was the same pale color as her skin, which was the same color as her teeth, which were the same color as her pillowy lips, like all parts of her had been soaked in a vat of Clorox. The only parts of her that bore any trace of color were her fingertips, rosy from her chewing on them constantly, a nervous habit. To shield her pigmentless nearsighted eyes from the sun she wore prescription sunglasses. Behind her back other students called her Casper the Friendly Ghost, Snow White, and Fluorescent Face, but I personally found her very attractive.

"So," she said to me, "you're Dwaine's new leading man?" She had a faint southern drawl. A southern Albino angel.

"Why? Have there been others?"

"One or two."

"I thought Dwaine was a new student?"

She shook her head. "He's been here half a year at least."

"Really? I haven't seen him around."

"He's like an owl, he usually only comes out at night."

"What happened to the other leading men?"

"The usual," she answered with a shrug. "Thrown off of buildings, hacked to pieces, overdosed, lobotomized, riddled with bullets…" She curled a strand of white hair with a white finger. "On film, that is. In real life I guess Dwaine just sort of wore them out."

We were sitting on the steps of the dormitory, next to the spot on the pavement where a dummy stuffed into my character's clothes lay in a pool of dashed calves' brains and other organ meats donated by the local Gristedes, doused with fake blood. Venus threw me a smile. I couldn't get over how pretty she was. The only other albinos I had known were ugly: the Hoppenthaler Twins, Kevin and Keith. They went to my high school. No one liked them, mainly because they loved each other so much and didn't seem to care about anyone else, but also because they were so fantastically ugly, with their long drooping faces and noses like melting vanilla ice-cream cones and hair like corn silk. We called them the Double-Headed Vanilla Monster, though never to their faces, since they were as short-fused and strong as they were hideous. To equate them with Venus was absurd, yet I couldn't help doing so.

I asked, "How long have you known Dwaine?"

"Since the start of last term, when he asked me to be in one of his movies."

"Were you always interested in movies?"

"Not really. I used to want to be a ballerina."

"What happened?"

"I couldn't stand on my toes."

"Why not?"

"It hurt. I have delicate toes."

We watched Dwaine arrange the camera for the next scene.

"Where does Dwaine get the money for all this?"

"The film department supplies him the film."

"And the rest?"

"Beats me. You'd have to ask him that, though I doubt he'd tell you. In case you haven't noticed, he can be very secretive."

She smiled. I imagined her looking deep into my eyes, wanting me. With those dark glasses on her I could imagine whatever I liked.

8

When *It's So Good Don't Even Try It Once* had its premiere in Dwaine's filmmaking class, I saw myself transformed. That was me, Nigel DePoli, up there on that pull-down movie screen, me writhing as the dope needle drew my suffering fake blood, me being chased across a rooftop by a fat bearded guy in a white Mister Softee uniform with a machete, me plunging eighteen stories into the white arms of an albino angel. Only it *wasn't* me, not the usual me; as a matter of fact I hardly recognized myself. I looked bigger, taller, stronger, with broader shoulders and a thicker, sturdier neck. The guy up there on that screen looked less Italian, more American, as if the process of being filmed at thirty-six frames per second had flushed away some of that olive-oily immigrant blood. No, it wasn't me up there; it wasn't *Nigel DeDago, Nigel De-Wop, Nigel DeGuinea* of Barnum, Connecticut.

It was someone bigger, better.

As we stepped out of Dwaine's film class he threw his arm around me. "So, babe," he said, "still want to major in advertising? Don't answer too quickly. Think about it. After all, someday you just might sell somebody the perfect underarm deodorant, or the ideal laxative, or the ultimate brand of toilet paper. *Try New Improved Bottom's-Up brand toilet tissue: soft as air, sweet as honey. You can't wipe your butt with it, but so what?"*

He jiggled his weird tooth at me.

9

We kept making movies.

In *Pig Iron Junkie* I played a bodybuilder. I used my own set of rusty barbells, which kept company with the dust bunnies under the bed in my room in Captain Nemo's apartment. Whenever I did curls and Navy lifts with them the barbells made a noise like an old-fashioned printing press. The movie consisted entirely of close-ups of clanking barbells and sweating, bulging, straining muscles, recapitulated *ad infinitum* thanks to a clever arrangement of mirrors installed by Dwaine in his one-room apartment. Between sweaty close-ups (some of the sweat mine, the rest faked with glycerin drops) Dwaine spliced in subliminal fake newspaper headlines:

MAN WEEPS ON STREET CORNER
BUTTERFLY SEEN IN CENTRAL PARK

In *Dust Off* I played an exhausted Army medic who can't see what he's operating on because a punctured artery keeps squirting him in the eye.

In *Toothpaste* I played a guy who brushes his teeth to death.

While brushing he pulls out a loose tooth, then another, and so on, until he's spitting out handfuls of teeth and gobs of foaming bright fake blood.

In *Blood Tickets* a botched pawnshop holdup left me riddled with bullets and bleeding to death under a window stuffed with used cameras, Spanish guitars, and saxophones. (To my bullet-riddled Clyde Venus played Bonnie.)

We dubbed ourselves—or Dwaine dubbed us—the Proto Realist Filmmaking Society. Our mission: to make movies so damned realistic (meaning so damned grim and violent and horrible) that you couldn't tell them from real life. We went through gallons of fake blood, which in real life looks a lot more purple than red, and dozens of squibs: miniature explosive devices filled with fake blood, taped to the skin under my clothes and detonated off-camera to produce gorily realistic bullet holes. Dwaine said I bled beautifully.

I wondered why Dwaine's movies were all so violent, and guessed it had something to do with his wartime past, with Vietnam. Personally I had never known any real soldiers, had never known anyone who had been to war. My father avoided fighting in both of the World Wars that he'd lived through. The whole concept of war was as foreign to me as the dark side of the moon. I longed to ask Dwaine outright, "What was being in a war like? What did you do? What did you *experience?*"

One day I put it to him straight. I asked him, "What was it like?"

Dwaine said, "What was what like?"

"The war."

"Which one, babe? There are so many."

"Vietnam," I said.

Dwaine blew a smoke ring. He was an expert at blowing them. We were sitting against a wall in his apartment, the one with the mirrors on it. I watched the smoke ring waver up and dash itself into the ceiling light fixture. "What was it *like?*" he said. "What was it *like?* An exploding dog, that's what it was like. Vietnam was like an exploding dog."

And that's all he would say.

10

As clam-mouthed as he was about Vietnam, Dwaine could be voluble on the subject of movies. "What is the dream of every red-blooded American boy?" he asked us all one day coming home from a day of filming.

"To be President of the United States," Venus guessed.

"Wrong. Try again."

"To pitch for the Yankees," Huff tried.

Dwaine shook his head. "One more guess."

"To cure cancer," I said.

Dwaine made a buzzer sound. "Wrong again. The dream of every red-blooded American boy is to make movies."

We were crossing City Island Bridge. We'd just wrapped up *Buster Gets Axed*, my fifth Dwaine movie, about a short order cook suffering from post-traumatic stress disorder who suffers a flashback when a customer orders a runny egg on his breakfast sandwich.

"Forget Methodist, forget Baptist, forget Lutheran, Episcopal and Congregational and even Seventh-Day Adventist," Dwaine said. "Movies—they're are the only valid form of divine sacrament left to us in this culture, the only church worth going to anymore."

It's dusk. To our left the sun sinks like a burning ocean liner into the waters of Eastchester Bay. To our left the lights of Manhattan twinkle in bluish-gray crepuscular light, a Whistler nocturne. Dwaine walks slightly ahead of us, making me wonder if that's what born leaders do, walk slightly ahead of everyone else, if that's what *makes* them born leaders.

"When people go to the movies, it's like a form of prayer," Dwaine asserts. "The theater's the cathedral, the screen's the altar, the colors flickering across it are the modern equivalent of stained glass windows. In medieval times that's how the church told Bible stories, through stained glass."

"What are the people praying for?"

"They're praying that in an hour and fifteen minutes or however long the movie is when the lights come back up and they leave the theater, they'll still be in a movie. The streets, houses and buildings will look real, but they won't be; they'll be made of plaster and plywood." In the dim air above us gulls wheel and shriek, their squawks blending with Huff's locomotive chuffs as he labors alongside us in three-piece suit and Burberry trench coat. Through the bridge's steel mesh dead fish and brine smells rise.

"What about all the people in the streets?" Venus asks.

"Extras," Dwaine submits.

"All of them?"

"All of them."

"And the sky and the trees?" says Huff, puffing.

"One big rear-screen projector fake."

"And the sun burning in the sky?" I say.

"A crane-mounted Musco light. The thing is," Dwaine continues, not really wanting or needing to be interrupted, "for the average moviegoer, the whole point is to escape from reality, because reality is unbearable. So they run off to the only place they can afford to run off to, which is the movies, which is why no one ever gets anywhere or learns anything. Which, by the way, is exactly how the church works, how it's always worked. People keep going and nothing ever changes, which as far as the church is concerned is a good thing, since if people were to really change, if they were to actually find anything like salvation, the church would go out of business, wouldn't it?"

"You've got a point there," says Huff.

A foghorn moans. A boat whistle toots. The brine smell grows stronger as the tide ebbs (or does whatever tides do).

"Salvation may be good for something," says Dwaine, "but it doesn't make the world go 'round. Anyhow nobody really wants to be saved. They want to be lost. *That's* why they go to the movies: to lose themselves in some totally made-up bullshit that has nothing, absolutely *nothing*, to do with real life.

"Ah," Dwaine adds wistfully, "but supposing—supposing the movie *was* about something real? Supposing it *was* convincing?—so convincing it could change a person's whole life? Consider the possibilities! Instead what have we got? Mindless corny bullshit! Flagrant wish fulfillment. Sentimental escapism. Full-length, big-budget car commercials! The world's most powerful artistic medium being used as a pacifier!"

"It's a shame," says Venus.

"It is! It's a crying shame! But we Proto Realists are going to change all that, aren't we?" He puts his arms around me and Venus (Huff being way too big to hug). "We're the four greatest filmmakers in New York."

11

I got to know a little more about Dwaine. I learned that he had no family, none that he had anything to do with anymore, that he'd disowned them, or they disowned him—I couldn't tell which. "Don't you miss them?" I asked.

"About as much as I miss having scarlet fever," he replied.

He called himself "black Irish," a term that intrigued me so much I went to the campus library to investigate it. According to one encyclopedia the phrase described a race of dark-complexioned Irish people descended from the Spanish Moors. Another source maintained that the black Irish were a legacy of African slaves imported from the island of Montserrat in the British West Indies. Yet another source claimed that the expression was a derogatory one applied by Irish Protestants to Irish Catholics and had no ethnic origins whatsoever.

I knew that he'd studied for the priesthood, briefly, and that he'd been a champion ice-hockey player—which is how he lost his real front tooth, which he kept at the bottom of the same mayonnaise jar that held all those pens. A dentist replaced the lost tooth with the removable, rattle-able, single-tooth bridge, but obviously didn't match the color very well. (Had my Papa been consulted, the false tooth would have matched perfectly, for he would have availed himself of *The Identikon*, his invention for comparing the color of false and real teeth.)

And I also knew that he drank. I saw the brown Budweiser quarts lined up next to his bed and, while scrounging ice cubes one day, the Smirnoff pint tucked deep into a glacier of freezer frost. Neither of my parents drank. The bottles of vermouth and gin that my mom kept in her closet grew thick mantles of leaden dust. Beyond what I'd gathered from movies like *The Lost Weekend* with Ray Milland and *The Country Girl* with Bing Crosby, I was totally ignorant of the ways of alcoholics.

About his love life Dwaine was as tight-lipped as he was about Vietnam. One day I asked him if he had a girlfriend. We'd gone to Hunter's Point, to the rail yards there to shoot some B-roll footage. We were taking a short break, sitting on the ends of a pair of boxcars facing each other when I put the question to him. Dwaine threw his head back and laughed. The sun was angled low in the sky. Its coppery rays burnished the laugh lines in my director's face, making him look all of his twenty-six years. He said he had "no time for all that stuff."

I asked, "What stuff?"

"Holding hands, eating out in fancy-ass restaurants, buying flowers and birthday presents, whispering to each other in squeaky cartoon voices between bouts of predictable sex. Besides, when it comes to women, this city is one big psycho ward."

"It *is?*"

"Are you shitting me? Man, open your eyes, look around you."

I looked around, seeing nothing but rows of boxcars and gleaming rails. Between one set of rails a pair of mongrel strays frolicked in the low-pitched sunlight. One of the dogs was missing a leg. The other dog sniffed at the legless dog's hindquar-

ters, making it hop away. Dwaine made an exasperated sound
and shook his head. I realized then that it was a stupid question.
Girlfriend indeed! For a guy like Dwaine, a genius with so many
more important matters to attend to, to waste his time in pursuit of the opposite sex would have been crazy indeed: it would
have been practically if not criminally irresponsible, I told myself, and felt ashamed for having put the question to him.

12

Unlike Dwaine, I had yet to rise above my own trivial pursuit
of the opposite sex. On the contrary, my crush on Venus grew
stronger by the day. And though I tried getting her to go out
with me, it was no use. I was too young, she claimed, though less
than a week divided our birthdays. Her resistance only amplified my desire. For some reason I liked everything about her,
from the sheer cotton skirts that she wore draped to the pavement (so when she walked she appeared to float on clouds of
fabric) to the endearing little chip on one of her two front teeth
(suggesting impulsiveness and hard candy) to the sweet pale vanilla smell that she gave off and that, along with her skin, made
me think of white chocolate.

"You're a late bloomer," she told me in response to one of
my many failed efforts to woo her. "Ten years from now, I bet
you'll be ripe for picking then."

"So I'm some sort of fruit, now, am I?"

"Not that you're not a perfectly nice person, Nigel; you are;
I like you a lot. It's just that you're *so* young."

"The spurned lover will now disembowel himself."

"You just need a little more time, is all."

"You misjudge me," I said. "I'm much older than I look. My
wrinkles are all inside. My internal organs look like a box of
stewed prunes."

"When you're twenty-eight maybe try me again."

"I'll phone you dead and decomposed from deep down in my grave," I said.

"'Age is the price we pay for maturity.' I'm not sure who said that, either Brigit Bardot or my mother when she was half sober and still living."

"'Give me chastity and continence, but not yet.' Saint Augustine."

13

We were interrupted by Dwaine, who ordered us back into bed to complete our lovemaking scene-in-progress. We were shooting our sixth movie, titled *In Flagrante Delicato*, about a seminarian who gets caught having sex in his dorm with a girl from town. Huff played the sanctimonious resident priest who catches us in the act, and offers his silence in exchange for a roll in the hay with my date, whereupon I castrate him with the machete that hangs on a hook over the door of my room.

To kiss Venus with Dwaine watching us through a series of camera lenses, yelling out orders, telling us what to do with our hands, our eyes, our lips and other body parts, would've been strange enough, but doing so knowing that Venus was only acting while every fiber of my being ached for the genuine thing was a special torture, exquisite and unheard of. The paradoxical result being that her performance was much more convincing than mine.

"Come on, babe," Dwaine yelled from behind the camera. "Put a little French into it! She's not a nun, for chrissake. And you're not a priest—yet!"

14

When I asked him what he did for money, Dwaine said he worked as a location scout for a small, independent film company. Pressed for details he said he couldn't divulge any, that he'd been sworn to secrecy, that if he said anything more his ass would be grass.

Secrecy notwithstanding, on several occasions he took me location scouting with him. From the Battery to its northernmost tip (where, as Dwaine pointed out, the city was still a green mound of virgin forest just as the Reckgawawanc Indians had known it) we explored the world's most famous island. Dwaine showed me the rusty swing bridge by which New York Central line trains traveled from the Bronx into Manhattan over the turbulent waters of the Spuyten Duyvil. In Brooklyn, in the Arabic shops sprinkled along Atlantic Avenue, we sampled sticky halvah and plump figs crusted with sugar, and from there rode the A-train to its terminus, to watch snowy egrets soar over the mudflats of Jamaica Bay.

Dwaine loved the city where he was born. For him it was like a humble backyard, while to me it remained as exotic and daunting as the control room of a nuclear submarine. Though I had visited New York with my father as a child, the city seemed entirely different to me now. Before it had been a museum of ocean liners looking like gargantuan banana splits in their berths, and skyscrapers lit up like Christmas trees. At the cut-rate hotel where my father and I slept, a black lady with fire engine red hair let me man the elevator whose caged brass doors opened at each floor to reveal different patterns of hallway carpeting. I remember how each of those carpets was like a city unto itself, its teeming arabesques of pattern and color mirroring the thrilling, multi-hued chaos outdoors. It had been so thrilling for me back then, the city, so modern yet so old, its hydrants and fireboxes layered with thick coats of time, its skyscrapers leaping into tomorrow, the subway's roar as fierce and rank as a lion's. Now, though, the city crushed me under the weight of its excesses, made me feel hopelessly, helplessly small, inept and orphaned. I had no idea how to exist there. Not a clue.

Dwaine showed me the curious parts of the city, its intimate shadows and nooks, the parts that, had the city been a woman, you would have most wanted to kiss. As if it were a confection he had spent his whole life concocting he shared his hometown with me. He taught me to savor the city's garlands of scent, from shoe polish to Xerox toner to the smells of money and fear wafting off people's bodies in the subway. He could even distinguish between doughnut smells, from old-fashioned to honey glazed. From dry cleaner chemicals to brass polish, he had a nose for every city odor. Walking down Broadway from 125th to Wall Street, he could name every business on every block with his eyes closed.

At the Russian baths on East 10th Street we doused each other with buckets of ice water and flailed each other's bare backs with oak branches holding crisp brown leaves. While doing so, I noticed the two quarter-sized fat cysts on Dwaine's back. His "Lucky Lumps," he called them.

15

When summer came around I decided to stay in the city. It was my first summer alone in New York, my first summer away from home anywhere. It happened to be the summer of the Son of Sam, that moonfaced postal employee who, on orders from a neighbor's barking dog, shot his victims dead in parked cars while they necked at sundown. When my mother heard about it on the TV news she phoned me up immediately, hysterical, begging me to please come back home. It took me over an hour to convince her that the odds of this particular psychopath drawing a bead on her precious *creatura di dio* were small indeed—especially given that I had no car to smooch in, and no girlfriend to smooch with.

"Okay, fine," my mother said. "Do like you want. Maybe someone come here an shoot me, if I lucky. Maybe then you come home to see me to my funeral, if it no asking too much, if you no too busy. *Pffff.*"

"Mom, please—"

"*Eh, va bene:* I no give a goop."

16

Some good movies came out that summer. Dwaine loved *Black Sunday*, but hated *Close Encounters of the Third Kind*, especially the last part where the dumb heavenly chandelier descends. And while *That Obscure Object of Desire* bored me stiff, Dwaine pronounced it a masterpiece (he was right, of course).

And though I never found a movie so bad I had to walk out on it, Dwaine walked out of many. Halfway through *Star Wars* (which he condescended to see in the first place only because I wanted to), as the Death Star loomed into view, he stood up, said, "That does it," and made a beeline for one of the Exit doors.

I caught up with him in the street.

"What's wrong?" I asked, panting.

"Nothing. Nothing's wrong."

"So why did you walk out?"

"Because: fuck that shit, that's why."

"Why? What was wrong with it?"

"Oh, babe, you know you really disappoint me at times, you know that?"

"Why?"

"Do I really have to explain?"

"Yes! I mean, what was the problem? What didn't you like about it? It was entertaining, wasn't it? And it wasn't stupid. Was it?"

"Fine. Then go on back, if that's how you feel. No one made you leave." All this time he kept walking, fast, with me keeping up with him, or trying to. "It's a free country, that's what they tell me, anyway."

It was late afternoon, but dark clouds hung all over the city, making it look like evening. I wore the button on my lapel, the one they had given us in the theater lobby, the one with the words MAY THE FORCE BE WITH YOU printed on a sky blue background. I caught up with Dwaine.

"What didn't you like about it?" I asked.

"It's a goddamn blockbuster," is all he said.

"So it's a blockbuster. What's wrong with that?"

He stopped walking then and faced me, burning me with those gray metal shards in his eyes. "Are you serious, babe? Are you *truly* serious? Mindless entertainment? Cunning escapism? *That's* what you want, huh? That's all you care about, isn't it?" I stood there. "Christ," he said. "Well *you* may go to the movies to have the brains sucked out of your skull, but I don't. I go to be *redeemed*. I guess that's the difference between you and me, babe. You want to escape from your sins; I want to be redeemed from mine. But that's not what I hate about that movie. A little harmless entertainment now and then isn't so bad. Only what we just saw in there wasn't harmless. What we just saw is a doomsday juggernaut, the cinematic equivalent of a gigantic shopping mall. Someday, movies like that are going to take over *everything!* They're like Godzillas flattening the landscape. And when they do, trust me, there won't be a thing left for the likes of us, of you and me."

He smiled then, as if to make light of it, but it was a tight, castigating smile, a smile blending pity with scorn. Then he turned and kept walking.

I hurried to catch up.

17

That was also the summer of the famous Blackout of '77. For twenty-four hours starting on a sweltering July evening the whole city went as dark as the sheets of newsprint Professor Crenshaw made us blacken with charcoal. In the forced darkness old people sat listening to themselves breathing in chairs, lovers embraced by candlelight, kids pulled fire alarms, looters smashed store windows and shouldered frozen turkeys and TV sets.

When the lights went out I phoned Venus. I had a bottle of Chianti in my room that I'd been saving for just such an occasion, and asked her if she would care to share it with me by candlelight. Predictably she made up some excuse. Rebuffed, I took the bottle with me over to Dwaine's place.

With no lights on anywhere the whole city felt like one of those sensory deprivation tanks. I couldn't see the sidewalk under my feet, or tell where the curb was, or say for sure what block I was on, or even what city I was walking in, in what country, on what planet, in which universe. I felt like an astronaut spacewalking without a lifeline.

When I got there I pressed Dwaine's lobby buzzer, which of course didn't work. So I stood in the street looking up at his third floor window, which framed more darkness. I was about to give up and go when a gloomy shape stumbled toward me on the sidewalk. He stumbled right into my arms.

"Jesus," I said.

Somehow I got him upstairs to his apartment. All the way up the dark stairs he kept on making terrible sounds, his breath rattling through the snot or whatever it was that clogged up his nose. I took his keys out of his pocket and let us both into his apartment, where I found some candles in a kitchen drawer. By their light I saw the blood draining from his nose and from his eye—real blood, not the fake stuff. Plum-like bruises ripened on every branch of his face. I said, "Jesus—what happened?"

"Get—get the camera," he said.

"What?"

"The camera," he said. "Get it."

He wanted me to film him bleeding.

The camera had its own battery-powered light. It felt weird, filming him, like Dwaine and I had traded places, with me seeing him as he had so often seen me, bleeding profusely through a series of lenses. I kept saying, *Should I stop now? Is that enough? Do you want me to keep on filming?* I exposed a whole roll.

I took off Dwaine's shoes and stretched his serape over him. I tended his wounds with cotton and iodine. Then I sat there, on the edge of his bed, not sure what to do next, watching his face by the candle's guttering glow.

He said, "What the hell are you doing, babe?"

"Nothing. Just sitting here," I said.

"Stop feeding on me!"

"Huh?"

"GET OUT OF HERE! GIVE ME SOME AIR!"

I was halfway home, walking through streets as black as a coal mine when I realized where I'd heard those words before.

Paul Newman, *Cool Hand Luke.*

18

September. School had started again. We spent the whole day shooting at the Bronx Botanic Garden, at the Enid A. Haupt Conservatory—a scene from *Bottle in Front of Me*, our latest masterpiece, about a mental patient whose sinister psychiatrist (Huff) talks him into getting a frontal lobotomy to cure him of his murderous rages. We spent most of the day shooting the nightmare sequence (all of Dwaine's movies seemed to have nightmare sequences), wherein the protagonist dreams that he has turned into a hothouse flower. An orchid.

I was headed home, carrying our new/used movie camera—a beautiful Beaulieu 16-millimeter bought with my mother's money (its chrome-accented body parts anodized to a milk chocolate brown) along with a shopping bag full of exposed film. The sun was setting, deepening in color as it crouched behind a bank of unimportant buildings. A gang of kids rushed me, all wearing ski masks. They came at me out of nowhere with nudges and shoves that seemed almost playful at first. Then they were all over me, branding my body with red-hot fists, kicking it with burning feet until I let go of the camera. Then they took off.

When I opened the door to where I lived Captain Nemo stood there, holding a Medaglia D'Oro coffee can with a yellow dishwashing-gloved hand and a disgusted look on his face. He said, "Do you mind explaining this?"

"It's a Medaglia D'Oro coffee can," I observed shrewdly.

"I know it's a coffee can, Nigel. I'm well aware that it's a coffee can. Can you tell me why there happens to be urine in it?"

"There happens to be urine in it because you never let me use the goddamn bathroom, that's why. You're too busy trying to scrub the mortal sins off of yourself, or whatever the heck it is that you do in there." I was not inclined toward tact.

Captain Nemo shook his fuzzball head. He wore a puffy mound of frizzy gray hair that made his head look like a dandelion gone to seed. I stood there tasting my blood. He started to say something, but before he could I pushed past him and his antique organ into the apartment. I went straight to the phone. I had no idea who I was going to call. The cops? My mother? Dwaine? I knew he'd never forgive me for losing that camera, which cost us a hundred dollars. True, my mom's money paid for it, but what difference did that make? It was still Dwaine's camera, just like they were his movies; he called them ours but they were Dwaine's, and he and I both knew it. I just acted in them. That's all.

I held the receiver to my lips, getting blood on it, trying with no success to remember Dwaine's phone number when it dawned on me that he had no telephone.

A nasty thought came to me then. It grew like a tough weed out of Captain Nemo's Persian rug, reaming its way up through the souls of my sneakers, climbing my legs into my guts. Captain Nemo was yelling at me for getting blood all over everything. I put the phone down, pushed past him again and hurried back out the door.

19

The last traces of light had vanished from the sky. I squeezed Dwaine's buzzer. No answer. I stood in the street yelling like Stanley Kowalski up at his black window:

"DWAINE! DWAAAAIIIINNNE!"

A man came out of the Chopsticks Express. He wore a white apron and had a square head. He looked like Odd Job in *Goldfinger.* He asked what I was yelling about. Just then a woman in a boiled wool coat stepped out of the building. I squeezed past her and let myself in. The Chinese man followed me as I ran up the stairs. Dwaine's door wasn't locked. I stepped into his apartment.

The desk was still there. So was the *Taxi Driver* poster. So were the wires strung across the room for hanging strips of exposed film. But all of the film cans and editing equipment were gone. So was the poster of Robert DeNiro. So was the machete. So was the rubber bullet, and the mayonnaise jar, and the pile of notebooks. And the aluminum trunk. I felt all of the planets of the solar system spinning out of orbit.

I staggered to the chair in front of the desk and sat there, head in hands, hearing but not understanding or really listening to anything the Chinese man was saying as he stood in the doorway, panting, telling me all kinds of things. All I heard was *He gone! He gone!*

Eagle
Electric
(Film Noir)

A few weeks after Dwaine disappeared and two shy of his graduation, Byron Huffnagel left New York for Boston. He had gone up there hoping to raise the money for a movie he wanted to make about Collyer brothers, the famous shut-ins who, in 1947, made headlines when their decomposed bodies were discovered in a Harlem mansion crammed with newspapers and junk. Huff's family lived in Boston, including an uncle who worked in the carting industry and had mob connections. Less than a week after Huff took off, Venus's coalmining father suffered a massive stroke, and she left to care for him down in Virginia.

I was on my own.

2

I took a job in lower Manhattan, at a tavern called the Rosinante Grill, where I peeled potatoes, washed dishes, wiped off the beer and soda taps, and patched holes in the cement floor of the basement where, on any given day, no fewer than two half-dead rats twitched in traps set by the owner, Graham, an Australian. He would point to the bloody furry lumps and say to me, "Right, there, mate: let's get that cleaned up, for a start."

I tore the collars off my shirts, I wore a dark vest, I bought a black hardcover notebook. I smoked Newports. I wandered the city just as Dwaine and I had wandered it together, but minus our strong sense of passion and purpose.

Without Dwaine the streets and avenues lost all of their meaning, practically. What little significance might have attached to them was sealed off and indecipherable. It was like watching a foreign movie with no subtitles.

I considered going home, back to Barnum, but there was no home left for me to go back to, really. By then I had all but disowned my small-town heritage, my un-cinematic, passionless past. The past was a room I had vacated, swept broom-clean for the next tenant.

Between dishwashing shifts I'd scribble away in my black book. Graham, who carried the same smelly bar rag slopped over his shoulder day after day (his "lucky mung rang," he called it), was forever teasing me, saying things like, "So, Shakespeare, what are you scribbling on about now? To be or not to be? It was the best of times, it was the worst of times? Roses are red, violets are blue, I'm William Fucking Shakespeare and, uh, screw you?" (Oh how I yearned to break a bar stool over his head.)

Quite a few good movies came out during those days. *A Bridge Too Far*, *The Last Wave*, *The American Friend*, *Looking for Mr. Goodbar*... Sitting alone in dark theaters, I couldn't help wondering what Dwaine would have thought of them. I missed his lavish whispered comments and annoyed sighs and even his constant sharp elbow in my ribs.

3

The Rosinante Grill had an open kitchen, with the dishwashing station facing the bar. If a decent-looking woman sat in the last stool, I'd flirt with her, and sometimes end up in her bed. The women I met that way were mostly a lot older than me, some of them divorced, others married, their husbands away somewhere on business. Some had kids, in which case they would ask me to leave before daybreak.

Sleeping with those older women in their big beds with too many pillows, I'd think of Venus, of her soft pigmentless sweet-smelling skin and that chipped tooth smile, and feel miserable. As I lay next to whomever's lumpy, sour-smelling body, staring up at a strange ceiling, who could blame me for wishing Venus there with me instead?

One foggy night, having vacated some lady's midtown apartment, I stood on the sidewalk in the fog in front of her building trying to decide whether to schlep back to Brooklyn. The doorman, who had a big drooping mustache, kept casting me these evil glances, his arms buried under his scarlet cape coat. It must have been October, around Halloween. The spire of the Empire State Building was haloed in orange fog. The doorman went on staring at me, giving me increasingly suspicious looks. After the third or fourth look I spat a wad on the sidewalk and turned to him and said (in my deepest, most truculent voice), "What the hell is *your* problem?"

Then, for no reason at all that I can think of—unless it was to try and run away from the ghostly grayness that I felt spreading through me—I took off running through the fog. I ran over a hundred blocks, all the way down to the Fulton Fish Market, where men unloaded icy crates of fish from the backs of big white trucks. I stood at the railing of the Brooklyn Bridge, looking down through air frigid with the smell of dead fish, watching a gang of fishmongers warm gloved fingers over an oil drum fire. They wore black and red Terry Malloy jackets with metal hooks clawing their shoulders. As I stood there watching, Leonard Bernstein's theme to *On the Waterfront* coursed through my cold head.

4

I'm sitting in an East Village diner, eating a bowl of cabbage soup, when I hear *tap tap tap* on the glass and look up and there's

Dwaine Fitzgibbon. He wears sunglasses, a black fur-collared coat and a matching black fur cap. He looks like a paramilitary Eskimo. I'm thinking I must be seeing things, one of those rear-screen projections, or maybe a hologram. He breathes a gray ball of condensation onto the glass then presses his tongue into it.

It's Dwaine, all right.

I wave him inside.

"Babe, where the hell have you been?" he asks.

"*Me? Where have you been?*"

"Since when do you smoke?" He snatches the cigarette from my lips, puts it in his. "You'll give yourself cancer," he says, puffing away. Seeing my look he says, "Don't look at me like that, babe. It's too late for me to quit. I quit now I'll lose all my benefits."

He's lost weight. Dark circles pull down his eyes. He stares at my bowl of soup. I push it to the center of the table. I ask him what he's been up to. Where did he go? In answer he whips out his latest black book and flips it open to a page of photographs of the East Village, the same East Village where he sits slurping my bowl of soup, but at night. I don't see anything special about the photos. "Look closer, babe."

I look closer. Then I realize: it's not the real East Village at all but a scale model of the East Village made out of clay. Clay buildings, clay buses, clay taxis and newspaper kiosks, clay fruit stands and delicatessens, clay punks and babushkas jaywalking across clay streets. Dwaine explains how he spent two months holed up in a former firehouse in Venice West building the claymation set for a producer named Groon, who paid him pin money plus room and board, the rest of his payment to be deferred pending sale of the finished product.

Dwaine finger-whistles the big-boned, heavy-treaded Ukranian waitress, orders another bowl of soup. "Make this one a beef barley!" he shouts at her. He tells me more about Hollywood, about how, with nowhere to go and no money left in his pockets, he took to breaking into cars and stealing change from their utility trays, and how he broke into and slept in an abandoned bungalow on Venice Beach, until the cops finally nabbed him there. They arrested and charged him and put him in jail. While in the can Dwaine wrote his first full-length screenplay, *A Terrible Beauty*, about an ice hockey playing seminarian who becomes an IRA operative and ends up blowing his own father to bits in a Belfast hotel lounge. Before releasing him the cops confiscated the screenplay.

"'This ain't no fucking writer's colony,' the dickhead cop says as he throws my script in the garbage. But that's okay." Dwaine taps his temple with his pen. "I've got the whole thing tucked away safe right here, in the gray matter, where not even Sigmund Freud can get to it. Soon to be a major motion picture." He smiles his face-eating smile. "And you, babe? How about you? What have you been up to? Having fun without me, I bet? You've lost weight; you're skinny. Are you not eating well?"

5

We leave the diner and walk uptown. A cloudy late November day, the sun a pale festering wound in the wet, colorless sky. As we walk Dwaine tells me more about Hollywood, how it's so different from New York, how if New York is the country's brain or maybe its congested lungs, Hollywood is its perverse, decadent, oversized heart.

"The curbs are blood red," he observes with something approaching glee. "It's like living in a never-ending Fellini movie. Everyone gets to play a starring role in his or her own spiritual death. You should see it for yourself one day, babe. Really. You'd love it."

As we walk up Third Avenue Dwaine tells me how he rode a beat-up old train all the way out there, how his compartment had a little flip-down stainless steel sink and no air-conditioning, how in the desert just outside of Phoenix the train derailed, how he and all the other passengers nearly died of suffocation and dehydration while waiting for a bus to pick them up. He explains how, as soon as he got off the bus in Hollywood, he headed straight for Martin Scorsese's Arabian-style mansion on Mulholland Drive, intent on prostrating himself at the famous director's feet and asking him for a job, any job, on his next movie.

"And?" I say.

"Alas," says Dwaine, shrugging, "Marty wasn't around."

Frame by frame as we keep on walking uptown Dwaine narrates his screenplay-in-progress, gesturing to indicate camera angles, the cigarette in his mouth bobbing, threatening to set the collar of his fur coat on fire. I listen distractedly, not yet quite convinced that Dwaine is there, right there walking beside me. I should be angry at him for skipping out on me the way he did, without a word, but his very presence erases all traces of anger, along with any doubts and suspicions, forgives all past sufferings and sins. Cloudy sky or no cloudy sky, being with Dwaine feels like walking out of a dark movie theater where a depressing film is playing and into a bright, clear, sunny day.

6

At the corner of 34th Street a crowd gathers to watch a game of Three Card Monty. Dwaine asks me to loan him five dollars, then pushes through the throng. My eyes follow the three cards being swirled by nimble black fingers on a makeshift cardboard table. When they stop swirling Dwaine slaps the five down. And loses.

"Another five," he says, snapping his fingers.

"Forget it," I say. "You know these games are rigged. There's no way you can win."

"Just give it to me. Don't worry; I'll pay you back. Promise."

I give him another five. He slaps it down. And loses again.

"I told you," I say as we walk away. "Why did you do it? You should know better."

"Should me no shoulds, babe. Once you start lining up all

the shoulds in the world there's no end to it. Besides," Dwaine says. "Every so often a person has to do something crazy, or he'll go nuts."

7

Dusk falls. We stand on the overlook up at Beekman Place, looking out across the river, at the lights of Long Island City shattered in black waves. "If I ever get tired of this view," says Dwaine, "please do me a big favor and put a hollow point in the back of my neck. I'm dead serious." He mashes out the cigarette that he's been smoking, lights another, blows a smoke ring. I smell booze in the smoke. Though cloudy above us the sky may as well be encrusted with diamonds, that's how thrilled I am to be with Dwaine again. With him I feel safe, protected not so much from the world as from myself, from my lonesome insecurity and lack of passion.

"So, did you miss me, babe?"

"A bit, I guess."

"Only a bit? You *guess?* Hell, I missed you a lot more than that."

"You *did?*"

"I did indeed."

"So why did you leave without even saying goodbye?"

"Oh, that. Well, see, I owed some people a pile of money and—well, they aren't the sort of people you can argue about things like that with, if you know what I mean. I hurt your feelings, didn't I, babe? I didn't mean to. I figured you of all people would understand. You understand, don't you? Life's exigencies, and all that."

I say I understand.

"Anyway now that we're back together nothing will tear us apart again, ever, right, babe? I knew you'd find me. I knew we'd find each other."

I remind him that our "finding" each other was a sheer coincidence.

"The hell it was. Don't you know by now that there's no such thing as a coincidence except in bad movies and worse novels? What happened this afternoon was no coincidence. What happened today is called Destiny, otherwise known as Fate, otherwise known as Fortune."

He changes the subject then and asks me whereabouts I'm living. I've taken a Flatbush share with some former art students and tell him so. "What about you?" I say. "Where do you live now?"

He points across the river at the Pepsi-Cola sign, with its giant blushing neon soda bottle. "Behind the second smaller 'P' in Pepsi. That's where *we* live, as in you and me, babe. Or do you plan to spend the rest of your days cooped up with a bunch of skanky ex-art students?"

8

On the Queens side of the 59th Street Bridge, above a windowless industrial building, a barge-sized neon sign winks on and off, on and off, floating the motto of the Eagle Electric Manufacturing Company, reminding all within eyeshot that

PERFECTION IS NOT A ACCIDENT

Above the motto looms an imposing tin eagle, its silhouetted wings spread across the Manhattan skyline. From my window its talons seem to claw at the tops of skyscrapers. This is where I lived with Dwaine Fitzgibbon for some months starting in the winter of 1977.

Our apartment building is a block away from the Pepsi-Cola bottling plant on a street named Extra Alley, as if there had been just the right number of alleys in the vicinity and it had been thrown in for good measure. For its short length the alley parallels the tracks of the No. 7 elevated, so close that, from the same window that frames the Eagle Electric Company sign, I can read the lips of riders as they careen by amid showers of sparks and squeals of tortured iron.

Our apartment has three rooms, including the kitchen, where a shoe-shaped bathtub floats on a lake of cracked, spinach-colored linoleum. There's no bathroom, just a closet with a toilet. In summer the window sashes swell and in winter they shrivel, shedding chunks of pale putty and plaster that look like the droppings of constipated birds. What little heat the landlady provides radiates from a silver pipe that climbs up a corner of the kitchen and which, though hot enough at times to cause third-degree burns, fails to heat the place properly.

There are more than a few things I have to get used to in my new home. For starters it's the noisiest place I've ever lived. There are the elevated trains digging tunnels through my sleep, and garbage trucks bleeping and growling, and the caterwauls of coital cats, and stray dogs barking endless streams of monomaniacal Morse code, and radios blaring, and wailing car and burglar alarms, and the hissing of that damned silver pipe, so loud at times it sounds like a spaceship trying to blast off. And, rumbling away under all those other sounds, the steady drumroll of Dwaine's Promethean snores.

Then there are those nightmares, Dwaine's nightmares, the ones that typically end with his blood curdling cries, screams that wake me up thinking he's being stabbed to death in his sleep. I rush into his room to find him sitting wide-eyed up in his bed, his face glowing red with each flash of the Eagle Electric motto. "It's okay, it's okay," I say, holding him, his shoulders sticky with sweat. "You had a nightmare, that's all. It's okay, it's okay…" As his breathing returns to normal I settle him back into his bed, wondering what sort of nightmares make him scream like that, and if the flashing neon bloodies his dreams.

9

Living with Dwaine wasn't all darkness and nightmares. We had good times, too. Though we no longer owned a movie camera, it didn't stop us from making what Dwaine called Tibetan Sand Movies, with Dwaine filming away behind an imaginary camera and me acting out our carefully scripted scenarios. And though I longed for us to get back to making real movies, for Dwaine, who'd had his fill of ten and fifteen minute shorts, that prospect held no appeal whatsoever.

"I'm done making dippy-ass toy movies," he said. "The next movie you and I make is going to be a feature, or forget it."

Meanwhile we kept exploring New York—a city I came to equate more and more with Dwaine, as if he and it were one, and in ways they were. We walked everywhere, soaking in the city's most intimate aspects and features, honing our senses on its grindstone-gritty streets. Dwaine believed it was every artist's duty to sharpen his senses and keep them sharp. "You've got to look, look, look, and *keep* looking," he said. "You've got to pay attention as deeply as when the eye doctor says, 'Don't blink'—a level of concentration worthy of blindness."

Just what did he mean by that, I wondered.

"The central line must be pursued. To get there you've got to drill through the third eye; you've got to shoot the sleeping Cyclops in the brain. That's what I mean, babe, by *looking.*"

We studied the patterns made by torn bill postings on the sides of garbage dumpsters and plywood construction fences, the striped shadows hurled against a brick wall by the railing of a fire escape, the film-noir moodiness of streetlamp's reflections in a puddle after a rain shower. We studied people, too, the man in the raincoat dozing on the subway, the way his arm fell next to his side as he slept, the shiny little smudge of saliva next to his mouth; the lady walking her mutt schnauzer in Gramercy

Park; the guy selling chestnuts on the corner of Fifth and 49th, the way he shook the cold like a clinging cat from his legs. The cameras in our heads never stopped rolling.

But Dwaine's lessons weren't strictly visual, olfactory or geographical. Above all he wanted me, his tutee, to appreciate the fact that artists hold a unique place in society, a privileged place exempt from the conventions and restrictions imposed on other mere mortals. To prove this point, as we crossed Queens Boulevard against a murderous onslaught of traffic, he admonished me for slowing my gait to let a transit bus roar by.

"Babe," he said, "if you're going to walk with me please do us both a favor and do it like you own the goddamn street, okay?"

I protested. "Did you see the look on that bus driver's face? I swear the guy had a hard-on! He would have run me over!"

"You'd have died with dignity, at least. The point, babe, is to never, *ever* let them see you sweat. Dig?"

10

Still, and though I appreciated all the things Dwaine had to teach me, living with him posed certain challenges. Like those nightmares, for instance, and his mystery walks, excursions he undertook alone almost every night after dinner, usually not returning until after midnight, if at all. When I'd ask him where he was going he would respond either with silence or vaguely, saying he had personal matters to tend to.

And no, I could NOT go with him.

Was it pure curiosity or too many cold nights alone that made Dwaine's disappearances unbearable to me? Where did he go? What did he do? I had to know.

And so, out of frustration as much as anything, one night when he went out on one of his mystery walks, I decided to follow him. I waited until he was down in the street, spying on him through my window to see which direction he turned. Then I hurried down the apartment buildings' ill-lit and loosely treaded stairs, reaching the street just as Dwaine's shadow swung around the corner.

It was winter still. Dwaine walked with his hands deep in the pockets of his army surplus pea coat, his cigarette weaving a blue trail of smoke for me to follow. Through a series of increasingly dismal neighborhoods I shadowed him, past sleeping subway sheds and low buildings squatting under a cave-like sky. Once he turned and nearly caught me, and my heart fell like a stone in my chest. But then he kept walking, shoulders hunched, heading for the expressway overpass, where, among a sea of concrete pillars, I lost him.

As I stood there feeling more lonely and miserable than ever, wondering where my best friend had gone, suddenly he leapt out from behind one of the pillars, startling me so completely I fell back-first onto the icy sidewalk. Dwaine wasn't a big man. He was my height, more or less, about five-foot-nine, a bit on the short side if anything. Still, standing there with his face lit from below like a face in a horror movie, he loomed bigger than life.

"Sorry about that, babe," he said, helping me to my feet and even brushing me off a little. "I meant to scare you, but not that much."

"It's all right," I said.

"Good," he said. "I'm glad it's all right. Now supposing you tell me why you were following me?"

"I wasn't—" I began.

"Don't lie. You were following me. The question is *why?*"

I bit my lip. I was nineteen, but just then I felt much younger. "To find out where you were going?" I tried.

Dwaine's smile lit up the dark. "A good answer," he said. "And I appreciate your honesty. But don't follow me again, okay?"

To let me know there were no hard feelings, he jiggled his false front tooth at me.

Then he turned and kept walking, disappearing through the tall iron gates of Calvary Cemetery.

11

The kitchen tub was the center of life in our apartment, the Acropolis of our fourth-floor Athens. It was where we soaked and scrubbed ourselves, and where (using a salvaged door as a tabletop) we broke bread and had most of our dinner conversations, which revolved, as always, around movies. Dwaine did most of the talking, as garrulous when it came to movies as he was reticent when it came to just about everything else in his life, advancing his feelings and opinions as if they were facts, with me challenging him only when the things he said struck me as patently absurd. One evening he insisted that every time you see an orange in *The Godfather* it means that somebody is about to get rubbed out, that Francis Ford Coppola actually planned it that way, that the bright fruits symbolized violent death. When I dared to suggest that it was probably a coincidence, Dwaine gave me a sideways look as if to say *of course it's a coincidence, you ninny, I'm pulling your fucking chain, as usual.* On another occasion he theorized that in *North by Northwest,* when Cary Grant stands waiting at that dusty bus stop in the middle of nowhere—before the crop duster scene—the lack of any scenery (aside from a withered corn field) or background music was meant to express the barren void at the center of "our nation's collective conscience." This I doubted every bit as much as I doubted his Godfather "orange theory," only this time I didn't argue with him, feeling that he was in earnest (though with Dwaine you could never tell).

After a glass of wine or two or three, we would speak to each other thus:

Me: *My whole artistic life feels carved from soap.*

Dwaine: *Then draw a bath, babe. Get squeaky clean.*

Me: *I'm ashamed of my squareness.*

Dwaine: *To win admission into the Academy, Giotto drew a perfect circle; you draw a perfect square. Between ruler and compass the gods of creativity don't discriminate.*

Me: *I'd like to draw one perfect circle, or even a squiggle.*

Dwaine: *The perfect is the enemy of the profound. We're all flesh and blood, babe. You'd better go to work on loving yourself. When the sand drains in the hourglass it's time to turn the glass over.*

Me: *What will it take?*

Dwaine: *Wine, song, and all the good will you can muster.*

Me: *Will you be there?*

Dwaine: *Brother, do you see me going anywhere?*

Me: *My father never read to me. My mother never fed me her own milk. I never saw my parents hug or kiss or share the same bed. Your folks are drunks; they drained the Seagram's Seven; mine drained the cup of misery.*

Dwaine: *Do you plan to feel sorry for yourself all night long? Because if you do, I may need aspirin and earplugs, a violin to play and a pot to puke in.*

Me: *Sorry.*

Dwaine: *Don't apologize, babe, and whatever you do don't regret. Guilt and regret top the chart of useless emotions. Live with the consequences of the future you make as you make it. Does that make sense?*

Me: *What's it like, being an alcoholic?*

Dwaine: *Like a calm red eye at the center of a hurricane of murderous rage; a charmed state of siege against the City of Common Sense. And yet I'd give anything to be dry, almost.*

Me: *Almost?*

Dwaine: *Anything, that is, except booze.*

Me: *I get it.*

Dwaine: *I'm like a starfish. Dry me out and I shrivel up and die. Sober, I cease to be.*

Me: *I'm sober enough for both of us.*

Dwaine: *I believe you're right. And it's a great comfort to me, babe, it really is. A great comfort.*

Me: *We live in strange times.*
Dwaine: *That's hardly true or even fair.*
Me: *You don't think it's fair?*
Dwaine: *No, I don't think it's fair.* "*Strange*" *does too great an injustice to all other times, especially when you stop to consider that the times we live in now suck the big whazoo. Since their inception the 1970's have never ceased to suck, not once, not for a split second. The decade's sole redeeming features can be summed up in two words,* "*Martin Scorsese*"…

Dwaine did most of the cooking, too, bringing home bleeding steaks, London broils that he would season with pepper and garlic and panfry on our stove. To watch Dwaine cook was an intense experience, like love or war. Fork and peppershaker in hand, he presided over the frying pan like a priest with a crosier and a thurible. There was something coded and regimented about him, like a soldier's squared-off shoulders, until he'd burst out laughing or jiggle his front tooth and destroy the effect.

One night, Dwaine brought home a big bag of fortune cookies he'd found in a dumpster outside a fortune cookie factory, at least a hundred of them. We sat side by side at the tub/table, smashing them open like walnuts with our fists, reading the fortunes aloud to each other, adding the phrase "in an insane asylum" after each fortune, giggling like schoolboys. Those fortunes that captured our imagination we taped to the refrigerator door. The others we set on fire using Dwaine's cigarette lighter, turning the pale slips of paper into tiny writhing angels of colorless ash.

12

Though we no longer made our own movies, whenever we could afford to we still watched them, old ones mostly, at revival houses—the Thalia, St. Marks, Bleecker Street…Watching movies with Dwaine was a mixed blessing. On the one hand you benefited from his knowledge and enthusiasm; on the other you had to put up with his constant elbow-nudgings, and with a steady stream of critical and historical commentary much like the kind provided on DVDs today. Did you know that, when making *The Train*, Burt Lancaster actually pulled a ligament in his knee while playing golf between takes, and that's why he limps through the whole last third of the picture?—esoteric comments that could enhance my viewing pleasure. But even when I found it edifying, still, the others in the audience hardly welcomed Dwaine's erudition. They would shush him extravagantly to no end.

We'd come home with lines of dialogue lodged in our heads, tossing them to each other like Frisbees. Those movie lines that struck us as particularly apt or memorable we would, using a thick black Magic Marker, commit to the wall between the refrigerator and the kitchen stove. This became the Pertinent Movie Quote Wall. Whoever soaked in the tub would dictate while the other transcribed. We kept a gallon of Dutch Boy flat white latex handy to paint over the quotes we grew tired of. Some quotes ("It's lamb on a stick, you should try it!"—*Panic in the Streets*) lasted only a matter of days, while others ("I can't help myself!"—Peter Lorre, *M.*) survived all tests of time.

13

That Christmas I went home. I owed my parents, whom I hadn't seen in over a year, a visit. And to be honest I'd been feeling a bit homesick. I asked Dwaine if he wanted to come with me, but he demurred.

"No Chaldean rune worship for this fallen Christian," he said. "Besides, I hate Christmas so much I'm sure I'd spoil it for your entire family."

I recall riding the train home from Grand Central, the series of wind-up toys I'd bought for Christmas presents riding on the baize seat beside me, the winter landscape flashing by beyond the green-shaded window like frames in a movie. To the train wheels' steady *kachumps* my mind flashed its own mental movie frames, horrific images of Dwaine dangling from the light fixture in our kitchen, or half-floating in a tub cloudy with red water. Why these images came to me I had no idea; I had no reason to believe, back then, that Dwaine would want to harm himself.

14

I visited my mother in the bridal boutique where she worked. She made no effort to hide her displeasure at my having quit college and, as if that wasn't bad enough, choosing to stay in the city for no good reason rather than come home. She blamed Dwaine, of course, whom sight unseen she had taken a dislike to. "*Cretino*," she said of him, snatching a fistful of fake pearls from a cardboard box filled with them on her back room work-table. But most of my mother's accusations against Dwaine weren't made explicitly, using words. She preferred dirty looks, eye-rolls, shrugs, heavy sighs, and other gestures swelling with innuendo, a language she spoke (still speaks) much more fluently than she speaks English or Italian.

"I no mind. I am use to be left alone to worry about my son while he risk his life in dat *maledetto* city. *Per che cosa?* So he can be a movie star! Pfff! Maybe I come down there; maybe you friend he make of me a movie star, too. *Pffff!*"

"Mom, don't do this to me, I beseech you."

"Do what? I no do nutting. Is you life. *Ma figurati! Non me ne frega niente.* I no give a goop."

Of Barnum's nine thousand-plus inhabitants, my father and I alone were immune to the charms of my mother's Italian accent, as thick and pungent as a Genovese salami, and which, like a witch's brew, could transform *air* into *hair* (as in "first I put hair in my tire, then I go get an air cut,") and shirt *sleeves* into *leaves* (as in "roll up you leave when you go rake de sleeve.") When not abusing words on an individual basis my mom tortured whole phrases, turning *all of a sudden* Japanese ("allowassan"), and mangling "I couldn't care less" into the less grammatical but more onomatopoeic "I no give a goop." Together with her accent my mom's movie star looks—a fusion of Sophia Loren and Anna Magnani, with Magnani's fierce gypsy eyes and Loren's sensual lips—made her a local *cause célèbre*. Which might have been impressive had the locality been, say, Boston and not Barnum, possibly the dreariest town in the universe, with its crumbling hat factories and all-too-symbolic white elephant mascot.

I felt sorry for my poor Italian mother, trapped up there in that brick hellhole, sewing bridal headpieces for nitwits with nothing better to do than instigate their own weddings. With her good looks she could have been a real movie star. She could have been courted by exiled Baltic princes, or entertained aboard pale yachts captained by toad-faced Greek shipping magnates. Instead she married my bicycle-peddling inventor papa, who dragged her off to Barnum, to divide her days between the bridal boutique and the First National supermarket (her shopping cart a Venetian gondola, the frozen food aisle her Grand Canal).

15

I dropped into my father's laboratory, a stucco shack at the bottom of our driveway. My mother called it The Building, as if it were the only standing structure in the world, let alone in Barnum, Connecticut. A sign on the door said, "Please enter by window." The window was open. I climbed in and entered my father's laboratory to find him bent over his bench, working in a cone of dusty light, wearing his ratty cardigan and deerstalker hat and smiling the little potato smile he always wore when concentrating. I approached cautiously, my sneakers sending up ruddy puffs where they broke through floorboards.

"Watch your step, my boy," said my father. "This is one very holy shrine."

With its frankincense of solder smoke, sawdust, scorched metal, and orange rind, The Building *was* a kind of shrine, the place where as a child I came to worship my absentminded genius papa, to gaze in wonder and awe upon his Miracles.

"What's wrong with the front door?" I asked.

"Ah!" He lowered his soldering gun. "I'll show you."

He led me to and opened the vestibule door. There, sunning just inside the main door in a patch of light from the window, was a black snake at least three feet long. "He lives under the floor boards. I feed him a loaf of bread once a week. He seems happy and we leave each other alone." He closed the door and led me back to his workbench.

"Have I shown you my latest?" he said, nodding toward a device the size of a toaster, with a Pyrex dish suspended over a lens opening on top. The dish held a spoonful of a pasty brown substance that I recognized immediately as one forbidden to me as a child. "I call it the P-B Analyzer," my father explained. "It measures the color, texture and consistency of peanut butter. Loathsome substance," he added, grimacing. "Whatever its consistency, it is consistently loathsome."

As a boy I loved watching my father work. I especially loved watching him at the lathe, his metal-stained fingers curved over the spinning chuck, his other hand turning an array of chromium dials, guiding the bit that sliced like a clipper ship prow through copper, brass, and aluminum seas, spewing steaming turnings that I'd sweep up off the floor afterwards, saving the longest and brightest for a collection I kept in a little wooden box by my bed.

"Wasn't it Henry Thoreau," I noted wisely, "who said that all of our inventions are but improved means to an unimproved end?"

"Have an orange, why don't you, old boy?"

While peeling it I saw that my father's zipper was—as usual—

down. I pointed this out to him. "Ah, so it is, my boy, so indeed
it is," he said without looking up from the circuit he soldered.
"Well, as Churchill said, a dead bird never fell from its nest."

Like Churchill before him my father is a dedicated Sunday
painter. His latest work-in-progress rested against a table-
mounted easel, a landscape with a Mission style building with
white stucco walls and a red, clay tiled roof. Below the building's
bell tower there was an odd, star-shaped window.

"That's Hudson Priory," my father explained. "A monastery
in New York State. I go there now and then for the peace and
quiet. One thing I'll say for those Trappists, they know how to
keep their bloody mouths shut."

When it was time for lunch we walked up the steep driveway,
stopping along the way for a ritual piss. As we emptied our bladders into the milkweed and Queen Anne's Lace my father said
to me, "The last time I visited the monastery it occurred to me
that I ought to have been a monk. A few chores, a prayer or two,
a bowl of rice and a clean bed. Who could ask for more? ..."

Like brass turnings from his lathe my father's urine spun
and glittered. As a child I marveled at the thickness and height
achieved by my father's stream, at its lofty gleaming goldenness,
and wondered would I ever piss so high, so far? It was a mar-
vel equivalent to his inventions, and to the parts that went into
making them: the relays, the lenses, the capacitors, the tubes
and solenoids and potentiometers boxed and stored on shelves
in The Building's dusty back room. For me the parts in those
boxes were like the planets, moons and asteroids of the solar
system, with my father the sun at its center.

"That's what I should have done, isn't it, old boy?" my father
said, packing his uncircumcised tool away. "I should have been
a bloody monk. True," he added, pursing his lips and nodding,
"I would have had to believe in God and salvation and all that
crap. But I could have faked that. Most do, I'm sure."

With these words spoken in the equivalent of a sigh my
father wiped my mother, myself, and all future generations of

our family off the face of the earth.

Dear Old Papa: *why hast thou forsaken me?*

16

After two years in New York I found Barnum unbearable. I felt like a ghost wandering its streets, streets that reeked of the past—a moldy, dusty smell. I threw away the Christmas presents I'd bought for my old friends. I didn't even bother looking them up. What for, when every cell in my body had changed? Compared to those of New York, the streets of my hometown looked gutted and radioactive, as if a nuclear bomb had been dropped there, one of those bombs that levels dreams but leaves buildings and people standing. Compared to the streets of New York those in my hometown seemed deserted. The few faces that darted into them looked nervous and suspicious, like the faces one-armed Spencer Tracy runs into in *Bad Day at Black Rock*. There was nothing worth filming there. The houses were tombs; the stores were museums of empty shelves. The town's only movie theater, having shown porno films for a few years, turned briefly into a Christian Science Reading Room before closing its doors for good. It amazed me that I, Nigel DePoli, movie actor and best friend of Dwaine Fitzgibbon, had sprung from such inauspicious beginnings. After two days I couldn't stand any more.

I left Christmas on morning. I told my parents I was sorry, but that I had some important things to do. My father reacted with his usual absentminded indifference; my mother laid on the guilt, sobbing her way through a Puccini tragedy about a mother whose son has become a total stranger to her.

"Go, go! Leave me stuck wid your useless father! Go back to you *maledetto* friend! *Pfff! I no give a goop!*"

Then I was back on the train again, sitting on a lumpy baize seat watching the green world pass by, rewinding the film of my journey back to Grand Central Terminal, to Long Island City, to Extra Alley, to our apartment, the gruesome images of before drawing closer and sharper until they hung clear as movie stills in the theater lobby of my mind.

In place of a dead body and a suicide note I found a newspaper-wrapped package waiting for me on the tub/table, adorned with a ribbon made out of a yard of exposed film. Inside: a framed photograph of Marlon Brando as Terry Malloy in *On the Waterfront*. *To the second best actor in the world*, the attached note read. *Merry Christmas, Bud Brando*.

I hadn't gotten Dwaine anything. In a panic I rushed to the Strand, where, among the dizzying stacks of used dusty books there, I found something I thought he might like, an oversized coffee table book published by Time-Life, stuffed with pictures of movies and stars, titled *Life Goes to the Movies*.

I left it, gift wrapped, on Dwaine's bed.

17

But Dwaine's real present didn't come wrapped in anything. On New Year's Eve, after we'd eaten a shoplifted steak and drunk half a bottle of cheap champagne, as I was getting ready for bed expecting him to go off alone on one of his mystery malks, Dwaine stood in my doorway.

"What's up?" he said.

"Going to bed," I answered. "Why?"

"Get dressed. I want to show you something."

As we passed through the kitchen he pointed to the champagne bottle (actually *asti spumante)* on the tub/table.

"Grab the bubbly."

I had no idea where we were going, and didn't ask, aware that this was a time for blind faith. We both wore our pea coats, purchased at Guiseppe's Thrift Emporium, mine with blue plastic buttons, Dwaine's with shiny brass ones embossed with anchors. We walked into the harsh headwind that met us under the highway overpass, whose whooshing traffic sounds echoed ominously between pylons. Out of the darkness Dwaine told me about his brother, Jack. I didn't know he had a brother; he'd never mentioned having a brother before. Then again, he'd hardly said anything at all about his family. As we walked he explained that Jack had been one of the biggest narcotics dealers in the country, that he'd owned a huge compound in the Arizona desert, with a fleet of tractor-trailers, four Cessna planes, and a small army of paperless Mexicans. When Dwaine last saw Jack he had just gotten back from "overseas" (I assumed he meant Vietnam). On his way to New York from Oakland he'd stopped in Arizona to pay Jack a visit. Like his parents, Dwaine had been operating under the impression that his brother was an undergraduate philosophy student at the University of Arizona. Instead when he arrived there he found a compound patrolled by armed guards and surveillance cameras.

"One of the guards tells me my brother's waiting out back," said Dwaine. "I turn the corner and freeze. There's like a hundred people camped around the biggest swimming pool I've ever seen, all naked and smoking swagg. My brother, he comes out of the cabana hut. He's grown enormous, three hundred pounds, with a thick beard. He looks like Huffnagel. 'Meet my new family,' Jack says, throwing his fat arms around me. Just then this little kid with no clothes on walks over to the edge of the pool and pees right into it. My brother laughed," said Dwaine. "He thought it was hysterical."

Dwaine went on to tell me how Jack gave him a tour of the place, including the giant Quonset hut where a crew of paperless workers dried, cut and packaged cocaine paste, while a smaller group of University of Arizona chemistry majors synthesized Quaaludes and LSD. His brother handed Dwaine a sheet of windowpane acid, hot off the press. "'Take as much as you want,' Jack says to me. 'There's plenty more where that came from.'"

As we kept walking Dwaine lit a cigarette, offered me one. He knew I didn't smoke, but not wanting to break the air of intimacy between us I took it anyway. He even lit it for me, his fingers forming a cup of orange flame under my chin. He told me how, after his visit, while Jack drove him to the airport, he asked Dwaine if he cared to go partners with him.

"What did you say?" I asked.

"I said no thanks. My brother, he looks at me like I'm the dumbest ass to ever walk the face of the earth. I'd never seen such a disgusted look before, not counting my father's face after he found out about my Army discharge."

Dwaine fell suddenly silent then, like he'd said too much, or maybe it was just one of those dramatic pauses he was so good at, or maybe he just wanted to get past the sounds of cars avalanching on the expressway overhead as we walked under it. It occurred to me then that he drove my curiosity the way some people drive a car, flooring it or hitting the brakes, nothing in between. He pulled a shiny silver flask from his pea coat pocket, one that I'd never seen before, drank from it and handed it to me. The chilled liquor burned my lips and carved a warm tunnel deep down into my guts.

We jumped a spiked iron fence to land with solid thuds on the frozen cemetery earth, and kept walking, passing the shiny flask back and forth. When he started talking again I listened the way I always listened to Dwaine, as if every word was a door being opened to let in more of the world. Drug dealers! Compounds in the Arizona desert! To think I knew someone who knew, had known, such criminals; that my best friend's brother had been a world-class drug dealer. Dwaine might have said that he knew John Dillinger, or that Al Capone was his brother, or Buffalo Bill! The whole illicit country seemed to have spilled from Dwaine's lips and landed in a bright gruesome puddle like vomit at my feet. Only it was good vomit; it was All-American vomit, it was just the sort of vomit I craved, the corrosive kind that could completely dissolve my immigrant son's sense of being an alien nobody from nowhere.

The sky went from cobalt to Prussian blue. Maybe it was the booze in my belly, but the colors of that night seemed to generate their own light without any help from the mercury vapor lamps or the moon. Was Dwaine drunk, too? If so he didn't show it; he never did, while I felt every drop sloshing around inside my brain like Shelly Winters in a rowboat.

18

We crossed an ocean of fancy graves to drift into a bay of plain tombstones bearing mostly Irish names: O'Rourke, O'Connor, Doherty, Doyle, Fitzgerald…Dwaine picked up speed. Soon we stood before a grave with a Distinguished Service Cross sprouting like a bronze sunflower from it:

John Daniel Fitzgibbon
b: October 15, 1946
d: February 14, 1975
Beloved Son of Sean and Irene

"That's him?" I said, and Dwaine nodded. "Your brother was in the war, too?"

"Infantry," said Dwaine. "Two tours. Jack got drafted; I didn't. He always believed it was because of the color of his skin. See, he had darker skin than me. Black Irish, some people call it. It made no sense to me, but it did to him, and I think he held it against me, too, in his way. Jack was like that. When he got pissed off he'd call me a little Irish nigger. Projection, the shrinks call it."

"How'd he die?"

Dwaine's face went through at least three transmission shifts there in the dark before he answered: "Narcotics overdose related cardiac arrest"—as if it were something he'd been brainwashed into saying by ruthless Chinese operatives.

Then, unzipping his fly, he undertook what apparently was

the crowning ritual of his graveside vigils, and peed a steady stream onto his brother's grave mound.

"'Dwaine,' my brother said to me last time I saw him, 'if I ever overdose I want you to promise me you'll piss on my grave.' Well…" Clouds of steam rose from the wet earth as rivulets formed around Dwaine's boot caps. "A fitting tribute," Dwaine added, zipping his fly, "to a guy who pissed his life away."

19

We left Jack's grave. As we did Dwaine said: "Have you ever wondered, babe, why so many things starting with the letter D are bad?"

"Like what?" I asked.

"Like Death. Disaster. Despair. Depression. Disease. Denial."

"What about Dreams?" I said. "And Daylight?"

"…Disenchantment, Depravity, Drunkenness, Dishonor…"

"…Destiny, Delight, Determination—"

"…Destruction, Defoliation…"

"…Doughnuts? Dominoes?"

"…Destitution, Dogma, Divorce…"

"…Dogs, Daisies, Dill Pickles?"

"…Dysentery, Dropsy, Defenestration…"

"…Dolphins? Driftwood?"

"*Driftwood?*" said Dwaine.

"Driftwood's great! You light beach fires with it. It floats!"

"Sometimes you worry me, babe, you know that?"

20

By then I was staggering—the champagne, the late hour. With Dwaine's arm around me for support we made our way to the mausoleums. The family names on the bronze doors were mostly Italian. We gazed in awe through barred windows at altars glowing in whisky-colored light, at the stained windows depicting the Stations of the Cross.

"You Wops sure know how to die, I'll grant you that," said Dwaine.

"I wish our apartment were this nice," I said.

"Yeah. Some people have got it made."

We both laughed then. For the first time I felt us both on the same level, almost. It gave me a weird mixed feeling, the kind I'd get on Christmas mornings after opening all my presents and finding that the colorful wrappings had been the best part.

21

We came upon a freshly dug grave, the raw earth piled up beside it under a tarpaulin. The hole went at least eight feet down. An aluminum ladder lay stretched alongside it. I dared Dwaine. "Darers go first," he said.

So I climbed down. Being the son of an atheist, I didn't believe at all in heaven or hell, and had no reason to fear a hole in the ground. As I went down Dwaine made werewolf sounds.

"Very funny," I said.

"Not at all," said Dwaine. "In fact it's rather *grave*."

I reached the bottom.

"Step off the ladder," Dwaine urged, and I did. He withdrew it.

"*Good evening,*" he said with his hands cupped around his mouth. "*We hope that you are enjoying your stay at the Club Inferno. Tonight at midnight we will have bingo in the Seventh Circle Lounge with prizes complimentary to you. Free wailing and gnashing of teeth instructions are available. See Moloch in the cabana.*"

Suddenly Dwaine stepped out of sight. Still I wasn't afraid. What was there to be afraid of? In fact I thought it was funny, and started laughing despite not having been in so dark a place since my mother locked me in the attic for smashing a shaving cream pie in the family dog's face. Then my eyes adjusted to the dark and I saw something jutting out of the dirt beside me, a milled corner casting a slivery gleam of moonlight, a coffin's edge. I said, "Dwaine?" And then I screamed, "*Dwaaaainnne!*"

He peered down.

"You rang?"

"Get me out of here!"

"Why? Did you see Lon Chaney, Jr.?"

"There's dead people down here!"

"Who were you expecting, the June Taylor Dancers?"

"Goddammit, *give me that fucking ladder!*"

My feet hardly touched the rungs as I bounded. When I reached the top Dwaine pulled me out the rest of the way, Hercules pulling Cerberus from the infernal regions. I fell panting against a nearby tombstone.

"*How bold of you,*" said Dwaine, quoting Dante or Virgil or whoever, "*to descend into the depths where the futile dead live on without their wits.*"

"Screw you!" I said.

"Hey, come on, it couldn't have been that bad."

"How would you know?"

"Believe me," Dwaine said with a smile. "I know."

22

From there we rode the subway all the way to Times Square. I'd never been to Times Square on New Year's Eve, but had heard tales of crowds and muggings and of people getting shot and stabbed. Dwaine assured me that crowds wouldn't be a problem.

"Not where we're going," he said.

As much as Dwaine hated Christmas, he put great stock in New Year's Eve, as if the mere turning of a calendar page could usher in bright prospects while eradicating all evidence of the botched, abortive past. Having exited the subway, we made our way through the throngs already gathering along 42nd Street, passing below the bulky marquees of once illustrious movie theaters now gone to seed, the Empire, the Liberty, the Lyric, the Harlem, the New Amsterdam, the Selwyn…pagan cathedrals where, as Dwaine saw it, people went to be delivered from their dull, pathetic, and often painful lives, and had their prayers answered immediately, if only for an hour and a half. Now half of those grand old theaters were boarded shut, while the other half showed only porn and slasher flicks.

"Such a shame," said Dwaine.

As the crowds grew ominous and ambulances prowled the streets Dwaine pulled me off the sidewalk and into the arcade of a building where a disused subway entrance sat blocked by planks, several of which he did in with a swift kick of his boot.

"After you," he said, bowing.

We headed down a flight of stairs, dark and dripping, so dark I couldn't see my hand in front of my face. Dwaine lit his cigarette lighter. It hardly made a dent in the darkness. My legs shook.

"Don't be scared," Dwaine said. "Just pretend you're in a movie. *Beneath the Planet of the Apes.*"

At the bottom of the stairs Dwaine put out the lighter and took a small flashlight from his pocket. He pointed it at a mildew-covered mosaic on the wall. I saw the bite-sized tiles spelling 42nd STREET.

I asked, "How long has this been here?"

"Since '38. It was built as a crossover station just before the Second World War, but was never actually used."

"How do you know these things?"

"Hey, I live here."

Though windless the subway tunnel was as cold as the street. I shivered in my surplus pea coat. En route to other places trains roared through the station. Dwaine looked up and down the platform, then jumped down into the tracks, telling me to do the same and warning me to watch out for the third rail.

"They say one of the most efficient ways to commit suicide is to piss on one of them things," he said as we started walking, headed uptown. "Seven hundred volts up the urethra, zzzzzap!"

"I'll keep it in mind."

"Don't. Nothing's worse than the smell of fried piss."

A train light appeared, highlighting old newspapers and scampering rats. We flattened our backs into a maintenance notch. The train roared by. Dwaine walked another dozen yards then he stopped. A rusted ladder climbed toward a matrix of pink dusty light. He went up first and I followed him, into a crawlspace under a grating that lead us on hands and knees into a chamber about eight feet long by six feet wide by five feet deep. There was an old fruit crate there, so coated with wax drippings it looked like something growing at the bottom of the sea, and a filthy mattress, and a wooden box of candles—long, tapered ones. We stretched out on the mattress and looked up through the grate at the lights of Times Square, pulsing away like a heavenly pinball machine, tinting the air with bright circus colors.

"The Stonehenge of the New Millennium," said Dwaine, looking up. "Or the asshole of the world, depending on your point of view."

"Is this where you go when you don't come home?"

"Maybe. Sometimes."

"Don't you get bored? Don't you get lonely?"

"I *am* lonely, but what's that got to do with anything?"

"I mean what do you do down here?"

"What do I *do?*"

"Yeah, what do you do?"

"Nothing. I don't do anything, babe. That's the whole point. You're not supposed to do anything in a sanctuary, and that's just what this place is, a sanctuary. I come here to get away from all the crazies up there." He pointed up. "To be safe with the alligators and the sewer rats. Listen." He cupped a hand over his ear. "Hear that? That's the OM, the gut-rumble of the New World Order." (I listened; I didn't hear a thing.) "Listen…" He made the sound for me. And then I heard it: a steady hum, like the sound a refrigerator makes when it's on. "They say there's a

Moog synthesizer down here somewhere, right here in the belly of civilization. They say that it gives off a special frequency designed to calm human nerves. They say it's been humming that one note since 1971, since the day I signed a piece of paper solemnly swearing to defend my country against all enemies foreign and domestic. Right up there," he pointed, "in the Armed Forces Recruiting Station in Times Square, that's where I signed on the dotted line."

"Why?"

"Why what?"

"Why did you enlist?"

He shook his head. "I don't know. Because my father dared me to. Because I was sick of him calling me a pussy. Because I wanted to be John Wayne in *The Green Berets*. Or maybe it was the OM that drew me there, like a snake charmer's flute. It still draws me to this day. Listen." We both listened. "They say that OM is all that's holding this city together. Supposedly if it should ever stop for any reason the forces binding civilization together will dissolve and the citizens of Gotham will go wild, rampaging, screaming bloody naked in the streets, tearing each other's throats out like werewolves. Someday, babe, OM or no OM, it's gonna happen, the other shoe is gonna drop. And when it does, man, right here—that's where you'll find me."

"Here?" I asked.

"That's right, babe. Here."

"In this hole under the city?"

"You call it a hole now. But when the time comes it will be the closest thing on earth to Paradise, relatively speaking."

"You'll be here all by yourself?"

"Most likely."

"And you still won't be lonely?"

"On the contrary, babe, I still *will* be lonely, but again I ask you what that has to do with the price of fish in Kentucky?"

"Wouldn't it be better if you had someone with you?"

"What for?"

"I mean some company, some companionship."

"Oh, companionship. No, it wouldn't be better," Dwaine said.

"Why not?"

"Because there are certain things that should be experienced in private, alone. A walk on the beach is one, a good bowel movement another, *Last Tango in Paris* a third. The end of the world is one of those things. I wouldn't *miss* it for the world, and I won't share it with anyone, if I can help it. Least of all with all those murderous motherfuckers up there. As for being lonely, George Orwell said that loneliness is just another word for being part of a very small minority. And that's just what we are, babe, you and I. We're part of a very small minority. We don't fit into the system and we never will. We're type-B cells swimming around inside a type-A bloodstream. Of course we're lonely! Would you have it any other way?"

I shook my head; I wouldn't have it any other way.

The candle spluttered. Through the overhead grate I saw the gaudy Times Square colors shifting and swirling, like St. Elmo's fire. We lay there listening to the OM humming discretely below the sounds of fireworks of jubilation being set off high above our heads. The countdown began; the bright burning ball of *auld lang syne* or whatever the hell it was descended. When the moment arrived Dwaine took the half-finished bottle of champagne (*asti spumante*) and two plastic cups from the satchel he'd been carrying.

"To us, babe, the Two Greatest Artists in New York."

We toasted with Dixie cups of ersatz champagne, with me feeling as though we'd passed over a threshold, that Dwaine and I had at last entered the sacred space of true friendship. Sure, there were things wrong with him; there were things wrong with everybody, especially with artists; especially with *great* artists. And I believed Dwaine was a great artist, or would be someday, as soon as he saw fit to generate some great art. I needed to believe it in order to believe that I might myself be great in some way, which beat the hell out of believing that I was wasting my life.

"This will be our year," Dwaine assured us both. "Count on it." He held up his pinky, as in *We've got more talent in our pinkies than most people have in their whole bodies.*

22

Later that morning, as I drifted drunkenly off to sleep, Dwaine, naked and smelling of metabolized sweet alcohol, climbed under my sheets. At first I thought he was pulling some sort of prank. "What gives?" I said, laughing. "What the hell are you doing?"

But Dwaine wasn't laughing. He sat there, smiling in the dark, his features lit fitfully by the red neon sign winking across the street. I heard what at first sounded to me like plumbing noises, rumbles and gurgles, until I realized they were coming from Dwaine's stomach, like he was about to get sick. "Are you okay?" I said.

"I'm fine," said Dwaine, his voice hard to hear. "Fine."

I reached up then and switched on my lamp. A mistake. He screamed. "*Turn it off! Turn the goddamn fucking light off!*"

I did, but not before seeing the erection that Dwaine hadn't had time to cover up, its tip as red and glossy as a fireman's helmet. Grabbing my bed sheet and wrapping it around himself he rushed out of my room. By the time I said, Wait! he was already gone. For a long time I stood there, feeling the bones of my face, all sound (including that of the subway train which chose that dramatic moment to roar by) edited out of the scene as in a violent sequence where everything turns to silence and slow motion before going black.

There are times in our lives that change us forever, or could have. Had I not been a square insecure small-town kid from Connecticut this might have been one of them. Instead I had to switch on that light. Why? I should have let Dwaine get into bed with me; I should have let him do whatever it is that he wanted to do. Again why? Because it would have done no harm.

Because we were both lonely animals burrowing in the dark, seeking warmth, comfort. Because life is short and that night especially was going to be long, very long. And because, when you get down to it, aside from changing my life completely, it would have made no difference.

I stopped feeling the bones in my face and called tentatively into the darkness: "Dwaine?"

Stepping into his room I felt the breeze from his open window against my bare ankles. I climbed the fire escape to the roof where I found him wrapped in the bed sheet, huddled close to the edge, the remains of a dead pigeon like a sacrificial offering at his feet. He looked up.

"I'm not a homo," he said.

"Neither am I."

"But I am fucked-up."

"No, you're not."

"Yes I am, babe. You bet your ass I am. I'm fucked up and so are you. Only I'm too fucked up and you're not fucked-up enough."

A subway passed, its roar and lights splashing. Over our heads a police helicopter flut-flutted, the whole scene lit intermittently by flashes of red neon. Dwaine gave a weird laugh then and slid himself closer to the brink. I dove and grabbed him, pulling him into the stairwell shed where I held him close and he burst out crying.

"You're my only friend," he said through a stream of tears. "My only friend in the whole goddamn world. It's funny, isn't it? Don't you think it's funny, babe? I think it's hysterical!"

I held him, feeling the clammy patch of skin between Lucky Lumps. If he'd been a woman I would have kissed him then, oh yes, I would have. Instead I silently, secretly prayed to the eagle electric manufacturing company sign across the way, wishing it would swoop down and protect us, shield us with its tin wings.

IV

*The Two
Greatest Artists
in New York
(a Farce)*

P icture this: The Two Greatest Artists in New York sprawled on the sands of Miami Beach. It's five in the morning, something like that, and I'm awake, perusing the seascape, trying to decipher those mysterious blue shapes floating way out there.

Mountains? Waves? Whales?

We're wearing tuxedoes, Bull Duncan's tuxedos, a pair of return airline tickets to New York tucked safely in Dwaine's breast pocket, boarding passes to Mutiny.

Behind us: a wall of luxury hotels stretching as pale and frothy as the waves that break along the shore: the Hyatt, the Hilton, the Konover, the Fontainebleau...And the Hotel Paradise where, in a deluxe penthouse suite, Literary and Film Agent Bull Duncan dreams sweet dreams of exclusivity, oblivious to all conspiracies being hatched in the sand.

It's 1978. I'm barely twenty (though it seems old to me), barely a year out of art school. Subways and winter are both as far away as can be as I lie here, watching my best friend sleep, dreaming his own not-so-sweet dreams of sniper fire and ambushes (lips contorting, limbs bucking and twitching, forehead bubbling with sweat).

Suddenly a sound like a swarm of swirling kitchen knives slashes its way toward us down the shore, an airborne Cuisinart headed our way, intent on slicing and dicing us both to smithereens. It gets to us and stops, hovering right over our heads, spewing up a tornado that makes it all too clear why beach sand is used for sandpaper. Dwaine, my friend, my bosom buddy, cinematic Telemachus to my Mentor, lurches awake, wide-eyed and scared stiff as a stop sign, screaming an otherworldly scream to wake the Greater Miami dead.

The Cosmic Cuisinart shoots a cool blue beam down into our eyes.

From the heavens an amplified voice commands:

Get down off the beach! Get down off the beach!

Dwaine keeps screaming, aluminum-shard pupils popping from his skull as I hold him, saying, "It's okay, it's okay…"

The whirling death machine churns on, scattering light, sand, and terror down the shore.

2

We were going to be famous, that was the plan. Dwaine would write and direct movies, and I'd star in them. Like Scorsese and DeNiro we'd ride waves of simulated gore to cinematic fortune and fame. We'd serve up bleeding slabs of grim realism to a public starving on a rabbit diet of Mindless Entertainment. To famished moviegoers we would dish out that rarest of delicacies, the Unvarnished Truth, and get famous doing it.

But first we needed to make some connections.

3

I was sitting at a corner table at the Rosinante Grill, bits of dead lettuce, raw hamburger meat and squashed French fries clinging to the crags of my work boots, scribbling away in my black book between dishwashing shifts when a guy who looked like a stubby bearded Klaus Kinsky strutted over and handed me his business card. "Who knows?" he said. "You could be the next William Goldman."

The card showed a bull in silhouette rearing up on its hind legs, its tail switching back like a whip.

Bull Duncan's office was a den of bulls. There were bull ashtrays, bull bookends, bull paintings, lithographs, sculptures and bull bas-reliefs, bull tapestries, inkwells and paperweights, bull lamps, bull coffee mugs, bull coasters...On a bull-pelted loveseat winged bulls stitched in gold soared across the faces of fat red velvet pillows. A curio cabinet with beveled glass doors shimmered with bulls haughty and heraldic, furious and ferocious, pompous and proud, some encrusted with jewels.

Wearing a red silk kimono embroidered with bulls, Mr. Duncan sat behind his African mahogany desk carved with bull heads, doing isometrics while talking on his speakerphone. Before he had looked like Klaus Kinsky, now he was Claude Rains in *Mr. Smith Goes to Washington*, or *Notorious*, with his sly calm smile and white brushed-back hair, waiting for the poison in the tea to do its job. As the voice in the speakerphone squawked he looked at me standing there and said, "Talk to me. What credentials have you got?" I said, "I could be the next William Goldman." And he hired me.

For two-fifty an hour I read submissions, typed rejection letters, answered the phone, made post office, copy shop and Chinese laundry runs. Bull Duncan meanwhile spent most of his time on his speakerphone trying to land exclusive deals. "Exclusive" was one of his favorite words, second only to "deal," a spice he sprinkled on every other sentence he spoke. *I'm going for the exclusive. This calls for an exclusive. I'm only interested in an exclusive.* Though only forty, he wore dentures that slipped so whenever he said "exclusive" it came out "*exsclushive.*"

Another assistant worked for Bull Duncan, a Columbia postdoctoral literature candidate named Esther Schmidt. Duncan called her his "eyes." She read everything that came into the agency "over the transom," which was agent talk, I learned, for unsolicited scripts.

One day I had Esther read the latest version of Dwaine's screenplay-in-progress, the one he had been working on since he got arrested in California, the one about the hockey player who becomes a priest and winds up working for the IRA, then somehow ends up blowing up the lounge of a Belfast inn that his father happens to own. He had written six drafts. With each new draft, Dwaine gave his screenplay a fresh title. All his titles came from the same poem, *The Second Coming*, by William Butler Yeats. The first title was *A Terrible Beauty*. After that it was *Things Fall Apart*, then *The Widening Gyre*. The draft I gave Esther was called *The Center Cannot Hold*. I didn't tell her my friend wrote it. I wanted Esther's honest opinion.

Along with a pile of other scripts Esther took Dwaine's home with her that weekend. She did most of her reading stretched out in bed, she told me, with a cup of hot ginger tea with honey. The thought provoked me. I imagined her naked, sipping tea and turning pages. She was a good-looking lady, about thirty, I guessed, with short legs and a blond butch hairdo. She reminded me of my middle school teacher, Mme. Grover, who wore linen suits and dark pantyhose that I constantly peeled down with my eyes while seated in the front row of Level I French. Esther's oversized prescription glasses gave her a shocked feminine fruit-fly look that enhanced her scholarly sexual appeal.

As soon as I saw her again on Monday I said to Esther, "So, what did you think?" forgetting that Dwaine's screenplay was but one of a dozen she had taken home with her, and that she might not have even gotten to it yet. She went down the whole long list of screenplays and novels she'd read, telling me all about every one of them. Esther spoke in a whisper, no matter where she was or what she was doing, as if the whole world were a library presided over by a severe, bun-headed, bifocaled crone.

I had to bend close to hear her, which I didn't at all mind doing, since it gave me a chance to peer down into the tawny shadow of her cleavage, her whispers half-drowned out by the growls of a garbage truck parked outdoors.

Finally, she got to Dwaine's screenplay, the plot of which she summed up in a few deft sentences.

"And?" I said. "Did you like it?"

"Well, no, I wouldn't say *liked*."

"What would you say?"

"I'd say he has talent." I waited but she didn't elaborate.

"But?" I said.

"But *boy*—!" She shook her small head, its smallness magnified by the big glasses. A thought occurred to her then. "You don't know this person, by any chance, do you, Nigel?"

"Know him? No, no. I'm just curious, that's all."

"Did you read it?"

"Huh? Oh, yeah. I sort of scanned it. You know, quickly."

"What did you think?"

"I thought it was … interesting."

"*Interesting* is an interesting word. In my experience it usually means lousy."

"I didn't mean that!"

"What did you mean, Nigel?"

"I meant—interesting."

"Well, one thing is for sure, whoever wrote this is *very, very* angry." She gave the script a sharp slap, like a mother slapping a misbehaved child. "This reads more like a vendetta than a screenplay." She described the writing as by turns maudlin, sentimental, and pornographically violent. "I would not want to have the author over to dinner, that's for sure."

"But—I mean, is it any *good?*"

"It has power," Esther said. "It definitely has power. But so does a mudslide. So did Joseph Stalin. So did Attila the Hun. I certainly would not recommend it. It has zero commercial potential."

4

Two days later Esther was fired. Duncan arrived at his office one morning to find a human turd, still reeking and glistening, deposited in his vestibule like a votive offering. It might have been left there by one of the many homeless people who roamed that part of the city at night, or it might have been a symbolic gesture on the part of one of Duncan's more disgruntled clients; very possibly it was both. When Esther arrived Duncan ordered her to clean it up. This she refused to do, and so Duncan fired her. I saw the whole thing. It made me sick. It was like watching a lion tackle a gazelle on one of those nature shows.

A few days later I learned that Bull Duncan was putting together an entourage to take with him to the first ever Greater Miami International Film Festival. The festival would be packed with Hollywood stars and their directors, he told me. There would be nightly screenings, receptions and cocktail parties. Martin Scorsese would be there, so would Bobby DeNiro, according to Bull Duncan, who needed an experienced cameraman to round out his coterie. I said I knew just the right person, a guy who could handhold a 16-millimeter as steady as a Steadicam, who had his own equipment and who would work for carfare.

Three weeks later Dwaine and I found ourselves packed into the tail section of a Douglas DC-8, among colicky infants and people whose concept of high fashion was a T-shirt that said "I'm with STUPID." In the luggage bin over our heads: a brand-new/used Bolex H16-RX-V sprung from a Third Avenue pawnshop. Flying ahead of us in First Class Bull Duncan sipped a complimentary mimosa and stretched his stubby legs. Before leaving he reminded us that we would not be paid anything, that we would have our sustentative needs provided for, that our compensation otherwise would consist *exclushively* of the privilege of serving Bull Duncan, King of Literary & Film Agents.

We didn't mind. We were going to Florida; we were going to be Famous.

Famous and Florida: like champagne and orange juice those two words blended, forming Mimosas of the Mind.

5

While Dwaine dozed in the window seat I struck up a conversation with a man across the aisle, a Culligan water softener salesman from Des Moines, Iowa. When the steward charged him for a second Bloody Mary, a voice from nowhere hissed: *Fucking jerk.* Moments later, when the lady in front of him reclined her seat deep into his ample lap, the same tinny voice from nowhere sneered, *Eat shit.*

Finally, the salesman revealed his secret: a palm-sized device bought in a Las Vegas novelty store. The Insultomatic had three buttons, a red button, a blue button, and a green button. Each button was color-coded to a different affront.

"Take it," said the salesman, pressing the device into my palm. "I'm sick of the damn thing. Besides, I got something even better." Reaching into his attaché case, he pulled out a Fart Detector.

We landed in Miami to learn that a hotel bed did not qualify as a sustentative need.

"Sleep on the beach," said Bull Duncan.

I pressed the red button.

6

Gulls wheel under a dome of powder blue sky. Dwaine hacks city smog and cigarette smoke from his lungs. Strands of seaweed cling to our tuxedoes. The morning sun invests everything with a lemony, prehistoric glow, the kind of light that I picture dinosaurs trouncing through. With its bare dunes and mausoleum-like hotels the landscape feels oddly menacing, like walking into a De Chirico or a Dali.

We march up a dune toward the Paradise. As we do a man in a sombrero and mirrored sunglasses finger-whistles us to a halt.

"How did you get off on the beach?" the sombrero wants to know.

"You mean how did we get *on* to the beach?" Dwaine, a stickler for grammar, corrects him.

"No," says the man, "I mean how did you *get off on* the beach?"

"We're still on the damn beach," Dwaine tells him. "We didn't get *off on* anything. We've been on the damn beach all goddamn night." Dwaine's mood could stand improvement.

"That is not what I am asking you," says the man in the sombrero, who looks exactly like Lee Marvin in *Hell in the Pacific*, and whose voice sounds like a machine for grinding rocks. "I'm asking how did you get *off* on the beach?"

"We swam," I submit, flicking bladder wrack off Dwaine's tuxedo shoulder. "We're fish; we just decided to evolve. See? No gills." I lift up my arms, point to where my gills should be.

The sombrero is not amused. He asks to see our identification. We flash our gold V.I.P. First Ever Greater Miami International Film Festival Press Corps Passes. Their gold laminate fails to dazzle. The sombrero man asks us what hotel we're registered with. I point over the sand dune to the Paradise. He asks me which room number. "Thirty-two-oh-eight," I say, thinking fast. But not fast enough. The Hotel Paradise is only twelve stories.

"This beach is private property," says the man in the sombrero. "If I see you two out here again I'll have you arrested. Good morning."

7

Good Morning, Good Morning, a suntan-oil slathered feminine voice greets us over the hotel P.A. system. *We hope you are enjoy-*

ing your stay at the Hotel Paradise. Today at eleven thirty we're offering bingo in the mezzanine lounge, with prizes complimentary to you. Sailing and waterskiing instructions are also available. See Hank at the cabana to reserve your time slot.

We ride the express elevator to Bull Duncan's penthouse suite, where we find our boss sitting up on a king-sized bed, talking into a phone, saying *Right, Sheila, right: I totally understand, but a deal's a deal, right? You said exclusive, didn't you? That is what you said, isn't it?* Seeing us walk in, he buries the receiver in the folds of his silk pajamas, gold bulls charging over a royal blue background. "Gimme a second," he looks up and says to us. "I'm dealing with an Grade-A Class-1 Premium Deluxe pain in the ass here." *What's that, Sheila? Sheila, listen, sweetheart, I can't do this right now. I've got people here, very important people—.* He mimes jerking off. *Right, Sheila. Right, pussycat. Love you, too. Bye-bye.* He hangs up. "God, what a festering cunt! So, guys, tell me, how was the beach? Beautiful, right?"

A fourth body crowds the suite, the international component of Bull Duncan's press entourage: a short skinny photojournalist from Milan named Nando, his Italian accent as thick as my mom's. He wears striped pajamas with socks and looks like Italy's not very good answer to Don Knotts. He looks up at us from the floor by Duncan's bed where he has apparently spent the night. As Duncan goes back to his phone, Nando shakes his head and mutters, "Dis is a shit."

8

From the start the festival is a fiasco. Most of the stars don't show up, including Scorsese and DeNiro. The few stars that do appear are of such dim wattage they barely outshine our patent leather tuxedo shoes, which after three nights of sleeping on the beach are beginning to look like Hush Puppies.

Each morning Duncan loads us into a rental van and sends us

off with his benediction ("You three pussies'll have the *Enquirer* eating out of your hands!") to the airport to greet and photograph the arriving stars. Each day the three of us stand there, at the arrivals gate, Nando with his Nikon, Dwaine with the Bolex H16-RX-V propped on his shoulder, me with boxes of additional film stock, all of us keeping our eyes peeled for Hollywood stars or directors, or anyone dressed all in black and wearing sunglasses indoors. Meanwhile the flights from Los Angeles keep coming with no one at all famous aboard any of them.

"Christ," says Dwaine, watching yet another stream of unfamous faces deplane. "Get a load of all these nobodies! Man, how can they *stand* it?"

"We're not exactly famous ourselves," I remind him as the latest plane's ultimate passenger, an oxygenated old man in a wheelchair, rolls by.

"We are so famous, babe," Dwaine corrects me. "It's just that no one knows about it yet."

"Dis is a shit," says Nando.

9

We have a choice. We can fly back to New York, back to gray slushy streets and subways as windy and cold as Vostok, Antarctica, back to our drafty fourth floor Queens tenement with kitchen tub/table. We can fly back to the known misery of our lives, or we can stay in Florida and mutiny.

We mutiny.

We swim laps in the Hotel Paradise pool, sun ourselves in the cabana, jog along the beach that is our bedroom, breakfast on mini Danishes and espressos at the Veranda Grill, make appointments with the kayaking, the windsurfing, the bossa nova, the flamenco dance instructors. We avail ourselves of the hotel's full complement of skilled, courteous staffers, courtesy of Bull

Duncan, whose signature Dwaine forges masterfully on an end-less series of room service chits. To where I start wondering if maybe we're going just a tad too far.

"Hell no," says Dwaine. "That dick-faced ex-boss of yours owes us at least this much for dragging our sorry asses down here. Besides, man," he waves a freshly manicured hand across the cabana hut, "look around you, what do you see?" I look around, seeing other hotel guests stretched out on long chairs with puffy yellow cushions, sunning themselves, older people mostly, their faces as red as lobsters under snowy retired heads. "People with money," says Dwaine. "Too much money. And where do you suppose they got all of that money? Huh? *Huh?* They *stole* it, naturally," he answers before I can wager a guess. "Or else they killed for it, or both. Compared to these people, man, you and me are nothing but pilot fish swimming in a tank full of killer sharks.

"Trust me," he adds, sipping a grenadine and soda, "it'll take more than a manicure and a few tango lessons to catch up with these fuckers. Ease up on the cuticles a bit, miss, do you mind?"

I've never seen Dwaine looking better, suntanned and healthy, not drinking or brooding at all. He seems transformed, his rough edges softened by repeated soakings in Miami Beach saltwater, his dark moods brightened by the Florida sun. Since we arrived here he hasn't lit a single Newport, or swallowed a drop of booze. Those metal shards that normally swim around in his eyes? They look more like silver than aluminum now. I would even go as far as to say that they sparkle.

Yes, they sparkle, they really do.

The one surviving relic of the old Dwaine are his scream-ing nightmares, aided and abetted by the Miami Beach Shore Patrol, with it blinding blue tungsten beam and loudspeaker imperative:

Get down off the beach! Get down off the beach!

"It's okay, it's okay, it's okay…"

10

At pre-screening cocktail parties we gorge ourselves on jumbo shrimp dunked in silver tureens of spicy red cocktail sauce, and crackers or melba toast straining under mounds of *fois gras*, gray beluga caviar, and cheeses runny, stinky and crumbly, all washed down with ash-dry, nose-tickling champagne (me) or pale ginger-ale (Dwaine). Bellies stuffed, whistles whetted, gold V.I.P. passes pinned to tuxedo lapels, we step into the theater and head straight for the roped-off seats, where we sit and wait for the *hoi polloi* to mistake us for stars. They hand us their festival programs, ask for our autographs. We sign away, basking in fame's transitory glow.

But Dwaine isn't satisfied with such minor ruses. He starts naming pictures, elucidating their plots. "Our latest feature is called *Don't Lean on Me*," he tells a pair of starry-eyed snowbirds. "It's a tragicomedy about these two crippled con artists who escape from Sing-Sing. See, they each have one leg that's missing. Sam's missing his right leg, and Sid's missing his left leg, but they've got only one crutch between them, which they have to share, see, since they lost one during the escape, but still they somehow manage to get away with it because it's so hard for anyone to believe. See, the whole premise of the movie has to do with what's called the willing suspension of disbelief, and with how these two con artists have got it figured out that the more unbelievable a thing is the more people are likely to suspend their beliefs to *believe* it."

"Where can we see it?" one of the snowbirds wants to know.

"So far it's been released only in a few select theaters in the Republic of Tuva," Dwaine answers over his shoulder as we toss aside paper signs saying RESERVED and make ourselves comfortable. "But it should be opening in local theaters any—"

A bow-tied old coot of an usher points his flashlight at our un-famous faces. "Sorry, boys, but those are reserved seats. You'll have to move."

11

On offer that evening is *Night Vision*, an independent feature about two Vietnam veterans living on the fringes of Hoboken and insanity. In the pivotal scene Gus, one of the two vets, licks an ice cream cone while the other, Rufus, tortures and kills a social worker. Having disposed of her body in a garbage dumpster they sit side by side on their crumbling stoop, their faces as droopy as the pizza slices they're eating. After a few dreary beats Rufus turns to Gus and says, "What's eating you?" "I don't know," Gus replies. *"I just feel empty."* As the film plays on more and more people rise from their seats and leave. "Night *soil* is more like it," one disgruntled viewer mutters on his way to the exit.

By the time the credits roll only a handful remain in their seats. Dwaine stands up and shouts, *"Bravo! Bravissimo!"* I stand too, but only because Dwaine has nudged me up with his elbow, saying, "Don't you know a goddamn masterpiece when you see one?" (When it comes to movies I know better than to argue with Dwaine.)

As we leave the hotel bound for another night of sandy dreams, Dwaine falls into a reverent silence. I've seen him fall mute like that only twice before, after *Dog Day Afternoon* and *One Flew Over the Cuckoo's Nest*, movies that left Dwaine bleeding inside, with silence the next best thing to a tourniquet.

The surf roars. The breeze spits up cottony flecks of foam.

Dwaine grabs my hand and holds it. He does it nonchalantly, the way you might pick up a bright shell from the beach. I don't say a thing or react in any way, I'm too surprised to react. After a while it seems perfectly natural, him holding my hand that way, like we've been holding hands forever, since we were five years old, like we were born to hold hands, Dwaine and I.

We walk a quarter mile or so and then Dwaine stops and takes his clothes off, handing me cufflinks, studs, bow tie and suspenders, turning me into his valet there on the beach. He drops the rest and runs, plunging like a fullback into the surf, tackling waves, paddling beyond them toward the horizon, adding his mystery to the other mysterious blue shapes floating way out there.

12

Afterwards, as we lie dozing, Dwaine talks in whispers that blend with surf about *Night Vision* and why he likes it so much, how it combines Scorsese's street poetry with Peckinpaw's nihilism, Schlesinger's satire, Terrence Malick's starkness, and Truffaut's nursery school charm. As his voice fades into snores I ask myself: why do I like him so much? Is it that brooding whale of a forehead? Is it those Gary Cooper heat-seeking missile eyes? Is it the Technicolor nightmares that haunt his sleep, the dark terrors saturating his black Irish blood?

Unable to sleep, I wander off into the Miami night and find myself downtown, where deco buildings burrow under the same moonlight that winks off car hoods. Except for the all-night porno theater everything's shut down. The ticket clerk, the spitting image of the lady in the Palmolive dishwashing liquid commercials, refuses me admittance because a) I have no I.D. on me and b) I'm wearing my bathing suit. "But I'm twenty years old!" I swear to her. "Here, look at my wrinkles!" I insist, pressing my forehead to the Plexiglas, but this cuts no mustard with Madge. "I wish I could oblige you, dear, but I'd get my ass fired."

Madge directs me to an all-night coffee shop, one of those stainless steel marvels overflowing with grease and light. I've got my black book with me and sit staring through my reflection in the dark glass, wondering: will Dwaine and I ever really be famous? Are these but the inauspiciously dim early days of a dazzlingly bright future?

13

We're sunbathing in the cabana the next morning when Bull Duncan charges up to us, waving a fistful of forged room service chits.

"You snakes in the grass! I'll have your balls boiled!"

"Excuse me." Dwaine waves him away. "But you're blocking our rays."

Duncan catalogues a series of bodily threats, the majority of which involve dismemberment by hired professionals, all of which Dwaine shakes off like dew from the bull's beard. Emboldened by his effrontery, I rummage in my beach bag, where—after some deliberation—I press the Insultomatic's blue button. Wise to me this time, Bull Duncan pulls my hand from the bag, exposing the device, which he snatches from my grip.

"Nice," he says, dropping it to the cabana deck where he grinds it to smithereens with the heel of a white Bally. Then he storms off, only to return moments later with a bevy of hotel security personnel, including Mr. Sombrero. We're about to get the heave-ho when a voice blending Popeye and Cary Grant intervenes.

"One moment. These gentlemen are with me," says a stranger, handing Mr. Sombrero a crisp folded twenty.

Mr. Sombrero in turn presents our savior with the balance due on Bull Duncan's hotel tab, advancing a figure in excess of two hundred dollars. "Charge it to my room," says the stranger, showing his festival pass. "It's the least these bastards can do for dragging me down here."

Duncan and the security guards head back to their silos.

The stranger looks familiar. Then I realize: he's the star/
writer/director/producer of *Night Vision*, the guy who played
Gus. In real life he looks taller, gaunter, paler and balder than
on the screen. Even under the influence of the Miami sun his
pale features look like a mortician has had something to do with
them. He wears a Claddagh ring just like Dwaine's, but gold.
"Flynn," he introduces himself in the backhanded manner of
Mr. Bond. "Archibald Flynn. And what brings you to this sunny
cemetery?"

"We're filmmakers," I say.

"So you've entered a film in this farce of a festival?"

"Our movie's not made yet," Dwaine explains.

"It's a work in progress."

"We're shadows flickering across a screen."

"We came with Bull Duncan."

"We were part of his international press entourage."

"Right, and I'm a bloody secret agent."

Flynn reaches into his beach bag, pulls out a frazzled toupee
and slaps it on his head. "Have you two had lunch yet?"

We shake our heads.

"My treat. It's not every day I get a standing ovation."

14

From the lobby of the Fontainebleau, amid bellhops in fir-
ing-squad regalia and a swinging '60s decor of woggles, boo-
merangs and beanpoles, the maitre d' escorts us to our table in
the Côte d'Azur lounge. Soon as we're seated the sommelier
(Clifton Web in *Mr. Belvedere Blows His Whistle*) takes our drink
orders. When Dwaine asks for water he takes offense. "*Water?*"
The sommelier gives him a frown and gestures with his towel-
draped arm toward the ubiquitous ocean view. "*Monsieur*, there
is water everywhere, why would anyone want to drink it?"

"Water," Dwaine insists.

"It will grow fish in your belly! *It is for those who have sinned!*"

"I've sinned. Now bring me some goddamn water."

"Make it your best bottle," says Flynn.

Over crabs parysis, trout amandine and veal cordon bleu Flynn fills us in on his theatrical past, explaining how he first fell in love with American movies via Alan Ladd in *Shane*. "I wanted to be just like Alan Ladd, but taller," he tells us, then goes on to say how he had achieved half of his wish, sprouting to six-foot-four by his eighteenth birthday, when a wealthy octogenarian he'd been tending in a Galway nursing home went to her glory, leaving him enough cash to go to America and pursue the other half. "I became a United States citizen just in time to receive greetings from Uncle Sam."

Unlike Dwaine, however, Flynn got no closer to Vietnam than Fort Dix, New Jersey, where according to him he contracted alopecia areata from a recycled army helmet ("My war wound," he tells us, tapping his toupee). But Flynn's *real* war would be fought later in Hollywood, a war against the forces of stereotyping that saw him cast in dozens of bad-guy bit roles, his handsome Irish face ending up, more often than not, on the cutting room floor. Thirty-three years old ("like Jesus"), two-thirds bald and totally typecast, he bought a bottle of Cutty Sark and carried it up into the Hollywood hills, intent on jumping off the fabled sign.

"Which letter?" Dwaine asks.

"What difference does it make?"

"Oh, it makes a difference."

"I don't know. H for Hell, I suppose."

"Like Penny Entwistle!" I note with enthusiasm.

"So—then what happened?"

"I had a better idea." Flynn sips water, wipes his thin Irish lips. "Flynn, you old fool, I said to myself, why not make your own blasted film? And that's what I've done, gentlemen. All I need now is a bloody distribution deal, for which I must re-enter the belly of the beast."

"Back to Hollywood, you mean?"

"That's right. Back to Hollywood. Back to hell."

"When will you go?" I ask.

"Soon as I get out of *this* particular hell."

"I know two guys who would be glad to go with you," says Dwaine with a kick to me under the table.

"You do?" says Flynn.

"Two really good guys," I say.

"We could provide moral support," says Dwaine.

"Could you?" says Flynn.

"We could," I say.

"Be careful what you wish for," Flynn says. "You especially." He prods Dwaine's chest with a gaunt, stiff finger. "You think Vietnam was bad, do you? Don't look so surprised. It's obvious that you were there; I've seen that look too many times not to know it. Well trust me, friend, till you've done battle with the Victor Charlies of Sunset Boulevard, you don't know the *meaning* of war. Ambushes? Booby traps? Friendly fire? Hollywood's got 'em all *and* Walt Disney, that antichrist, him and his squeaky, verminous idol! People say this country is desolate. They're right: it's as desolate as a petrol station at night. But where desolation meets decadence—*that's* Hollywood.

"Make no mistake, gentlemen:

"Hollywood is a cursing, merciless tyranny!"

15

Dissolve to us barreling down I-95 in a stretch limo, blue sky above, blue water below, everything between a variation on a theme of pink. That's me behind the wheel, wearing a chauffeur's cap, while the chauffeur, Dominic, rides in back with the others, all of them laughing over some joke about the Pope driving a limousine. But they're also laughing because they think it's funny, me up here driving, and I guess it is, considering I don't even have a driver's license.

We hop from club to club, all with names like *Fifth Avenue, Central Park, California*... "Is it just me," Dwaine observes, "or do any of you get the feeling that the locals would rather be somewhere else?"

At a club called Gracie Mansion we run into Bull Duncan, burning us looks as we practice our bossa nova steps on two local girls named April and June ("How's that for a couple of *dates?*"—Dwaine). The girls are in a celebratory mood. They've just been hired as Playboy bunnies at the Miami Mansion. They tell us all about training week, about memorizing their liquor categories, learning bumper pool and the Bunny Dip and how to apply eyelashes and carry service trays in three-inch stiletto heels, knowledge likely to serve them well for decades. As fascinated as I am by their Playboy pedigrees (will they one day soon be airbrushed, folded and stapled?), I'm more intent on watching Dwaine flirt with them. I've never seen Dwaine flirt before; I've rarely seen him interact with the opposite sex, though he seems to be doing quite well at it, all bright smiles and devastating dimples. While I twirl June he cuts the rug with April, doing a salsa. The club is hot. Under the shifting lights June's cheeks glow with sweat. Unlike my three feet which never know what they're supposed to do, Dwaine's patent leather tuxedo shoes slide softly across the dance floor like shuffleboard disks. The music switches from whatever to disco as Nando, there with Bull Duncan, joins us on the dance floor, a piping brunette having tapped him for a tango.

"I can no stay long," he shouts at us over his partner's shoulder and the loud music. "Meester Duncan, *dat stronzo,* he want me to go to airport an photograph Mizz Brooke Shield."

"*Brooke* Shields?" says June.

"*The* Brooke Shields?" says April.

"Oh please please please please take us with you," says June.

"I'll give you all a ride if you do," says April.

"She's got a Porsche," says June.

"We've never been around any real movie stars," says April.

"Unless you count Dom Deluise," says June.

"Which we don't," both of them say.

16

We squeeze into the back of April's vintage Porsche, equipped with a Playboy metal bottle opener and tube radio. Nando rides on June's lap. Miami rolls by in waves of stucco and neon. By the time we get to the airport (having stopped on the way to retrieve the Bolex H16-RX-V from the Paradise safe) dawn glows as pink as the inside of a conch shell.

Paparazzi swarm the arrivals terminal. We jam our way through the outer banks of media parasites to run headlong into Bull Duncan, who asks us what the hell we're doing there.

"What you hired us for," says Dwaine, holding the Bolex high.

"And what's with the hookers?" Duncan points to our dates.

"They're not hookers," I note. "They're Playboy bunnies."

Brooke Shields arrives, flanked by her mother, her director, and a trio of double-breasted bodyguards. She wears a flamingo-feathered gown and smiles for the cameras, her teeth slamming back the lights of several dozen flash units. With the Bolex propped on his shoulder Dwaine pushes his way toward her and starts filming. Nando, eager to prove to the world that he's more than just Bull Duncan's sad Milanese flunky, rides my shoulders piggyback. He flashes away joyously, rapturously, orgasmically…until his Nikon jams.

"*Porca miseria!*" he says, his fingers squirming like worms as they try to unjam it. Dwaine meanwhile has vaulted over the security cordon to film within inches of the pert starlet's eyes. He keeps filming as Brooke Shield's bodyguards hustle her into a waiting Lincoln.

Dwaine tosses Bull Duncan the exposed reel.

"Don't say I never gave you anything."

17

I wake up in a cubist painting of body parts, arms, legs, bellies, all batter-dipped and basted with beach sand. Who's foot is that? Who's arm? Whose ass? I inventory my surroundings. No hotels or dunes in sight, no landmarks at all other than a concrete structure that looks for all the tea in China like the pillbox in *The Guns of Navarone*. Miami Beach is gone, washed away by a tidal wave. Or something.

Somewhere in this tangle of bodies Dwaine lies with me. I harbor distinct memories of sexual grunts and sighs blending with surf sounds. Dwaine's arm is around April's neck. A smile curves his lips. Seeing him smile I smile, too.

Dwaine snores, twitches, coughs. The surf makes a hushed sound like the murmurings of a movie audience. A smell of ozone hangs in the sea breeze. I feel us both in Vietnam, the beach our foxhole, flashes of distant heat lightning mortar fire, the enemy everywhere and nowhere, lurking in ambush, silent, cunning, deadly.

The Shore Patrol helicopter churns its way toward us down the shore. I brace for the bright tungsten beam, the sandstorm, the loudspeaker imperative, Dwaine's scream. Helicopters and blood: they're the stuff of Dwaine's dreams.

The helicopter flies right past us. It doesn't stop.

18

Back at the Paradise a thundershower erupts. Ominous clouds darken hotel facades. Raindrops pock dunes, bounce off cabana chair cushions. After the storm has blown out to sea a double

rainbow forms, arching over the horizon. "Did you know that
Van Gogh dreamed in color?" Dwaine says as we watch it from
the cabana. "It's true," he says. "To Vincent colors were a form
of prayer. Red and green for rage, blue for solitude, yellow for
madness and despair. The man painted himself into a state of
grace."

We've made up our minds: tomorrow morning we're flying
back home. There's nothing left for us down here in Florida,
nothing but cocktails, melanomas, and death.

"Please," says Nando. "No leave me here wid dat *stronzo*."

"Come with us," says Dwaine.

"Yeah. You can be our still photographer."

But Nando can't leave. Duncan holds his ticket hostage.

"Please," he pleads with us. "I no want to die in Florida.
Who will bring me flower if I die?"

Dwaine tells him not to worry.

He has a plan.

19

Swipe-cut to all of us making our way up a floodlit pier to the
Wet Dream, a seventy-eight foot twin-diesel-powered floating
dildo, her fiberglass hull twinkling with waterborne moonlight.
Reggae music braids dreadlocks into the marijuana-scented
dusk.

Halfway up the dock a security guard checks Archie's credentials. Shoulder to shoulder (Kirk Douglas, Burt Lancaster
and those other two guys in *Gunfight at the O.K. Corral*) we
march toward the gangplank.

Medium shot: the party in full swing. Men in breezy linen
blazers worn over pressed and laundered T-shirts, women in
skimpy cocktail dresses with shoelace straps. Close-ups of cigarette ashes being flicked into canapé and oyster shells. Quick-
cuts of Archie working the tennis set on the foredeck, Nando

frolicking with a pair of Cosmo-cover redheads on the poop deck, April, June and I bending over the starboard bow to watch a pod of dolphins leap by. Dwaine nowhere to be seen. All the while Bull Duncan casts us withering glances from amidships, Nando's ticket held hostage in his tuxedo pocket.

At midnight, precisely on cue, Nando wades into Duncan, demanding his airline ticket, which Duncan naturally refuses to surrender, whereupon Nando launches into a feverish tenor *recitativo* in Milanese dialect, of which Duncan understands not a jot. Which is where I come in.

"He says," I translate, "give me my airline ticket, or else."

"Or else what?" says Duncan.

"*This!*" Dwaine swoops down from the quarterdeck, grabs Duncan around the waist. Archie takes one leg, I take the other, and together we heave the son of a bitch overboard. But not before rescuing Nando's ticket from his pocket.

Cross-fade to Don Knotts, Cary Grant, Kirk Douglas and Burt Lancaster hightailing it down the long floodlit pier. Don Knotts brings up the rear, Nikon held high over his head, yelling: "I got *peecture!* I got *peecture!*"

V

The Pure
Truth
(Road Movie)

GREETINGS FROM
THE HOTEL MONTECIDO
Hotel of the Stars

The postcard shows a deco white hotel perched on a Hollywood hillside, photographed in sepia. A '36 Duesenberg Boattail Speedster with Gary Cooper—or someone who looks an awful lot like Coop—at the wheel, breezes up to the hotel's portholed doors, which are flanked by braided doormen. On the flip side the water-blurred message says: *Four days of cursing, merciless rain have drowned this Irish filmmaker's dreams. Offer of support accepted if still standing. Will provide means.*

Signed: Archibald Flynn.

Under the signature are two phone numbers, Flynn's hotel room in Hollywood, and that of a man in New Jersey with a drive-a-way car.

Our pockets stuffed with laundry quarters, Dwaine and I run through banks of dirty snow to the corner pay phone, where Archibald's flu-congested Irish brogue comes to us all the way from Hollywood. He says if he sells his movie (Dwaine tells me with the phone buried in his pea coat) he'll make us part of his new production team.

"And if he doesn't sell it?" I say. "How will we get home?"

Archibald's tinny telephone voice answers: "Tell your fine fickle friend to stiffen his backbone, come out with his dreams, and take his chances."

2

The next day at the No Name Café, the diner on 57th Street where I serve bland meals to a parade of geriatrics who slide, shuffle, wheel and otherwise convey themselves in from the retirement hotel next door, I can't seem to concentrate, my mind is so taken up with thoughts of Hollywood. *Warner Brothers, MGM, Paramount, Columbia, Twentieth Century Fox...* The famous names spin around in my head like a toy Lionel train around a Christmas tree. I screw up everyone's dinner orders, serve Father Lester Gringold his tea with milk instead of lemon, neglect to keep Miss Tyson's coffee cup refilled. The coffee shop's mirror-tiled walls compound and disseminate my copious errors. When I forget to rinse the stainless steel frappé container after serving Beverly the Weight Watcher her strawberry malted, the night manager, a hare-lipped Ozone Park lug with a passion for GTO transmission swaps, snarls, "You got your brains in your underwear DePoli, or *what?*" But it's no use. I can't get my act together. When I spew Redi-Whip all over Beverly's dietetic lime Jell-O, that's it, I'm history.

I find Dwaine soaking in our tub, doing his Moby Dick impersonation, surfacing, spouting, submerging.

"So?" I say when he surfaces. "Do we phone the guy in New Jersey, or what?"

"We'll be Archibald's slaves," Dwaine warns. "His palace eunuchs, sampling his food and powdering his concubines."

He points a dripping finger at the Pertinent Movie Quote Wall:

Supply List for Tinseltown Express
- Sunglasses
- Cigarettes
- Umbrellas
- Machete

- Grapefruit
  (pink Florida seedless)
- Dreams
- Chances

3

We roll across Pennsylvania, the drive-a-way convertible Bonneville's odometer having barely broken a hundred, its trunk filled with Indian River Isle of Merritt ruby red jumbo grapefruit, two hundred dollars in drive-a-way funds tucked into the glove compartment. Though it's mid-February we ride with the top down, warmed by our twin surplus pea coats and mutual enthusiasm, as shiny with optimism as the Bonneville's four hubcaps. The number in New Jersey looked like Wallace Beery and called where he lived *Sea*kawkus, as if to emphasize that it was by the sea, by the sea, by the beautiful sea, when in fact it was by the Holland Tunnel. We have three days to deliver the car to his daughter, a UCLA social sciences undergraduate living in Marina del Rey.

We're both wearing sunglasses. Dwaine wears mirrored aviators; I wear a pair of cheap Wayfarer knock-offs. Halfway across the state line into Ohio my right lens falls out.

Zooming toward Akron I peel Dwaine a grapefruit. He has boned up on the health-giving properties of grapefruit, how they increase circulation, tighten the skin, reduce fever, quench thirst, kill germs, promote salivary and other gastric functions, relieve constipation, reduce fatigue, prevent infectious diseases (like dysentery, typhus and enteritis) and also cure influenza, malaria, and scurvy.

I've never been west of the Water Gap. The whole western half of the United States of America is mythic to me, a land of buffaloes roaming and Conestoga wagons drawn into tight circles, a place to get ambushed and scalped. I long for spacious skies, amber waves of grain, fruited plains, and buttes, whatever they are.

We see America at eighty miles an hour, our vision hindered by the uncouth rear-ends of tractor trailer trucks (How's My Driving? Dial 1-800-EAT-SHIT), flying past land formations older than the dinosaurs. I picture our car as it might appear from space, a silver flea traversing the nation. May this highway never end; may it unwind forever. Meanwhile Dwaine drives with an elbow out the window and one hand on the steering wheel, looking totally unimpressed by the passing scenery, like he drives across the country for milk every morning.

4

While riding we swap movie quotes, with Dwaine's knowledge of contemporary films ("I'll give you a dollar if you eat this collie"—Martin Sheen, *Badlands*) trumping mine, while I'm more than a match for him when it comes to the classics ("You can't write good with handcuffs!"—Nick Adams to Andy Griffith in *No Time for Sergeants*).

"Man," he says (after I stump him with "They're makin' me run"—Gary Cooper, *High Noon*), "how can you stand to sit through all those boring old black-and-white movies?"

"Since when don't you love black-and-white movies?"

"Boring," says Dwaine.

"*High Noon*, boring? It's one of the greatest movies ever!"

"It's like watching grass grow without the benefit of color."

"You're nuts."

"Okay, so I'm nuts."

"Black-and-white has it over color ten ways from Sunday. Why do you think Kazan shot *On the Waterfront* in black-and-white? And *Streetcar*—and *Viva Zapata!*—and *A Face in the Crowd?*"

"Because he was too cheap to use color."

"Because it's more realistic! Because it's *grittier!* Same with Frankenheimer. *The Train, Seven Days in May, Bird Man of*

Alcatraz."

"*Bonnie & Clyde, The Godfather, Badlands*—those are gritty movies."

"Black and white is the color of drama. Not only is it more psychologically realistic, it's more *morally* realistic! White for good, black for evil. And every shade of gray. Black and white are the soul's true colors!"

"Horseshit," Dwaine says.

"Know what your problem is?"

"No, babe, what is my problem?"

"Your problem is you have no appreciation of the classics."

"Wrong. My problem is that you don't know what a classic is. *Badlands* is a classic, *Zabriskie Point* is a classic. *Blow Up*'s a classic. *High Noon* isn't a classic, it's a relic. It's the difference between a '62 Corvette and a ... a ... a ... "

"A Stanley Steamer."

"A Stanley Steamer. Exactly. Thank you."

"But it's not!"

"A Stanley Steamer: chugga chugga chugga chugga ... "

In spite of my biases and thanks to a keen memory I manage to guess where most of the lines Dwaine tosses my way come from, which infuriates him, until halfway through Ohio, when he stumps me with, "Everything is worth precisely as much as a belch, the difference being that a belch is more satisfying."

"Gene Hackman," I guess. *"The Conversation."*

Dwaine makes a buzzer sound.

"Brando? *Night of the Following Day?"*

More error noises.

"I'll give you a clue: it's a *classic* and it's in *black-and-white*."

"I don't know," I say.

"You don't know?"

"No, I have no idea. What's it from?"

"You don't fucking *know?"*

"Tell me, dickweed!"

"The Seventh Seal."

"Never saw it."

"*Seventh Seal?* Max Von Sydow playing chess with Death? You never *saw it?* And you call yourself a moviegoer? Hah!"

It takes Dwaine fifty miles to get over the fact that I've never seen *The Seventh Seal.* The whole way he doesn't say a word to me, he just stares through the bug-spattered windshield, shaking his head, smiling, sniffing and sighing ironically. He does this all the way to the Indiana border, where his fury at the state trooper who pulls him over for doing eighty replaces his disgust for me.

5

I've brought another item along for the ride, one of Dwaine's black books. For the last few weeks I've been secretly reading them, boning up on my best friend's background. One night while he went out for one of his Mystery Walks I looked in his room and saw one of the books lying there, spread open on his serape covered bed like a lover waiting for sex. I went in, picked it up and started reading. It was a bad thing to do, I know, but like Peter Lorre in *M* I couldn't help myself. Besides, the way he left the notebook lying there like that made me think he *wanted* it read, that he was giving me tacit permission to do so.

At first I told myself I'd read just one sentence, that's all. Then I read a whole paragraph, then another, then a page. Soon I was gulping down pages, bent over Dwaine's notebook like a graduate student with a candle burning and a mug of tea. The notebooks held a jumble of storyboards, notes and scenes for screenplays-in-progress, newspaper clippings, pen sketches and journal entries, most of the latter scrawled in jagged, hard-to-read handwriting, much of it barely intelligible, to wit:

March (on) 2ⁿᵈ, 1978. Never mind the date gap discrepancy (that will be explained later on down). This entry is declaratory[sic] in gender as I implode, this will not become the secret journal, written on

*the run and in the rain away from home, away from the paid space,
the co-inhabited space, the now in the process of becoming space, the
not yet shyed [sic] from space due to uncofortability [sic] and conflict of
interest, style, dress, purpose, aim, taste of environment for art space,
the 'who is chic and who isn't' question space, not yet and it won't,
can't, caint [sic], won't, because if it does, it will become a battlefield of
confestation[sic], and I won't let it be so.*

Like those mirrored disco balls suspended from dance hall
ceilings, Dwaine's notebooks whirled flashes of light more dazzling than illuminating. Still, I hoped that by reading enough of
them the individually puzzling entries would add up to something coherent, and reading them might help me gain some understanding of Dwaine's past, especially of what happened to
him in Vietnam.

Night after night with him gone off as usual I sat on Dwaine's
bed and read, piecing together the bones of his past like a pa-
leontologist piecing together a pterodactyl. And I learned a few
things. I learned, for instance, that he left the Army rather suddenly and under less-than-ideal circumstances, that he spent
time in an Okinawa brig before being packed into a transport
plane bound for Oakland, where he spent a night shivering on a
beach, gripping his balls to keep his fingers from freezing. Such
were the only direct references to the war, save for a yellowed
newspaper clipping from the *Daily News:*

Veteran Dies at War Memorial

TAMPA, Fla., Oct. 14 (AP)—Wearing a military jacket and clutching divorce papers, a veteran of Vietnam committed suicide Tuesday
at the foot of the Vietnam War Memorial in
Tampa. A police spokesman, Henry Crow,
said the 39-year-old veteran, John Desmond
Hurly, was found with a pistol in his lap after
shooting himself in the head as he sat on the
grass beneath a flagpole.

Under the clipping Dwaine wrote, "Just what is it, exactly, about the word 'mercy' that God can't understand?"

6

With Dwaine behind the wheel and the United States rolling by under and around me, I stretch out in the back seat, feigning sleep, turning pages. This book, taken from the aluminum trunk (the key to which I found in an orphaned sweat sock) finds Dwaine in the Peace Corps, stationed at a former R&R resort at Pattaya Beach, on the Gulf of Siam. This was where he met the pirates, the ones who gave him the machete. They lived on a junk moored in the harbor. In exchange for practicing their English on him the pirates taught Dwaine how to hand-roll the local sinsemilla and walk barefoot on the junk's sail booms.

Rising from the tropical mists a thousand yards from Dwaine's hut was a jungle-clad hill nicknamed Monkey Mountain. At dusk the monkeys would come down to the beach to scavenge for food. One monkey became Dwaine's pet. Dwaine named him Father Pike, after the man who tried to make a priest out of him, and kept him in his hut. This didn't sit well with Frank Sitwell, Dwaine's Peace Corps supervisor, whose name fit him to a 'T', since he did nothing all day but sit at his desk throwing darts at a board. He told Dwaine "get rid of the monkey" or it would be "disposed of."

Dwaine's Peace Corps duties consisted of handing out malaria pills and mosquito netting and lecturing locals on the evils of stagnant water. But Dwaine found the Corps highly disorganized, and little in the way of malaria control was achieved. When Dwaine complained to Sitwell, his supervisor suggested that he was suffering from exhaustion, that he should take a vacation. When Dwaine insisted that he felt fine the suggestion morphed into a standing order. "Come back when you're feeling better," said Sitwell.

Before leaving Dwaine asked his pirate friends to board Father Pike, which they gladly did.

And so where did I vacate to? Why, Udorn, where else. The scene of my former captivity. Except for a few rusting Quonset huts the airbase was gone, vanished, its tarmac broken and overgrown. It was like those closing scenes in Papillon, *showing the ruins of the prison buildings at Devil's Island, decayed and overgrown, with Steve McQueen's voiceover sneering, "I'm still here, you bastards!" I pitched a tent on the former grounds of the 498th, my old unit. And though I hadn't packed any weed and was stone sober, still, I dreamed more dreams than ever before in one night while getting bitten by the world's largest mosquitoes ...*

Two weeks later, when Dwaine returned to Pataya Beach, as he was driving up to the harborside in his Jeep, he noticed a thick plume of smoke rising from it. Closer, he saw the pirate's junk half sunk and burning. He jumped out and ran shouting toward it, only to be stopped by a line of Thai police armed with wooden batons. *("Okay, okay, take it easy, you fascist fucks!")* As they held him back Dwaine heard cries mixed with the pops and squeals of burning timber. He stood there feeling helpless, watching until all that was left of the junk were a few floating chunks of charred timber and swirling clouds of acrid smoke.

The next day Dwaine marched into Sitwell's office and tendered his resignation, which Sitwell gladly accepted. In exchange Dwaine was offered a one-way ticket to any destination of his choice.

"What's your pleasure, Fitzgibbon?" said Sitwell. "And don't take all day deciding, I've got other matters to attend to here."

Dwaine plucked a dart from Sitwell's dartboard, aimed it at a map on the wall over his desk, and threw it.

It landed in Belfast, Ireland.

7

East of Indianapolis Dwaine turns off the interstate and heads north on Route 31. I ask where we're going. "Oz," he says.

"We're following the Yellow Brick Road."

Soon we're hiking through a muddy plowed field. It's late in the afternoon, the sun burnishing everything, including the dome of the University of Notre Dame, copper. As we head toward the dome Dwaine tells me how Father Pike—not the monkey, the man—picked him up hitchhiking after his visit with Brother Jack. At the end of their ride, following a lengthy discussion of war, politics, religion, and art, Pike had Dwaine convinced that he might be priestly material, and encouraged him to apply to the seminary at Notre Dame.

"Which," said Dwaine, "I ultimately did."

Dwaine took to his theological studies well (he explains this as his boots and my sneakers make obscene farting sounds in the mud). "I plowed through Aquinas and Saint Augustine and made a fetish of Lao Tzu. I loved the whole idea of being a priest, of saving people's souls instead of their blown-up bodies." It's the first clue he's given me to his war duties. Saving blown-up bodies. So he *was* a medic. "Trouble was," Dwaine admits as we stand there, watching the dome's colors shift from brilliant copper to molten red, "there was this little requirement called celibacy that I was not terribly good at, in fact I confess that I failed at it miserably. That movie we made about the seminarian being found in his dorm with a townie girl? That was me, of course, only I didn't castrate the son of a bitch who ratted on me, though I should have. The next day I go into Father Pike's office. The look on his face, like I'd totally betrayed him. I had a knack for betraying fathers. Anyway so much for my becoming a priest. "

He bends down, picks up a handful of soil and holds it under my nose. By the light of the setting sun I see little metallic flakes sparkling in it.

"Bits of gold leaf blown off the dome by the prairie winds," Dwaine explains. "You could say this is very rich soil."

He lights a cigarette and smokes, blowing rings that float away like haloes in search of angels.

"Are you sorry about not becoming a priest?"

"Oh, I don't know. Like I said, the celibacy thing, that was a real sticking point. Besides, there's other ways of ministering. You know the old saying, 'Preach the gospel at all times, if necessary use words'? That's why movies are so great. You can preach without preaching. You can show people the light without telling them what to believe or how they should think or act or what they should do with their money or their dicks. Although I still hold a place in my heart for the Church. It's a beautiful thing. As a kid I fell in love with the stained glass windows, with the light coming through all those colors. Now I make movies, or anyway I plan to make them. And like I think I said before, movies are just another kind of stained glass window, only the windows keep changing: they tell a much more complicated story."

We stand there until the sun finishes setting, then head back to the Bonneville, the orange light of Dwaine's cigarette tip the brightest on earth.

8

West of Effingham we stop at a truck stop where the waitress calls us "honey" and "doll face" and wears a pencil tucked behind her right ear. As we lunch on twin burgers and milkshakes (Dwaine's vanilla, mine chocolate) from a pocket of his pea coat he withdraws a tattered, tea-stained document. "It's all here, babe—in black and white," he says, tapping it with a nicotine-stained finger. In fact the document is written in blue ballpoint on yellow legal pad paper.

"What is that?" I ask.

"My contract with Dexter Groon. Fucker owes me three grand."

"How come you never told me this before?"

"Because it's too *embarrassing*, that's why. The guy screwed me. And it gets even worse." Dwaine takes out his latest black book, opens it to another newspaper clipping, this one also from the *Daily News:* a list of Academy Award winners for 1977. Bottoming the list: *Alphabet City*, Best Short Animated Feature, Dexter Groon, Writer/Producer/Director.

"When we get to Hollywood, soon as we do, it's payday."

9

To keep each other from falling asleep at the wheel we devise a game called Pure Truth. Whoever sits in the passenger seat must answer truthfully, with total unblinking candor, whatever question the driver puts to him.

We get one question each.

Dwaine goes first. He wants to know about my heroes. I follow the rules and hold nothing back. I tell him all about my earliest childhood heroes, about Popeye and Soupy Sales and Diver Dan and Superman and Secret Service Agent James West of *The Wild, Wild West*—a James Bond/Western TV series notable for its plucky theme music and balletic fight sequences, whose hero wore muscle-hugging brocade vests. From small screen heroes I move on to the big screen, to Cagney and Bogart and Cooper, to Cary Grant and Burt Lancaster, working my way up to Brando, whom I first encountered in *A Streetcar Named Desire* on the Million Dollar Movie. At first the movie disappointed me, since it had nothing to do with streetcars. But Brando was no disappointment. With his torn sweaty T-shirts, his mumbling brutishness, and that upper lip frozen in a permanent adolescent sneer it took no time at all for him to jump to first place in my long line of heroes. "What was it about Marlon?" I wondered out loud. Was it that face of his, so like the map of America, grinning like a naughty boy one minute, smashing table settings and buttering Parisian assholes the next? But it was Brando's pure Americanness that won me over, his owing nothing to the old world. That more than anything else made me want to be like him.

The Bonneville hummed along, the moon a bright fingernail clipping up in the sky ahead of us. A coyote reamed the night with its howls.

"To think," I shook my head and said to the passing world, "of all the time I wasted trying to be Marlon Brando."

"Don't feel too bad," Dwaine said. "Think how much time Marlon Brando's wasted. And what does it say about us, incidentally, that the two greatest twentieth-century American icons of hip masculinity, Elvis Brando and Marlon Presley, happen to be, or to have been, save for the color of their skins, black men?"

"I hear they both have or had small dicks."

"Brother, Marlon and Elvis don't *need* big dicks; they *are* big dicks."

10

Then it's my turn. I'm thinking great, this is it, my big chance to fill in the Arizona Crater of Dwaine's past, to tap the source of those neon-stained nightmares of his.

"Tell me all about Vietnam," I say. "And don't say it was like an exploding dog, or any damn crap like that."

We ride in tight-packed silence for at least another twenty minutes, when suddenly Dwaine switches to an unpaved bumpy side road, battering the Bonneville and ourselves, passing by twisted old lady trees and mounds of aborted highway dirt.

"Now where are we going?"

He lights a cigarette with the car lighter and says nothing. We climb up into the foothills. There, in what seems like the middle of nowhere, Dwaine parks the Bonneville. From among quarters and Rolaids in the utility tray he grabs a pack of Juicy Fruit gum. I follow him up a trail to a series of bubbling soda springs. Steam rises from them into the dry desert air. It's just like Dwaine to know the springs are there. Only when naked and sitting in hot bubbling sulfurous water does he finally get down to talking.

"The dog was part Pekingese, part wolfhound and mostly mongrel," he says, folding a stick of Juicy Fruit into his mouth, handing me one. "It had been lying dead on that dry dusty street in Udorn for days, putrefying under the tropical sun. Day after day I'd pass by and the carcass would still be there, still lying in the same place, getting more and more bloated. Don't ask me why, but the natives, they refused to touch it, like it was cursed, like it was the hundred-headed dragon of the Hesperides. One day I'm walking by it on the way to a cafe and KA*BOOM!*—the thing explodes like a booby trap. All the rest of the way down the street I'm picking maggots out of my face and hair."

The water smells of sulfur and is very hot. Steam floats up into my nose, burning my nostrils. It's twilight. The desert sky is the color of an overripe peach, the earth purple below it.

"That's it, babe. I'm sorry, but that's the best answer that I can give you. That was Vietnam."

"No GODDAMN FAIR!" I say. "You're supposed to tell everything! I followed the rules! I told you everything! Now you do the same. Fucker! Fair is fair!"

Dwaine nods, conceding.

"Okay," he says. "You're right, babe. I'm sorry. Let me try once more."

He waits a moment or two before beginning again.

"You know those dreams I keep having? Well, it's always the same dream. I'm falling out of a helicopter. In the army I was a medic. I rode in helicopters all the time. We'd pick up the wounded in them. My job was to patch them up while door gunners strafed the jungle canopy for sappers. Anyway—" He lights and drags deeply on a cigarette. "—one day me and these two other medics, we really *did* fall out of a helicopter, no shit. They tried to come back for us, but the jungle canopy was too thick and there were too many snipers around. Long story short, babe, soon me and my fellow medic were taken prisoner by the V.C. They brought me and Stevie—that was the other medic's name—to this bamboo hut built over a river. And that's where they tortured us."

"You were *tortured?*"

"You want me to tell the story or not?"

"Sorry."

He clears his throat. "They took us one by one from this holding pen underneath the hut, dragged us up through a trap door and sat us down at a table where they made us play Russian Roulette. We could hear the snap of the pistol hammer hitting an empty chamber, and then the explosion when it found a bullet, and then we'd see the blood dripping down through the bamboo floorboards."

I'm thinking: *huh, this sounds familiar …*

"When it was our turn they brought me and Stevie up and took bets on who'd get the first bullet. I'm sitting watching Stevie put the pistol to his head saying, 'Stevie ya gotta do it! Stevie if ya don't do it you're gonna die, they'll throw you in the pit. C'mon, Stevie. Go ahead, go ahead Stevie, go ahead. Go a*head!* Show these bastards, these cocksuckers, show 'em! Don't worry, Stevie, don't worry kid, don't worry—' "

"*Deer Hunter!*"

Dwaine goes under, blows bubbles.

VI

Greetings
from
Hollywood
(a Western)

> "It's the climate, I've been drinking
> too much orange juice."
> —W. C. Fields, *Million Dollar Legs*
> THE PERTINENT MOVIE QUOTE WALL

At first glance Hollywood is all that I hoped it would be. There's something thrillingly one-dimensional about this place, with its overexposed lighting and pastel shades straight out of a Bugs Bunny caper. The air shimmers with fraudulence. Everything looks like a movie set waiting to be boxed up for storage or burned. The pedestrians walking the sidewalks are all extras outfitted by Western or American Costume. Which is fine with me, since I've always felt that movies and all things associated with them are (or should be) fake, that their purpose in life is to make life less real, less boring.

My view, of course, is antithetical to Dwaine's. Dwaine believes that movies should make life *more* real, *less* phony, that not only are they capable of changing the world, movies *should* change it.

As for those record-breaking rains Archibald wrote to us about in his postcard, we see no sign of them, just a cartoon blue sky tinged by what Dwaine assures me is a customary layer of butter-colored smog. A transit bus (we have delivered the

Bonneville, minus three hubcaps and spattered with insect guts, to its undergraduate owner in Marina del Rey) rolls us through the brothy haze, past muffler and lube shops and storefronts with carnival signs hawking GUNS and AMMO.

The bus merges onto Sunset Boulevard, where it jockeys among bumper-to-bumper herds of Mercedes SL convertibles, each driven by someone with a car phone and a leathery suntan. Everything glitters with gold like a Klondike stream, or anyway it seems to. Only the sleepy-eyed Mexican day workers crammed into the back of the bus offset the general impression of Paradise Regained.

The bus pulls up to a red painted curb in front of a Chinese restaurant conflating itself with a movie theater, or vice-versa. Dwaine taps my shoulder. "This is it," he says. "Tinseltown."

We hopscotch down the trail of pink terrazzo stars embedded in black squares, reeling off the legendary bronze names as we go, bound for Musso & Frank's restaurant, where we find our host sitting alone among tables packed with men wearing nice polyester shirts and sports coats. "Moguls," Dwaine leans close and whispers to me.

Archibald blows his nose, adjusts his road-kill of a toupee.

Mr. Flynn watches with transparent anxiety as we stoke our stubbled furnaces with eggs Benedict, assorted grilled breakfast meats, and fruit compote. We haven't shaved since St. Louis, haven't brushed our teeth since the Arizona Crater, haven't eaten a square meal since our drive-a-way funds expired in Needles, California. When the tab comes Dwaine jumps on it.

"On us," he says, and is about to slide the check into his black book and bolt when Archibald stops him.

"Let's have none of that out here," he says.

As we head for the hotel rain clouds roll in, pig-shaped with dark bellies. Archibald reaches a hand out, catches a raindrop.

He sneezes.

2

Since then it hasn't stopped raining.

In the suite's vast kitchen I ram a thick carrot down the vegetable juicer's throat while Dwaine halves a grapefruit for the citrus juicer. The juice is all for Archibald, who lies in one of a pair of twin squeaky Murphy beds surrounded by over-the-counter cold and flu remedies, his toupee sprawled in a puddle of grapefruit juice freshly squeezed. A hot water bottle sucks starfish-like at his bald head. The suite reeks of Vick's VapoRub. It rains, Hollywood melts.

Meanwhile the three steel film canisters holding *Night Vision* gather darkness and dust in the tuck-a-way ironing board closet. They've been sitting there for four days. Archibald has yet to arrange a single screening. He considers the rain a bad omen. Until it stops, he refuses to do business in Hollywood.

"Where's my juice?" he wheezes. "I need more juice!"

Dwaine has brought his machete along for the trip. Using it he whacks a grapefruit in half, then he twists both halves into the citrus juicer's maw, like he's James Cagney and the citrus juicer is May Clarke's face. A tumbler fills with bubbling pink grapefruit juice. On a silver tray with a sullen butler's air Dwaine delivers the juice to Archibald's bedside. "This is fucked," he says back in the kitchen. "*We're* fucked. We shouldn't have come." He whacks more grapefruit.

"It can't rain like this forever," I say. "He's got to get out of bed eventually."

"Bet?"

Once the toast of Hollywood hotels, the Hotel Montecido ("the Hotel of the Stars") has since fallen on hard times. Graffiti filigrees its vanilla stucco walls. The swimming pool is a dry jungle of vines. These days the hotel's fray-braided doormen greet more muscle cars and pimpmobiles than Deusenbergs and

Mercedes. Be that as it may, ours is one of the finer suites, a deluxe maisonette with flocked fleur-de-lis wallpaper, rabbit-eared TV, tuck-a-way ironing board, and a candlestick phone straight out of Sam Spade's office. Yellowed back issues of *Billboard* and *Variety* share the desk drawer with Gideon's Bible.

As for the stars, those yet lingering here are as faded and threadbare as the hallway carpeting, as rusty as the water that farts brown from the hotel's sink and tub taps. Two days ago I saw Chuck McCann, the former kiddie show host, talking downstairs on the lobby phone, wearing a white T-shirt with the sleeves rolled up. And just yesterday I rode the hotel elevator with one of the stars of *Car 54 Where Are You?*, the one who goes, *Oooh! Oooh!*

At least those stars are still alive. It's the dead movie stars that worry me. On my way back from buying a paper in the rain this morning I saw a man step out of the next-door suite. When he bent down to pick up his complimentary copy of *Variety*, I caught a glimpse over his shoulder of Cathy O'Donnell, the actress who plays Wilma in *Best Year of Our Lives*, ironing clothes. Then the man looks up and (I swear!) he's the dead spit of Eddie Robinson in *Little Caesar*, down to thick lips ringed with shaving cream.

"You've been watching too many of those old black-and-white movies, that's what your problem is," is Dwaine's take on things as he smokes yet another in an endless series of cigarettes out on our balcony, which offers a Cinemascope view of Hollywood Boulevard, a flattened rainbow of gas stations, drug stores and fast food joints. At a stretch we can see the Pacific Ocean. Taking center stage is the twenty-four hour porn theater, the marquee of which flashes

PINK PUSSYCAT
PINK PUSSYCAT
PINK PUSSYCAT

—night and day, day after day.

3

From the same balcony we watch local rats doing trapeze acts, flying through the air with the greatest of ease as they swing from palm tree to palm tree, building their nests in the fronds.

"Star rats," says Dwaine, watching them, smoking.

"That's a whatchamacallit," I say.

"An anagram."

"Not an anagram, the other thing. You know, Madam I'm Adam. A man, a plan, a canal, Panama."

"It's called an anagram, babe."

"No it's *not*." (We're getting on each other's nerves.)

"More juice!" cries Archibald.

4

We walk in the drizzle down to the Boulevard, to join the bit players in the local Jack in the Box, and where, as I sip a Coke, Dwaine shows me the contract again. A single paragraph choked with faux legalese.

"There's no date," I note. "You can't have a contract without a date."

Dwaine snatches the contract back. He studies it, gray eyes toggling back and forth. Through the plate glass window two neighborhood bums share a meat food snack. Under a dripping parka one of them looks exactly like Clarke Gable in *The Misfits*. The other bears a striking resemblance to Jack Palance in *Man in the Attic*.

"Big deal. So there's no fucking date. So what? A contract's a contract."

"Tell that to Dexter Groon," I say, "and he'll laugh in your face."

With quarters liberated from Archibald's dresser top we ride the bus to Venice Beach, where Dwaine leaves me lying in a patch of wet grass under a date palm. As I gaze up through its fronds at the cloud-stuffed sky people young and old zip by on roller skates. A housefly lands on my arm. It amazes and disappoints me to see a common housefly in California. A half hour or so later Dwaine returns. He doesn't look triumphant.

"I showed Groon the contract," he says.

"And?"

"He laughed in my face."

Back at the Montecido, Archibald sits up watching a special news report on the rabbit-eared television set. The rain has broken all records. Floods and mudslides everywhere. Governor Brown has declared a state of emergency.

"Where were you?" Archibald asks.

"Reconnaissance mission," Dwaine answers.

"From here on," says Archibald, "no leaving this hotel without my express authority, is that understood? If you don't care for those terms, then by all means leave, but don't come back."

Dwaine's forehead smolders, the metal shards swirl in his eyes. Gently I escort him to the suite kitchen to whack more grapefruit.

"I may be rancid butter, but I'm on your side of the bread."

"Gene Kelly," says Dwaine, whacking. "*Inherit the Wind.*"

5

Seven straight days of rain and then: a miracle.

Sunlight streams in through the balcony doors. Archibald, risen from the dead, points to the candlestick phone.

"Call Columbia! Call MGM! Call Paramount! Call Universal! Ask for Shapiro!"

"At which studio?" I say.

"All of them!"

Within an hour I've booked eight screenings. The canisters holding *Night Vision* come out of the tuck-a-way ironing board closet and get loaded into the coffin compartment of a 1968 Cadillac hearse. Having run out of vans and station wagons the rent-a-wreck agency offered the hearse to Archibald at an irresistible discount. "I've always felt dead in this town anyway," he said as we pulled out of the rental lot.

6

Universal, MGM, Fox, Warner Brothers, Screen Gems—all turn *Night Vision* down. But Paramount still beckons and hopes are riding high. Dwaine and I are dressed in our Sunday best—Archibald's Sunday best. Dwaine wears his seersucker suit, I wear his rancid corduroy blazer with leather elbow patches, our trousers cuffed and bellies sucked in to accommodate Archibald's scarecrow physique. We wear Archie's cowboy boots, too, mine with snakeskin tops, Dwaine's of ostrich hide. Dwaine's slip, mine pinch.

Sunlight spears the hearse windshield, making Dwaine's dreamridden eyes look even dreamier, cataracted. I ride shotgun, Archie stretches out in back with the cans.

Halfway to Paramount a plump raindrop plops like a rotten berry on the hearse windshield. It starts pouring. The Santa Monica Freeway turns into the Nile, the rent-a-hearse into a funeral barge. Archibald points to a mansion sliding down a hillside like a pat of butter melting in a frying pan. "Irwin Allen's house," he says, pointing. Tottering by the side of the highway a soaking-wet hitchhiker is a ringer for Joel McCrea in *Sullivan's Travels*. We pass Henry Fonda and the rest of the Joads in their truck and keep going.

7

A security guard in a pith helmet checks our names against a roster and swings the gate open. Dwaine rolls the hearse into the Mercedes sculpture garden that is the visitor's parking lot. As Archie waits in the car Dwaine and I lug the heavy canisters through gray sheets of rain toward the screening trailer, where a sign beneath a burning red light bulb above a blue door says:

SCREENING IN PROGRESS

We wait soaking for the light to go off. When it does we knock. A scowling man in porkpie hat and pale trench coat (the coequal of Richard Widmark in *Kiss of Death*) answers.

"We're moguls," Dwaine tells him. "Hand over the cans, babe." Film canisters in hand, Madigan recedes into the dark depths of the screening trailer.

The red light goes back on.

8

Dwaine rolls the hearse onto the studio back lot, where giant fans whip raindrops into a storm at sea for what appears to be yet another remake of *Mutiny on the Bounty*, with masts snapping like twigs as mutinous stuntmen plunge to their air-cushioned deaths. We drive on, passing a Wells Fargo stagecoach, a wooden submarine, King Kong's left foot, and the upper two-thirds of the Eiffel Tower.

We roll past plaster brownstones on a fake New York street.

"Dumbass Californians," Dwaine says shaking his head. "They even got the Johnny pumps wrong! They're black with silver tops, not fucking green! Everyone *knows* that! What the fuck is *wrong* with these fucking people?"

We round a corner and the world changes. Suddenly we're in a western frontier town, saloon, general store, dry goods, blacksmith, livery stable, arranged tidily along a muddy thoroughfare. Except for the rain the set conforms perfectly to my obstinate view of the wild, wild west. Dwaine pulls up to the Dry Gulch Saloon.

"Spotcha a whisky, pardner?"

We twist through barbed wire and NO TRESPASSING signs. Bowlegged and ready to draw we stagger through the swinging doors to find ourselves in a dripping void of pavement and sawdust. We belly up to where the bar isn't but ought to be. Slamming his fist on it, or pretending to, Dwaine orders rotgut while I, his trusty sidekick, settle for Sarsaparilla. We draw pretend six-shooters and gun each other down and live to laugh about it.

Somewhere out in the rain a dog barks. Through the gap in the swinging doors I see a wet black animal charging toward us, its teeth bared, only to jerk, yelp and strain at the end of a runner chain. A security officer in canary sansabelt pants bounces after it in an umbrella-covered golf cart—Broderick Crawford in *The Last Posse*. Before he can arrest us we hoof it back to the rental hearse, where Archibald checks his wristwatch.

"T-minus twenty minutes and counting."

By then the moguls have gotten to the scene where Rufus murders the social worker. If they get past that, I'm thinking— we're all probably thinking—there's hope.

Oh please distribute Archie's movie! Fill our jars with moonbeams!

We roll on past a series of hangar-sized soundstages and circle back to the screening trailer. The three film canisters sit on the sidewalk in the rain.

The red light over the blue door is dead.

Archibald sneezes.

9

PINK PUSSYCAT
PINK PUSSYCAT
PINK PUSSYCAT

10

We've just about lost hope when the candlestick phone rings. Thinking it's the brass at Columbia, the one studio that sat through all of *Night Vision*, calling with an offer, Archibald lurches out of bed to answer it. But it's not Columbia. It's the hotel manager telling us to report at once to the lobby, that there has been "an incident."

The elevator is out of order. I rush down the stairs to find Dwaine seated in an upholstered lobby chair with the manager and the concierge standing nearby, his right arm swaddled in a bloody towel. Shards of glass dazzle the lobby floor below where a fist-sized crater ventilates one of the front door's port-hole windows. Scattered among the shards are what look like the pages of a screenplay.

"I saw him," says Dwaine.

"Who?" I say.

"Marty," he says.

"Scorsese?" I say.

"No, *Marty* starring Ernest Borgnine. Yes, Marty Scorsese."

"And?"

"I asked him to read my screenplay."

"Cool. What did he say?"

"He said fuck off, what does it look like he said?"

11

Archibald gives us twenty-four hours to vacate. Between us Dwaine and I don't have candy bar change.

Dwaine's not worried.

He's got a plan.

12

The lights of the firehouse burn softly. We wait on a bus bench.

"Describe him to me again."

"He's bald, fat, with no neck and a face like a gopher."

"Gotcha."

An hour passes. In the shadow of a billboard for *Apocalypse Now* we take turns emptying our bladders. Ducks quack in a nearby canal. A faint rustling of palm fronds clings to the breeze.

"Maybe he left town."

Dwaine shakes his head. "He's here. I can smell him. That faint earwax odor? That's Dexter's smell."

Another hour oozes. We're about to give up when a tomato red Austin Healy pulls up to the curb. The driver wears a camouflage fatigue jacket and looks familiar.

"That's him," Dwaine nudges me. "That's Dexter Groon."

No it's not, I say to myself, it's Peter Lorre.

Dwaine nudges me again.

"Okay, okay: I'm going; I'm going."

I proceed with The Plan, my part of it. The Plan: I get Groon to open the firehouse door. Dwaine will do the rest. I straighten the knot in Archibald's necktie, then cross the street as casually I can, noting, in so doing, that the streetlamps in Venice West are different in color from those in New York, that they're cooler, more blue, less pink. I also notice that the Austin Healy has an unorthodox hood ornament, a toy Oscar welded there like a gunsite. Seeing me approach, Groon eyes me warily but without apparent concern. I toss him a smile: a mistake. My smile must tip him off—or maybe it's Archibald Flynn's reckless taste in men's neckwear—but all of a sudden Groon's softboiled eyes go sunny-side up and crying, "My God—no!" he takes off.

Peter Lorre or Dexter Groon, he's not built for speed. Yards from the firehouse door I catch up with and grab hold of him.

"I just want to talk," I say, gripping the sleeve of his fatigue jacket.

"Well I don't!" he says.

"Well I *do!*"

"Well I *don't!*"

Shouting, "Help, police! I'm being *attacked!*" Groon breaks away and runs into the street, the fatigue jacket sliding like something greased, along with a blue Hawaiian shirt, off his shoulders into my hands. I'm standing there like a fool holding his clothes when it occurs to me that I've just assaulted a man, that he is summoning the police, that at any moment now they will arrive, sirens blaring, guns drawn, shooting first and asking questions later. My stomach churns. As it does a man leaps from the shadows and stands there, slicing the air where Dexter Groon stood with a tarnished machete.

"What the hell happened?" Dwaine asks.

"He got away from me."

"And you *let* him?"

"What was I supposed to do, bust his kneecaps?"

"As opposed to doing absolutely nothing, yes."

"Jesus Christ, Dwaine, we're artists, not muggers."

"Don't be splitting hairs on me, babe."

A siren jellies the air. We split and run.

I've run a hundred feet when I realize I've still got Groon's clothes. I toss them into the bed of a Toyota pickup truck.

13

I'm first to arrive at Buffalo Chips, where we agreed to meet in case we were forced to split up, and where a ceiling matrix of piano wire snares everything from a covered wagon to a fiberglass bison. I go to the bathroom to take a leak and end up puking my guts up, squatting there on the smelly floor, arms wrapped around the old-fashioned toilet, like the one Al Pacino takes the gun out from behind in *The Godfather*, with a wooden box with a handle dangling from a beaded chain.

Everything having whooshed out of me in an ochre flood I rise slowly, my eyes coming level as I do so with a publicity shot of Randolph Scott in *Ride Lonesome*. I look at Scott's face in the photograph (tanned, squinting, chiseled, heroic) then at mine in the men's room mirror (curly-haired, layered with baby-fat, flecked with butterscotch-colored puke) and bend to heave into the bowl again.

At the bar Dwaine joins me, slapping my back.

"You were *gawjuss*, babe, absolutely *gawjuss*. A regular hooligan. An Italian Burt Lancaster."

With stolen tips he buys us both beers. We're about to drink a toast when Dwaine's eyes go blurry and his nostrils start twitching.

"Earwax," he says.

We swivel in our stools. A half-naked, shivering Peter Lorre stands there.

"May I please have my jacket back?" says Dexter Groon. "You Easterners may not realize it, but L.A. can get damned chilly at night."

14

It takes us a while to find the Toyota pickup truck. Dwaine hands Dexter Groon his clothes.

"My keys," says Groon, rifling the fatigue jacket's pockets. "I had a bunch of keys in here."

Dwaine dangles them.

"What do you want me to do, write you a check?"

"Hell no. Your checks bounce as much as your belly, probably."

"What, then?"

"Oscar," says Dwaine.

"Oscar?"

"Oscar."

"*My* Oscar? Is that what you guys are after?"

"No, shithead, we're after *my* Oscar! I built that set with my two bare hands while you sat around scratching your balls. That Oscar is mine; it belongs to me! Your Best Short Animated Feature is your dick."

He carves the air in front of Groon's face. Groon cowers, but not nearly as much as Peter Lorre would have.

15

Inside the firehouse: a wooden floor marked with duct and gaffer tape. A push broom leans drunkenly against varnished wainscoting. The fire pole gleams.

"Where's the set? What did you *do* with it, fucker?"

"Relax," says Groon flicking a light switch. A bay door opens. There's the Lower East Side, from 14th to Delancey, running the length of a hook and ladder, all made out of clay. Dwaine's eyes go misty. Then the set's profane new centerpiece, a McDonald's with golden arches gleaming, comes into view and his shard-wreathed pupils narrow to disdainful slits.

"Don't look at me like that," says Groon. "I needed the money. Hell, just because I won an Oscar doesn't make me Onassis."

Dwaine orders the set lights switched on. Groon obeys. A thousand Christmas bulbs gleam in as many windows, headlights and streetlamps. Dwaine pries off Archie's cowboy boots and tiptoes in ventilated socks down Second Avenue, the machete swinging at his hips, squatting to read 6-point *Daily News* headlines, squeeze BB-sized clay cantaloupes, and greet tiny clay cabbies.

"*Hey, there, little guy. How's it going?*"

"Come on, Dwaine," I say. "Let's get this over with, okay?"

16

In Dexter Groon's office, the former fire chief's office, on a steel desk dating from the Eisenhower Administration, there it stands: the golden phallus, the Academy of Motion Picture Arts and Sciences Award. Dexter Groon writes out a receipt and hands it to us to sign. "If you don't mind," he says.

He's just about to turn the statuette over when Dwaine snatches it, gripping it to his chest like a BaMbuti tribeswoman suckling her newborn. He's holding it like that when a shrill insistent bleating echoes through the firehouse.

"You guys didn't think I'd just let you walk out of here with it, did you?" says Groon with a watery Jell-O smile. "Use your heads."

About now is when I wish I were in a plush theater seat with a tub of buttered popcorn in my lap. This time, though, in my opinion the movie is *too* realistic. As for whether it's a comedy or a tragedy, that remains to be seen. It depends on the ending. Will the two protagonists come out smelling like roses—like Paul Newman and Robert Redford in *The Sting?* Or will their exploits culminate in a freeze-frame of them running, guns drawn, into a hail of municipal bullets—like Paul Newman and Robert Redford in *Butch Cassidy & The Sundance Kid?*

With my eyes closed I mull over these and other intriguing possibilities, and open them in time to catch Oscar's reflection in Dwaine's pupils as, gripping the statuette in his bandaged claw, he lifts it high into the caged fluorescent lights and swings it in a golden rainbow onto the back of Dexter Groon's skull.

Groon does an actor's fall and lies there. And keeps lying.

"Dig this fucker, acting dead. Now *that's* worth an Oscar!"

"Jesus, Dwaine, now what have you done?"

I kneel and cradle Groon's neckless gopher head, its short hairs tacky with bright blood. But it *can't* be blood, not *real* blood. Nothing out here is supposed to be real, right? On the other hand the blood lacks the telltale purple color of the fake stuff, meaning a concussion at the very least, while leaving open the possibility of paralysis, brain damage, aphasia, coma, manslaughter. Mandatory jail sentences. Does California have the death penalty? Holy shit, we've gone and murdered a man!

Dwaine takes Groon's pulse, pries open an eye.

"He'll be fine," he says.

"How do you know?"

"I was a combat medic, remember?"

"Damn it, Dwaine, this isn't Vietnam!"

"That's what you think."

17

Groon stirs, moans—just like in the movies. In a glaze of fluorescent light his gopher head twists back and forth. Dwaine finds a roll of duct tape, winds it around him. Help me out here, he says. But I don't, I stand there, I can't move. I'm stuck in my plush seat watching as Dwaine drags Groon's mummified body down Avenue A and deposits him in a vacant lot at the corner of East Houston Street. With what's left of the duct tape roll he mummifies Oscar.

We're about to haul ass out of the firehouse when, as the alarm keeps swooping, Dwaine doubles back to flatten the McDonald's, removing golden arches, crowning Dexter Groon with them.

Then we're off, hightailing it down the rollerskating path, hoofing it past overflowing storm sewers and canals, down boulevards flanked with stereoscopic palm trees. Night rises in blue waves over Hollywood, over the studios and sets and soundstages, over Schwab's Drugstore and the Garden of Allah. Pale rats dust the soggy heavens as stars scurry to build their nests in palm fronds. We run until we find ourselves by the ocean, lying in wet sand looking up at where the stars are supposed to be, seeing nothing but the bottoms of clouds. Dwaine hoists the swaddled statue up into the dark air and—panting, doing his best Cagney doing *his* best George M. Cohan—says: "My mother thanks you, my father thanks you, my sister thanks you, and I thank you!"

Then he grabs and kisses me, hard.

"What was that for?"

"Because you're beautiful, Ollie, that's what. We're both beautiful. It's why everyone wants to fuck us."

He kisses me again, harder.

Like lovers in a cheesy old movie we gaze into each other's eyes. His sparkle: there's no other word for it. I'm pulled in by them and almost want him to kiss me again when he starts laughing and so do I, I can't help it.

We're cracking up laughing there on the dark wet Pacific sand. My gut hurts, I'm laughing so hard. We have to hold onto each other, that's how hard the two of us are both laughing. I'm still laughing when I lurch away to puke in the sand.

VII
The
Horror Movie
Man
(Horror Movie)

DON'T GIVE UP!

Such is Madame Helena's advice, and she should know, hailing from the Land of Miracles. According to the slim yellow flyers taped to lampposts, mailboxes and phone booths, strewn like ginkgo leaves along sidewalks, one short visit is all it takes to HELP THOSE WHO'VE BEEN DOUBLE-CROSSED, HAVE FAINTING SPELLS, CAN'T HOLD ON TO MONEY, WANT LUCK, WANT THEIR LOVED ONES BACK, WANT TO STOP NATURE PROBLEMS or WANT TO GET RID OF STRANGE SICKNESS and/ or WISH TO GAIN FINANCIAL AID, PEACE, LOVE and PROSPERITY.

The rest, presumably, are left to their own devices.

"Don't worry, babe. Things will break for us. And soon."

So saying and using a small magnet Dwaine fixes one of Madame Helena's yellow flyers to the door of our refrigerator, which, save for a dozen triple-A flash unit batteries, a jar of B-12 vitamins, a bottle of extra-strength parasiticide, an ice water-filled quart grapefruit juice bottle with a half lemon floating jellyfish-like inside, three plastic tubes of duck sauce, a jar of Mrs. Fanning's Bread & Butter Pickles (juice only), and a rubbery celery stalk, is empty.

We're six weeks behind in the rent.

Dwaine refuses any work not having to do with movies. "We don't do shit jobs," he says. "We're the Two Greatest Filmmakers in New York, remember?" And holds up a symbolic pinky.

Since coming home from Hollywood we've been unemployed. Dunning notices darken our tenement mailbox, chilly legal instruments laden with phrases like "affidavit of service" and "admission of liability" that prod my chest like a stern lawyer's stiff finger.

True, I could appeal to my parents in Connecticut, to Mamma Lasagna and Dear Old Papa, they'd bail me out. Better still I could toss in the towel and go home, back to Barnum and dead brick hat factories.

But what about Dwaine? He has no family to run to, no ripcord to pull in case of emergency, only the hard city pavement to land on, splat. Besides, he's my pal, my buddy, my chum. I can't just abandon him, can I, just like that? No. I'd rather live out the starving artist myth, Rudolpho and Marcello huddled in their Long Island City garret, feeding masterpieces to the wood stove.

Only we have no wood stove.

And no masterpieces to feed to it.

We were two mountain climbers roped together, Spencer Tracy and Robert Wagner in *The Mountain*, our rope wound from the frayed stuff of artistic dreams.

2

Sometimes the movie of our lives together was in sunny color, sometimes in black-and-white. Lately it had been bluish-gray: the grainy gray of an old black-and-white movie; the blue of Technicolor past its prime. The blue-gray of a damp November sky. Or of cheap cigar smoke.

The cigar belonged to one Demitris Demetropoulos, a.k.a.

The Horror Movie Man, who hired us to make posters for the horror movies he produced and that had their single yet highly profitable runs in those once glorious but gone-to-seed theaters lining West 42nd Street.

"Okay, fellas, let's see what you've got."

The Horror Movie Man's office is in the old Paramount building, overlooking Times Square. Where visible through eddies of cigar smoke its walls are covered with horror movie posters, their titles oozing green slime and dripping red blood. Staggered piles of scripts with covers of all different materials and colors crowd the room, leaving just a narrow path for Dwaine and me to approach the Horror Movie Man's desk: an old-fashioned rolltop behind which the Horror Movie Man sits in his high-back black leather Herman Miller lounge chair, his hairy fingers laced over the pinstripes of a double-breasted Nathan Detroit suit. Arabesques of bluish smoke rise from the cigar clamped between yellow teeth to dance around his flat, Boris-Karloff-as-Frankenstein head. A cubic clock radio dispenses stock quotes and classical music.

Bearing the cardboard portfolio we advance.

We've been up all night long working on the poster by candlelight, the ghouls at Con Edison having nixed our electricity. Dwaine took charge of the background while I concentrated on the poster's focal element: a partially decomposed human hand bursting through a mound of graveyard dirt, shedding loose gray slabs of flesh like chicken parts left too long on the boil. In the background, as I worked on the hand, Dwaine rendered other zombies in various states of putrefaction rising from their graves, all trailing hideous bits of themselves. Background and foreground alike are lit by a pus-colored moon.

When we finished, by the light of the morning sun as it rose over the East River, we stood side by side admiring it. There could be no doubt: our poster for *Dawn of the Delirious* was a masterpiece. It had better be, we both agreed as grayish dawn brushed the tin eagle sign next door, since the first three posters we'd done for Demetropoulos were all rejected. The vampire's fangs in *Eve of the Eviscerated* weren't sharp and bloody enough; the werewolf's palms in *Dusk of the Decayed* weren't sufficiently hirsute; the lagoon-dwelling creature in *Twilight of the Drowned* didn't ooze and drip enough slime and muck. In all three cases The Horror Movie Man paid us a kill-fee of fifty dollars (out of an agreed-upon three hundred) and insisted on "holding onto" the posters in question for "matters of copyright." ("You understand, now, don't you, Fellas?")

Before packing it in the portfolio, to protect it from the freezing rain that's been soaking the city for two days now, we sealed the poster with layers of garbage bags and duct tape, so it takes some doing to unveil. In the meantime The Horror Movie Man snuffs out his cigar in a novelty ashtray, takes another from a cedar box on his desk, decapitates its tip with a gold-plated miniature guillotine, and lights it with a silver lighter in the shape of a coffin. Hands folded in front of him again, he sits back at his desk.

(That rolltop desk, by the way, is the one tidy thing in The Horror Movie Man's office, no coffee rings or cigar burns, a can of Scott's Liquid Gold kept handy for the occasional quick polish.)

The last wrappings finally come off. The Horror Movie Man scrutinizes our latest effort, working the stogie from one end of his square mouth to the other. He squints, snorts, sniffs, makes little uncategorizable groaning sounds, taps a gold fountain pen against his desk blotter, sits back again, re-laces his fingers, sighs, shakes his head.

"Fellas, I'm sorry, but it ain't exactly what I'm looking for."

We look at each other, Dwaine and I.

"It's the hand," the Horror Movie Man decides. "The fingernails —they're too long. It looks like a *broad's* hand."

"You wanted realism!" Dwaine protests. "Fingernails and hair keep growing after they bury you! We know; we looked it up!"[1]

---

[1] Fingernails and hair do not keep growing after you die; we hadn't looked up anything.

"Fellas, I'm no scientist. All I know is it don't look right. Tell you what: I'll make it a hundred this time." He slides open his desk drawer, pulls out a check ledger. "Remind me, who do I make this out to?"

That's when I see the look on Dwaine's face, the one that tells me he's about to do something we'll probably both regret, or I will, anyway. By now I know the look well; God knows I've seen it enough times. And I know once that look comes into his face there's not much—in fact there's not a damned thing—I can do to stop whatever's about to happen.

3

Dissolve to us taking turns dragging a sopping cardboard portfolio along West 42nd Street in the freezing rain.

"Damn it, Dwaine. What did you have to do that for? We could have used that hundred dollars! We could have paid the electric bill! We could have paid some of our overdue rent!"

We're stopped at the traffic light at Seventh Avenue, our shoes sloshing in gray storm sewage. For the first time I feel myself truly at odds with Dwaine, thinking that maybe our friendship isn't the best thing for my financial and mental well-being. But there's still that frayed rope connecting us.

"Don't you see, babe? If we let fuckers like him walk over us, then what's the limit, huh? We've got to stand up for ourselves!"

"You call that standing up?"

"What do you call it, sitting down?"

"I call it climbing on someone's desk and pissing on it!"

"Well—he deserved it!"

"That is not the *point*, Dwaine."

"Of course it is; of course it's the point."

"No—it isn't."

"Yes, it is! Don't tell me what the point is or isn't, babe. You saw what that motherfucker tried to do! And not for the first time, either! And it's not just us that I'm thinking about. Nossir. It's not just myself I stood up for. It's all artists everywhere. It's you, babe. I did it for you."

"Spare me," I say.

"Hell, babe, you think for a second that Greek ghoul could've drawn that hand? No way! That Hellenic whoreson couldn't draw his way out of a wet paper bag! That Demonic demon couldn't draw bees with honey! That Athenian asshole couldn't draw water from a wishing well with a two-gallon galvanized bucket! That Peloponnesian pudthumper couldn't draw a crowd in Times Square with the Rockettes high-kicking buck-ass-naked—"

"All right already, I get the idea!"

The light changes. I take off, splashing through puddles.

"Good," says Dwaine following me. "Because to tell you the truth I was starting to worry."

I pick up my pace, pretending that Dwaine's not right there behind me, wishing that I'd never heard of Dwaine Fitzgibbon. Dwaine *who?* He grabs me by my pea coat sleeve.

"Without us, babe, the Bull Duncans, the Archie Flynns, the Dexter Groons, the Demitris Whatshisnames—they'd all be nothing, *nothing!* Don't ever forget that. In their heart of hearts they want to be artists, just like us, but they don't have the time; they're too busy getting in touch with their inner stockbrokers. Do you see what I'm saying? Do you? *Huh?*"

"Yeah, yeah, I see what you're saying. *Jesus…*"

"They're the real zombies; they eat the flesh of human dreams!"

All this time he's tugging at my sleeve. I pull free.

"Fine!" I say. "But did you have to piss on his desk?"

"What can I say, Ollie. Nature and duty both called simultaneously. *Mea culpa, mea maxima culpa.* Tell you what, I'll give you one Our Father, six Hail Marys, and a novena. Will *that* make you happy, dear artificer?"

We've stopped at another intersection. He grabs my sleeve

again and gives it a tug. I turn around and face him, our chins almost touching, so close I can feel his winter breath on me and see his razor burns and feel the heat as he lasers me with those aluminum-shard eyes of his. When he looks at me like that I swear he could shoot his tongue out and swallow me like a lizard swallowing an insect, whole.

"Know why they want to fuck us, babe? Huh? Know why?"

"Because we're beautiful," I submit dully.

"Exactly: Because we're beautiful."

Umbrellas blot out the sky. As I hurry along Dwaine falls behind. I turn and see him standing on the opposite curb, rattling his tooth with his pinkie high in the air: *we've got more talent*, etc., Dwaine's pep-rally cry, the life saver he throws overboard in times of strife. Only I'm not grabbing it, not this time, uh-uh, not taking the bait, nossir. I keep walking, ready and more than willing to leave him behind, abandon him to catch pneumonia or whatever it is that a person catches from standing like a fool in the frozen rain, and start to do just that when my resolve melts and I turn and he's still there, still standing there rattling that goofy front tooth of his. I shake my head, re-cross the street. As I get to him he does an about-face and peers into the window of a Hoffritz knife store, his breath frosting the glass as he admires a flotilla of Swiss Army knives.

"Check it out, babe. Third one from the left. Can opener, cigarette lighter, hacksaw, jumper cables, back hoe..."

By the arm I escort him back to the curb. As we get there a taxicab passes, heaving up a puddle of water that broadsides the cardboard portfolio and soaks us from the waist down in brown storm sewage. Dwaine throws his laughing head back.

"And—CUT!" he says.

VIII

A
Pre-Victorian
Bathtub
(Adult Feature)

> "Made it, Ma. Top of the world!"
> —James Cagney, *White Heat*
> THE PERTINENT MOVIE QUOTE WALL

Smoking in the tub, combing the classifieds in *Variety* after a meal of garbanzo beans and chopped celery in soy sauce, Dwaine chances upon the following notice:

> Wanted: experienced artist/ designer to work on independent feature film. Contact: B. Huffnagel, Production Mgr, Priapus Pictures.

"Huffnagel!" In a deprecatory smoke cloud Dwaine expels the name of my erstwhile antagonist. "Do you believe it? That fat fucking slob is a production manager and we're eating garbanzo beans!"

"It's movie work," I say.

2

We meet Huff at Joe Allen's in the theater district. Since our student days he has lost most of his excess weight, down to a feathery two hundred pounds. He's trimmed the Rasputin beard, too, and traded his horn rims in for contact lenses. But his breath still smells like dead worms in a jar. And he still looks like a central casting heavy.

"It's an adult feature," he explains, downing a Rolaid with his diet ginger ale. "You guys will be in charge of sets, props, clean-up."

Dwaine pounds a fist on the table. "The fuck we will. We're the Two Greatest Artists in New York. No way are we doing grunt work on a goddamn skin flick!"

"It's not a skin flick," says Huff. "Please do not call it that. We're producing an adult feature."

"It's a lousy smut film, is what it is."

"Fine, if that's how you feel about it."

Huff tosses a twenty down on the tablecloth. With a wailing scrape he pushes his chair back. He's about to go when I grab his camel hair sleeve and turn to Dwaine, my eyes speaking eloquently of dunning notices, unemployment agencies, and garbanzo bean suppers eaten by candlelight. "It's movie work," I remind him under my breath.

"How much does it pay?" Dwaine asks Huff.

"Ten an hour," says Huff. "That's five a piece if I hire you both."

"Make it twenty and we'll think about it."

"Five," says Huff.

"Ten," says Dwaine.

"Five."

"We'll take it," I say and turn to Dwaine who says nothing.

"You'll see," says Huff. "It'll be just like the old days."

"The dark ages, you mean," says Dwaine.

Huff heads for the door.

"But no clean up!" Dwaine shouts after him. "We're not standing around with hot towels and garbage bags. Got that?"

"Fear not," Huff says from the breezeway. "I won't ask you

guys to do anything I wouldn't do." And leaves.

"That's what I was afraid of," says Dwaine.

3

Dissolve to the temporary headquarters of Priapus Pictures, a series of unplastered office spaces at 1600 Broadway. The Two Greatest Artists in New York sit at a folding table, collating the shooting script for *Angels in Heat:* a stack of index cards in no special order, indicating the number and gender of cast members, set and lighting specifications, props (if any), and giving a brief summary of the action:

ANGEL #1 and ANGEL #2 give ANGEL #3 a BATH

I hand Dwaine an index card. He enters the card's number into a ledger, puts a check mark on it, then sends the card fluttering down into a cardboard liquor box on the floor. A nearby shelf sags with soundtracks to old movies.

"Look," I say, pointing to one of the soundtrack cans. "There's the soundtrack for *Midnight Cowboy.* I wonder what it's doing there?"

Dwaine doesn't answer. He's not speaking to me. He hasn't spoken to me since I talked him into taking this job.

In an improvised reception area out in the hallway interviewees await their interviews. While waiting they share cigarettes and gossip.

Did you hear about what happened to Johnny Holmes?

Oh, isn't it awful?

Accused of six murders!

Yeah, and they say he only killed three!

So unfair…

I hand Dwaine another index card. He checks it off and sends it fluttering into the cardboard box.

4

At a warehouse in Corona, Queens, we meet the First A.D., Huff's sister-in-law, who has a Long Island accent and looks like she'd be more at home on the set of a Hellmann's mayonnaise commercial. She shows us around inside the warehouse.

"This," she says, pointing a frosted fingernail at a pile of canvas flats stacked up against a wall, "is going to be the Fantasy Room. It gets painted flat black, with mirrors and day-glo lights." Dwaine and I both nod. "This here," she points to another pile of flats, "is going to be the Jailhouse. It gets painted battleship gray with lots of splotches and graffiti. And this—" she points to a third set of flats piled in a corner—"is going to be the locker room. It gets painted green."

"What shade?" says Dwaine.

"Use your imagination," says Mrs. Huffnagel. "And this," another corner, "will be the Whorehouse. Painted whorehouse red, naturally."

"Naturally," says Dwaine.

"And last but not least…" the First A.D. points to a big mound of chicken wire and bags of *papier-mâché*. "Over here's gonna be Hell. You need to make it look like underground walls, textured and sponged. You also need to get hold of a pre-Victorian bathtub. Don't ask why. It's what herr director wants and it's what herr director is going to get."

5

We spend the rest of the afternoon hauling, hammering, painting, plastering and papier-mâchéing. We're especially proud of our underground walls and jailhouse graffiti, trump l'oeil stuff (with a nod to Max Ernst and the Surrealists).

Clothes spattered with black, gray, green and red paint, we

step out into the Corona dusk. Walls of bloated black garbage bags crowd the sidewalks. The sanitation workers have gone on strike. Rotting food smells taint the cold damp air.

At the local doughnut shop we squeeze in among the blue collars at the counter and order doughnuts, Dwaine's chocolate, mine honey-glazed, with our coffees. A radio splutters. *Shah's Nephew Slain in Paris. Picasso Mural Found. Sanitation Workers to Go on Strike. Pope John Paul II to Visit City. Blizzard Predicted.* We cross ourselves.

"Think they'll throw the Pope a parade?" I ask Dwaine, who is speaking to me again, thank God.

"Not unless they can get all the garbage off the streets."

"Maybe the Catholic Church will help."

"The Catholic Church doesn't pick up garbage, it only dispenses it."

Dwaine, who still dips into philosophy now and then, has brought along a paperback book. "Thus Spake *who?*" the off-duty transit cop on the stool next to him asks.

"Zarathustra," Dwaine tells him. "He's a prophet who comes down from the mountains to tell people God is dead and teach them how to be Supermen. *Whatever will break in our truths, let it break. Many a house has yet to be built.*"

6

The next day it starts snowing. I sit in the double-parked production van on Broadway, waiting as Dwaine and Huff do stuff in the office. In the driver's seat, sipping a container of tea, I watch pedestrians through the snow-blurred windshield. A few yards down the block businessmen in trench coats slink in and out of the Circus Cinema, where a double feature, NASTY NURSES and TALK DIRTY TO ME, plays. Under the big marquee letters a smaller sign announces:

NOW HEAR THE SOUND OF LOVE
IN DOLBY STEREO

I'm reminded of the first porno film I ever saw, back in Barnum. The X-rated cinema had recently opened its doors to vociferous protests. Among the protesters out front my best friend Clyde and I, who had just turned seventeen, recognized quite a few faces, but inside we recognized quite a few more. The title of the movie had the word Beethoven in it. Of it's plot I remember absolutely nothing, though I wouldn't soon forget the face that first demonstrated to me, on a wide screen and in glorious full color, the precise meaning of the word fellatio, with giant lips encompassing a male organ the size of a sequoia.

Suddenly everyone on the sidewalk is a porno actor or actress—businessmen, secretaries, children, bums and cops—no exceptions. The whole city is one big porno set. Everyone out there is having sex, or is about to, or has just finished doing so. I'm obsessed. I can't stop thinking of Sex: X-rated Sex, Times Square Sex, Sex that leaves a film over the eyes. The cameras haven't even started to roll yet and already I'm delirious. I try telling myself it's just a job—a degrading, demeaning, deplorable, detestable job. But the libido has its own way of seeing things. So I sit here with a hard-on pulsing under my jeans, sipping tea from a to-go cup, mulling over the potential irony of jerking off into a vessel marked IT IS OUR PLEASURE TO SERVE YOU.

Dwaine takes my place. Up in the office Huff hands me a pile of call sheets and tells me to go to a certain address on Eighth Avenue to have them photocopied. I run down streets already painted with snow, looking for 630 Eighth Avenue. 629, 632, 634. No 630. I run into the Film Center Pub and ask the ruined souls slouched there if any of them by any chance know where 630 Eighth Avenue is? The ruined souls all stare. I run back to 1600 Broadway and take the elevator up to the office where Huff yells, "*It's six-thirteen, not six-thirty!*" and out I go again.

It's freezing out. I left my pea coat back in the van. By the time I get to the address I'm shivering so hard my teeth chatter. A lady in a body-hugging, black leather Emma Peel outfit answers my knock. Something about her eyes, the bend of her jaw, the angle and shape of that upper lip, reminds me of someone. Then it comes to me: she's the star of the first porno movie I ever saw, the one in Barnum, the one about Beethoven. Only it can't possibly be her. *Can it?* She looks older, of course, more sophisticated, less careless, like she's since gone on to raise a family and earn a degree in one of the social sciences.

"Can I help you?"

"Byron H-H-Huffnagel sent me. T-t-t-to ph-photocopy the-the-the c-c-c-call sheets." I hand them to her.

"Where's your coat?"

"Oh. I g-g-g-guess I f-f-forgot it."

"Poor thing, you must be freezing. Come on in."

She shuts the door behind us and takes the call sheets over to the copy machine. I watch as she bends to load in a fresh ream of paper into the paper tray, her tight leather clothes stretching to accommodate the full roundness of her body. My cheeks prickle and flush. Must be the cold. "You want 'em collated, sweetbuns?" she asks.

The copy machine has no collator. Next thing I know we're on all fours next to each other on the gray industrial carpeting, slapping pages down. I feel the gusts of animal heat radiating from her body as it works next to mine, our parts all but touching to sounds of pages slapping and the swishes of skin-tight leather. Now and then on its way to deliver a sheet to its pile her hand and mine intersect, bolstering the hard-on I've been carrying around with me ever since leaving the production van. I picture the same hand reaching over to undo the clasp of my belt, sliding the zipper of my Levi's down, springing my swollen dick from the damp jungle stockade of my Fruit of the Looms, and guiding it gently, oh so gently, between…

"Here you go, sweetstuff."

Having plopped the collated, staggered call sheets into my arms, with a wink suggesting that I haven't fantasized alone, Mrs. Peel sends me and my boner back out into the cold.

7

When I get back at the double-parked production van I find Dwaine eating a slice of pizza, a droopy bridge of mozzarella connecting him to it. In his free hand he holds his paperback. *Do you not smell the slaughterhouses and ovens of the spirit? Does this town not steam with the fumes of slaughtered spirit?*

8

On the way to the warehouse the next morning we swing by Astoria to pick up the costume designer, none other than Veronica Wiggins, a.k.a. Venus. "Fancy meeting you two here!" She wears a fur-collared winter coat, the same reddish purple as the fake blood Dwaine and I spilled in many a Scorsese-inspired movie: blood on snow. Her hair is cut in jagged blue spikes, like she lost an argument with a pair of hedge clippers. A punk albino angel.

She carries a notebook in her shoulder satchel. "I think it's every artist's obligation," she says climbing into the production van, "to experience some form of degradation, don't you?"

"*I prefer the disagreeable to the agreeable,*" says Dwaine, "*and this is the sane part of me.*"

"We're in it for the Degradation," I say.

"Another D word," says Dwaine.

"What?" says Venus.

"Nothing."

"Mind you, I've got nothing against pornography, per se," Venus informs us while wriggling her way onto the transmission hump. "It's vulgarity I can't stand."

"Nothing is alien to us," I offer.

Dwaine blows smoke rings.

"So—how did you guys end up here?"

"It's a long story," I say.

"We're between pictures," says Dwaine.

"We just got back from Hollywood," I say.

"Hollywood? What were you doing there?"

"Rubbing shoulders with moguls and movie stars."

"Really?"

"Yeah. It was great."

"Great," says Dwaine.

"I see. And now you've rubbed your way into this?"

Dwaine floors the gas pedal, lays a long patch of disgruntled rubber.

It has stopped snowing, at least for now, though the forecast calls for ever more lavish spectacles of snow. From a landscape of two-family brick homes packed like encyclopedias on a shelf the van rumbles into one of truck lots and welding sheds, the sort of place where mobsters routinely drop bodies dead. While it rumbles Venus fills us in on how, shortly after graduating from art school, Huffnagel produced his first movie, the one about the Collyer brothers. When the movie didn't earn back a dime its shady financiers, associates of Huff's Boston laundry (or was it carting?) service uncle, conceived the present, uhm, enterprise as a means of recouping their losses.

"They've given Huff fifty grand and five days to win himself back into their good graces," Venus explains with a queasy smile.

"Or else?" I say.

"Or else…" Venus mock slits her snowy throat and then she smiles. I'm pleased to report to myself that she still has that endearing little chip in her front tooth. I want to make love to her, but then I've always wanted to make love to her; I've never stopped wanting to make love to her.

9

With the sets (except for the pre-Victorian bathtub) complete, we wait for the director to arrive. Cast and crewmembers smoke cigarettes, drink coffee and mineral water and huddle around the portable TV set up in an improvised lounge.

Squatting on the Whorehouse floor, Dwaine, Venus and I play Scrabble on Venus' travel edition, equipped with a textured board to keep the tiny wooden letters from drifting.

"Quahog," says Venus, reading from the small dictionary that comes with the game. "A thick-shelled American clam."

While playing Venus tells us how she went back to Virginia to tend her dying father, president of the second biggest coal mine in the state and one of its wealthiest citizens. "Also one of its dumbest," she says. "See, Daddy inherited the mine, he never did a thing to earn it. He couldn't hammer a nail or count to ten without using his fingers. But he could carry a tune. In fact he could remember just about any song ever written, from an obscure aria in Wagner's Ring cycle to the theme music for *Run, Buddy, Run*. Remember that TV show? About a guy being chased around by the Mob after overhearing the words 'Chicken Little' in a steam room? The guy who played Buddy—what was his name?— the lead trumpet player for the Johnny Carson band. Anyway, my dad was probably the one person left on earth who could still hum that tune." Venus hums a few bars. "That was it, his one talent. Now he's gone and so is the money (he cut me out of the will, wasn't that sweet of him?) and all that's left is that silly tune going around in my head."

"Is 'pigging' a word?" says Dwaine.

"He couldn't stand me, my father. Couldn't stand to touch me. It made him cringe. It was like he was afraid to sully me with those coal-stained hands of his, or maybe he was afraid that my white skin would stain *him*. He never looked me in the eyes. I never figured out what he was so ashamed of. If it hadn't been for his stroke we'd have never gotten to know each other, then it was me touching him, feeding him with a spoon, turning him over in bed so he wouldn't get sores, wiping him. By then he'd already written me out of his will. He left everything to my sister, who also won't speak to me. Oh, well." She shrugged. "I never wanted any of his dirty old coal money anyway."

Dwaine says, "I say we dig him up and kick his teeth in."

At last the director arrives, rolling across the studio in a motorized wheelchair. His name is Hamilton Banes Driver, but those who've had the dubious honor of working with him before call him H.B., as in Hamilton Beach, as in blender, he so likes whipping things and people around. His wheelchair makes a high-pitched whirring noise and gives off a tangy, electronic odor—not always, but on occasion and in concentrated blasts, as if wheelchairs, too, need to fart.

To hide his incipient turkey gullet Driver wears a puffed silk ascot, its loose ends tucked into a leisure suit. From a distance he looks like someone's annoying but benign uncle, the kind that blows raspberries into your ticklish neck, the type of character played to a fare-the-well by Jason Robards or Burgess Meredith. Through an old-fashioned megaphone with his initials (HBD) painted on it he shouts his directions:

"Listen up, boys and girls. The Blizzard of '79 has flattened most of Saskatchewan and all of Manitoba and is headed this way. So how about we get things rolling here, huh?"

Scene One takes place in the Fantasy Room. The First A.D. calls for quiet on the set. Venus and I join the semicircle of crewmembers gathered to watch. With cameras rolling, following a few lines of poorly improvised dialogue, the cast members shed their clothes. I feel like a spectator at a nuclear bomb-testing site, positioned there by the authorities to calculate the effects of the blast: impact, windburn, fallout. My mouth goes dry as desert dust; my legs turn into watery reflections of legs; my brain imitates sculpted Kleenex. I forget what breathing is for. It's not that I *like* what I'm seeing, not really, it's just that I can't

seem to take my eyes off the spectacle, as if the sight of bodies
fucking has its own irrepressible magnetic aura, like a bonfire
or a car accident, turning us all, the rest of the cast and crew,
into rubberneckers at a fleshy demolition derby. (Wasn't it Rilke
who said *beauty is nothing but the beginning of terror we're still just
able to bear?*)

We watch until things get boring. When Mrs. Huffnagel
calls for the "money shot" we brace ourselves for the white-hot
aurora, for the blinding, billowing dome. On detonation Venus
takes my hand and squeezes it, hard. *Did thee feel the earth move?*

As hot towels and plastic bags are distributed we go off in
search of Dwaine, who has vanished. We find him lying supine
on a lumpy jail cell cot, deep into his Nietzsche.

*My foot is a cloven foot, with it I trample and trod over sticks, and
I am happy as the devil while running so fast.*

10

The set of a porno film is a strange place to fall in love, yet that's
just what we do, Dwaine and I: we both fall for Venus. I see it in
Dwaine's metal-shard eyes, in how they light up at every whisper
of her name, and in his smile when one of us catches the other
thinking about her. On the third day of the shoot, between the
Jailhouse and Locker Room scenes, we have to leave the warehouse, we're both tittering so hard, our titters occasioned by the
director's wheelchair—which, depending on our mood, we've
taken to referring to as either the Electric Farting Contraption
or the Atomic Stinkmobile. But the underlying cause of our titters is our shared crush on Venus, a crush that has turned us into
giddy grade-schoolers.

"Admit it!" Dwaine threatens me with a fat wet snowball. "You're
smitten, all right. I saw you both holding hands in there."

"That was just a nervous response."

"So is love, babe; so is love."

A half-foot of snow has fallen on the city. We've stepped out into the winter wonderland of a full-blown blizzard, the flakes swirling around fireboxes, fluttering among the elevated subway's hodgepodge of girders. We fall into a bank of freshly plowed snow and tussle like twins, powdering each other's faces, laughing. A voice calls to us and we look up and there's Venus, standing in the yellow rectangle of light that is the warehouse side entrance. She steps closer, her face as pale as the snowflakes. She smiles her chip-toothed smile. "*Now* what are you two troublemakers up to?"

The three of us make snow angels, on our backs with the snow falling gently on our faces, melting on cheeks, tongues, eyes, lips. We're back in first grade. Our teacher, Mrs. Szost, sits at her desk inside, waiting with crayons and construction paper and a map of the United States of America, each state a different removable colored piece of wood.

The warehouse door swings open. Mrs. Huffnagel fills the yellow rectangle: "Hey, Snow White, get your frosted buns back in here! Driver wants you to whip him up a fluffy muumuu!"

11

Day three and we still haven't found the right bathtub. The director insists that it be pre-Victorian. No other tub will do. We've been to antique stores, plumbing supply depots, salvage shops. We've searched all five boroughs and beyond, into parts of New Jersey and Connecticut. We've seen every kingdom, phylum, class, order, family and genus of bathtub imaginable. But no pre-Victorians, none, not one.

"Without that tub I'm dead," says Huff, kicking a set flat. "Driver says he won't shoot the Hell scene without it. He calls it the film's centerpiece. Fuckin' A-hole thinks he's Cecil B. DeMille." Huff swigs Philip's Milk of Magnesia straight from the cobalt blue bottle. "I may as well shoot myself right now," he observes, though the closest thing to a firearm on the set is a dildo dangling from the end of a fishing pole.

In desperation he offers a three hundred dollar bonus to anyone who can locate a pre-Victorian bathtub.

12

Having driven the rest of the cast members home to their door-manned Manhattan apartment buildings we double back to Astoria to drop Venus off at her place.

" 'Night," I say and kiss her on the cheek.

We watch her walk up the stairs into her building.

"Man," says Dwaine, watching.

"She's really great, isn't she?"

"Oh, man. Oh, *man.*" He puts the van in gear and drives off, still shaking his head.

"What? What's the matter?"

"When will this torture end, that's what's the matter."

I ask him what torture? What's he talking about?

"Man, do I have to draw you a map, print you out a circuit, write you a manual? Or should I act out a goddamn charade?"

I still don't get it.

"For God's sake, the least you could do is take her in your arms, swap a little spit, box tonsils—but *noooo*, you go and kiss her on the cheek like a goddamn blushing choirboy!"

"Fuck you!"

"Hey, I'm just saying that's exactly what you did, isn't it?"

"At least I did *something.* You just sat there."

"You're the one who's in love."

"Says you."

"Am I wrong? Huh? Am I?"

"Eat me."

"So I'm not wrong."

"None of your business."

"You're in love, all right."

"Kiss her yourself if it means so much to you!"

"Listen to you. You'd think I was asking you to eat worms or sit through another Fassbinder film."

We ride the rest of the way home in silence, through tunnels of garbage bags. Along the way Dwaine takes his silver flask from the glove compartment and drinks. It's the first time I've seen him drink in a long while. Back in our neighborhood he parks by the river, in front of the Pepsi-Cola plant where, before we head home, he stops as usual to admire the view across the river through the chain-link fence. As he does a stiff gust blows, sending Dwaine's military beret Frisbee-flying over the fence and into the river. Next thing I know he's climbing the fence, chain links rattling. "Dwaine, what the hell—?" But he keeps climbing, up and over. Soon he's making his way down an old pier, his boots breaking through the rotten wood every few steps. When he gets to the end he strips off his coat and stands there, arms swung out wide as he leans further and further forward over the black, freezing water.

I go after him, stepping through the same rotten holes, and get to the end of the pier in time to see him dangling by one arm from a piling, swooping out over the gelid waters like sopping Gene Kelly swinging blissfully from a lamp post.

"Just getting my hat," he tells me when I've grabbed and pulled him back from the brink, slapping the sopping beret against his knees. "Just getting my fucking hat."

13

I dream of bathtubs chasing me in herds like porcelain elephants, to be woken by Dwaine on all fours in our kitchen, yelling. "Eureka! I found it!"

Dwaine has torn away the surrounding wooden frame used to support an eating surface, revealing a tub of a different nature. We squat to scrutinize it. No legs, a bottom as flat as a boat, a rolled brim like a derby, raised at one end like the back of a shoe. No question, a pre-Victorian. "Do

you believe it, babe? It was here all this time—right under
our noses and other body parts!"

"How can it be? This building's not that old."

"Don't look a gift tub in the mouth."

It takes all morning and a half-dozen hacksaw blades to free
the tub from its plumbing prison. Then bump-THUMP, bump-
THUMP down five flights to the street where the van waits.

Cheers rise as we carry the tub into the warehouse. Huffnagel
hugs us. Driver circumnavigates the tub like Magellan, caress-
ing its porcelain curves with a moleskin-gloved finger.

Per his instructions we paint it: pink.

14

Time to shoot the Hell Scene. It's the coldest hell on record,
with a blizzard blowing and a wind-chill factor of five below—
and the temperature inside the warehouse, which isn't insulated,
not much higher.

"Imagine hell freezing over in our lifetime," Venus reflects.

Crewmembers huddle in winter coats; cast members shiver
under robes and packing blankets. All but a few of the men can't
perform. "This is supposed to be hell, goddamn it," the director
shouts through his antique megaphone. "I won't have breaths
condensing in the underworld!"

We raid every hardware store in the neighborhood, returning with seven portable space heaters, four electric, three kerosene. By three o'clock the warehouse is an inferno.

"That's more like it," says the director.

Wearing angel and devil costumes designed by Venus, the
entire cast converges around the pink-painted bathtub. Smoke
machines billow. Red and yellow lights simulate fire and brim-
stone. The lead cameraman circles his fists. The first A.D. says,
"Action!" The director yells, "Cut!"

"Now what?" says Huff.

"Devils. I need more devils!" says the director. "There are

PORTER SQUARE BOOKS

Porter Square Shopping Center
25 White St.
Cambridge, MA 02140
617-491-2220
www.portersquarebooks.com

192596 Reg 2 6:39 pm 06/17/09

S LIFE GOES TO THE	1 @	16.95	16.95
SUBTOTAL			16.95
SALES TAX - 5%			.85
TOTAL			17.80
CASH PAYMENT			20.00
CHANGE			2.20

Booksense
An Independent Bookstore for
Independent Minds

too many angels and not enough devils!" In fact there are an equal number of both, but Driver feels the scales should be tipped in favor of the Common Enemy. Volunteers are offered a hundred dollars extra pay each.

Dwaine turns to me. "It's movie work," he says.

15

Dissolve to the Two Greatest Artists in New York wearing devil costumes. When the First A.D. yells, "Action!" we're supposed to climb into the pink tub brimming with soapsuds and angels and do suggestive things to them with our velvet tails and foamcore pitchforks. The tub is frothed full of bubbles. The angels climb in (careful to keep their wings dry). The First A.D. demands quiet on the set. The lead cameraman rolls his fists around each other.

"And—action!" says the First A.D.

I start toward the tub, the camera lights so bright in my eyes I can't see anything beyond them, just a semicircle of dark heads and shoulders watching. When I arrive at the tub's brim I stand there frozen, foamcore pitchfork in hand, devil's tail between my legs, not sure what I'm supposed to do, exactly, or that I'm willing or prepared to do it. After standing there for what seems like days (with all sorts of people shouting orders and other things at me), I do a one-eighty and walk off the set.

Out of the corner of my eye, through clouds of artificially colored artificial smoke, I see Dwaine doing what devils are supposed to do to angels, prodding one with his pitchfork, snatching her tin foil harp and tossing it away, whipping her vigorously with the point of his pointy tail. A ravenous leer floods his eyes. Every few steps I turn to watch him while slipping deeper and deeper into the shadows, until I'm standing in the dark outer circle of watchers beside Venus, watching with her as Dwaine goes at it with two angels at once, tearing off their silk wings and pipe-cleaner halos, straddling one in the pink tub, peeling the straps of her bra back as the other glides slowly down the length of his velvet devil's pants, unzipping him, with him meanwhile casting glances—at me? At Venus? At both of us?

"He's good at this, isn't he?" Venus observes.

I turn away. I can't look.

16

I wake up pitching and swaying and seasick in the Fantasy Room waterbed. Dwaine and Venus are up, seated in the glow of a kerosene stove, watching a fuzzy broadcast of *Dr. Zhivago* on the cast's portable TV.

I take my blanket and join them. Soon we're all huddled together watching Omar Shariff trying to write a poem in that frozen mansion. To the haunting carousel theme I fall back asleep, only to be woken later by the sounds of Dwaine and Venus kissing, their shadows and sighs mingling in the dark. They're trying to be quiet about it, which of course only accentuates every sound. I close my eyes, pretend to keep sleeping, lying there listening, a sexual spy. Dwaine grunts.

"Shhh," Venus says.

They both fall silent as I get up, taking the blanket with me. Wrapped in it, I step outside to watch the snow as it piles up on car hoods and on the elevated subway station's pagoda rooftop, darkening as it colludes with sooty buildings and grimy streets. The snow and soot, I tell myself sleepily, are two sides of the same argument: black vs. white, angels vs. devils, love vs. hate, innocence vs. experience. The extremes cancel each other out, turn everything into gray slush, what I feel like inside.

17

Dawn. The warehouse phone rings. Huff wants one of us to drive up to Nyack, where the director lives, and pick up a vial of prescription drugs from his partner. I remind him that there's a blizzard out there.

"Do it," says Huff, "or you're fired."

"Kiss my ass," I say and hang up.

"What did you just do?" Dwaine stands there wearing a blanket.

"I got us fired, what does it look like?"

"Call him back."

"You call him. I quit."

I grab my coat.

"Babe, where are you going?"

"You'd kill your own mother if it landed you a movie job."

"Only if they let me rape and torture her first."

"You have no morals. You're sick. You'd eat the sludge out of a vampire's belly button if he had one."

"You know what they say, preach the gospel at all times, if necessary use words."

"You should be put back in the womb and fucked for again!"

"*What have I ever done to make you treat me so disrespectfully?*"

"Shit head!"

Then I'm gone, out the warehouse door, running straight into a blizzard, each frozen breath an ice pick to my lungs. I don't know or care where I'm going. My boots kick through snow. I've run at least four blocks when a horn sounds behind me and I turn. High beams blind me. Then I see the production van. The passenger door flies open.

"Get in," Dwaine says.

Venus slides over onto the transmission hump. All around us black plastic garbage bags mount up to the snowy sky. The van radio splutters. *Pope's visit postponed. Mother Theresa wins Nobel Prize.*

Dwaine drives us back to our apartment, helps me pack my things. He knows where I'm going; he doesn't have to ask. Back to Connecticut, to Barnum, to the land of picket fences and hat factories. We stand in the detritus where the bathtub used to be, an oval patch sprinkled with copper filings. A smell of burned bridges hangs in the air.

18

We're just about to cross the Brooklyn Bridge when Venus points out the inverted triangle of smoke filling the salmon-colored eastern sky. Dwaine makes a U-turn and heads for it. Back in Corona, swirling red lights ring the burning warehouse. Venus chews her fingernail. "Know what? I think I may have left the kerosene stove on." I see the burning wings of angels rising with the flames that lick the stars.

We sit watching until the roof caves in, then Dwaine throws the van into reverse. We're crossing the East River again when the sun breaks rapturously through clouds.

The Blizzard of '79 is over.

At the 125th Street Metro North station Dwaine helps me with my things. As he does I apologize for calling him immoral.

"Apology unnecessary. Of course I'm immoral." He shrugs. "I'm a product of the times."

He grabs a box of Jujubes from the glove compartment and hands them to me. "Little going away present," he says. "Each colored bead contains water from the miraculous Fountain of Lourdes. Guaranteed to cure gout, lameness, and non-specific, twentieth-century malaise."

We take turns hugging. The van radio splutters on, announcing the end of the sanitation workers' strike. Within a fortnight the city will return to its original state of filth. While hugging Dwaine I look down and see him and Venus holding hands. The train whistle blows. As I rush up the station platform stairs Dwaine shouts: "Politicians, ugly buildings and whores all get respectable if they last long enough!"

"John Huston," I shout back, running. "*Chinatown!*"

part **TWO**

IX
The
Building
(Home Movie)

I n Barnum I worked for a company called Chem-U-Solve. I
wore a scarlet jumpsuit and drove a yellow truck from gas
station to gas station, exchanging used drums of parts cleaner
solvent for supposedly brand new ones. At the end of the day,
with the sun setting and mosquitoes feasting on my spaghetti
sauce flavored blood, I'd empty the drums into a scummy ditch,
wipe them clean with a rag, and refill them with filtered clean-
ing solvent from the same scummy ditch.

I took courses at the state university, working toward my degree in advertising. I made a dwelling for myself in my parents'
basement. Though moldy and thick with furnace fumes, I preferred it to my bedroom upstairs, with its ocean liner curtains
and other frayed relics of my childhood.

When not working or studying I wandered around. Towns
and cities look different when you no longer know anyone
there. My hometown was a Picasso cubist painting in browns
and grays that I colored in with my loneliness, an exotic loneliness that bubbled and swirled like those Maurice Binder cred-
it montages that opened the early James Bond movies, with
naked women undulating in plasmas of shifting spectral color.
Somewhere out there men sailed the Greek Islands, swam the
Hellespont, parachuted from strutted biplane wings, and awoke
with naked lovers on balconies facing the Bosporus. If I walked
long and far enough sooner or later I'd join them.

Though I missed Dwaine and our desperate bounding about

in search of artistic fortune and fame (the Bohemian Rhapsody of our shared days), I tried not to think too much about it. I tried to see our friendship for what it was, or what it had been: a passing young person's phase, something to look back on with a wan indulgent smile.

I missed Venus, too. God I missed her. I even dreamed about her. In one dream we're walking down a street like the streets of Barnum, but with every house painted a different bright primary color. As we pass them by Venus's pigmentless skin turns the same colors as the houses: red, blue, yellow. We come to an open field. Against the open sky her forehead and cheeks blush sky blue. Clouds float across her eyes.

2

Dwaine sent me letters. My father, who still pedaled his rusty Raleigh to the post office and back, would bring them home in his handlebar basket. Some were long and rambling, others no more than a few quick lines on a postcard.

Occasionally Dwaine would attach newspaper clippings, a random sampling of which might include Virgin Mary sightings, an elderly couple arrested for clamming in the waters of Jamaica Bay, men caught having sex with kidnapped chickens in a Mississippi motel room, and Aborigines attacking Australian police with frozen kangaroo tails.

He teased me for quitting New York in favor of small-town life, a move that he insisted could not possibly be permanent. *Seriously, babe,* he wrote, *when are you coming back home? This is your home, after all, or do you plan to spend the rest of your life in that scummy little guppy tank up there? New York misses you, I miss you! So ditch the Nutmeg State and get your city-slicking ass back down here, okay???*

O.O.T.T.G.A.I.N.Y.*
*One Of The Two Greatest Artists in New York**

**Other famous showbiz teams: Martin & Lewis, Nichols & May, Abbot & Costello, Burns & Allen, Ozzie & Harriet, and Rosey Grier and Ray Milland in THE INCREDIBLE TWO-HEADED MAN.

3

One day a larger than normal parcel arrives in my father's handle-bar basket. Inside it is one of Dwaine's black books, one I've never seen before. No letter, no explanation, just the black book.

I'm in the middle of finals. I have two papers due, one on ethics and problems in advertising, one on the principles of marketing statistic analysis. With no time for it I put Dwaine's black book aside. I tell myself whatever's inside can wait; I'll get to it later.

But after twenty minutes of boning up on discriminant function analogues and stepwise multiple regression, or trying to, I shove my schoolwork aside and pick up Dwaine's notebook.

4

Though the pages still look fresh and white, the notebook is dated 1974, with the words BELFAST, IRELAND written in thick marker across the top of the first page. The notebook contains the usual motley mixture of drawings and newspaper clippings, interspersed between scrawled entries, some plain and clear, others illegible, indecipherable, or a mix of both.

So I await the train to the ferry, with blind drunkenness not suited [sic] alternative to the cold, my goals right now being to weather a third cup of tea from the Indians at the counter and take charge of the Euston Station day, still a good three hours from daylight in this magnificence [?]

Dwaine arrived in Belfast on Easter Sunday, 1975. As his Irish luck would have it he got there just as the Protestant

Orangemen were gearing up for their parade.

Yes, lads, the Tims and Huns have broken out their colors to loudly proclaim the history of their tireless faith in colorful clashes and killings via fresh clashes and killings. That's Easter in Belfast for you. And here I am, folks, one American with a camera around his neck [illegible] Orangemen get it up for their parade of force, thunderous drums, torch-like plumes, and other boisterous intimidations readily[sic] guaranteed to drive many an Irish Catholic saheeb back to the black hole of Calcutta…

Dwaine arrived to streets teaming with police, soldiers and armored vehicles there to protect the loyalist marchers…*Now the parade has started, and the drumbeats ring through the streets, and the orange plumes burn, and teenage girls in the sidelines scream, "koooo-kooooo"—grinning at the decked-out patriots. Do mine eyes decieve[sic] [?]there more soldiers and armored vehicles guarding here than ever I saw in Vietnam?…*

Eager to see the Catholic version of the Easter festivities, Dwaine ran ahead of the marchers to a place called the Cowley House, headquarters of the Greenmen, who had gathered for their own demonstration, their leaders giving speeches from a podium set up on an appropriately green patch of lawn in front of the house.

A fellow named Sam Steele, the Irish American chairman of NORAID, the heavily banned, super-militant faction of the IRA, is going to make a speech guaranteed to, shall we say, liven up the festivities? So cheer up, Virginia, there really is an Easter Bunny.

But it seems I'm getting ahead of myself, or rather ahead of the parade, here, running out of patience, camera clutched to my chest to keep it from swinging wildly into some Brit gob face, eager to get a glimpse (while I can) of Mr. Steele, who's easy enough to glimpse. If provocateurs were paid by the pound Mr. Steele would be one very wealthy provocateur. He's tall, too. One of his henchmen has to adjust the mike for him. Then the speech begins.

It's a fine speech, lads, a very fine speech, and effective as gasoline on a banked fire. Someone cries, someone curses, someone throws a rock, someone kicks, someone punches, someone smashes a window, someone sets a car on fire: yes, lads, a typical peaceful demonstration in the North of Ireland ... The police stop slapping their batons against their black leather gloved palms and bring them down on Catholic heads, breaking shoulders and skulls at random as the Brits roll in their halftracks ... [Illegible matter.]

... the rubber bullets start flying, with the cops targeting five- and six-year-olds. I see one boy get struck point-blank in the chest. As he's being picked up and hauled into the Cowley House I see the blood pooling on his green shirt.

And that's when it starts getting scary, lads. See all this time I've had my face buried in my camera, shooting away, not really thinking that anything that I'm seeing is actually happening. But now all of a sudden things get, uh, real. The iron side gate to Cowley House opens. A woman sticks her head out. Good-looking, red hair, a fresh face decked out with freckles. She yells, "Does anyone out here have any medical experience?"

And damned if she doesn't look straight at me. Next thing I know I'm being helped through the crowd and led into what was the Cowley House living room, only now its[sic] a MASH unit packed with injured bodies, mostly by rubber bullets, with everyone crying, screaming, hysterical. Broken arms, burn and puncture wounds, broken legs. It's like a doll reject factory, or a slaughterhouse for human cattle. I help a girl whose forearm is broken, a compound wound that spurts bright marrow blood. Meanwhile Mr. Steele, the big-bellied blob who set this whole thing off, through the window I see his handlers hustling him away. Then the cops go wild, shooting baton rounds through the windows, the rubber bullets leaving thick welts where they ping off the walls. I'm on top of this little girl, not doing what you think, you gutter-minded fucks. I'm protecting her, pushing her down to keep her from getting shot, her face and mine to the floor, waiting for the baton rounds to stop, thinking for sure we're all going to be killed, yes, lads, every one of us: tomorrow morning the rest of the world will eat us for breakfast in the papers.

Then, just when I'm thinking things can't get worse, the soldiers and cops start with the smoke bombs. CS, they call the stuff. Method of transport: grenade. We're pulling our sweaters and shirts over our heads, coughing and gagging into them.

Then the shooting stops, the smoke clears. Nobody moves. A door smashes open and soldiers and police storm in, their rifles drawn, telling us all to freeze, like we're not frozen already. They throw me in a chair and slap my face until I whip out my passport, God Bless America, and wave it in their faces, shouting, "Back the fuck off, Jack!"—or something to that effect. Which must have worked, babe, because they let me go.

So then it's back out to the Fall Road again, with me stumbling past broken glass and burning overturned cars like a scene out of god knows what, with no idea where I'm going or why, like I even give a shit. I just keep walking, feeling as twisted up and upside-down as I've ever felt in my life (oh, and by the way, the cops took my camera, yes they did, they tore the film out of it and then they kept it for good measure: such considerate blokes). You see, lads, by then I was in what they call a state of shock. And then I see this blue door. Tell me, what is it about blue that's so inviting in times of stress? The blue of the ocean, of the Caribbean on a warm breezy June day. So I knocked, and kept knocking, until this lady answers, a nice lady, a very nice lady who just happened to be blind: worse, she had no eyeballs in her head, none at all, just these two sunken bowls of wrinkled flesh where her eyeballs should have been. "Who is it?" she says. "What do you want?" I say, "I'm an American, a friendly American, and I'm scared." "Come in," she says. I spend the next forty minutes there, having shortbread cookies and tea, listening to her talk all about her son, David, of whom I apparently remind her, though she can't see me. He was killed the year before in an identical riot, the same riot that left her blind. A rubber bullet passed through her skull from ear to ear. She had the scars on both sides of her head to prove it. I kid you not. Right, lads: I couldn't believe it myself.

That rubber bullet, the one that passed through her head? She showed it to me just as I was about to leave, she hands it over to me, a souvineer [sic]. I said, "Are you sure?" She says, "What do I need it for? It's done with me."

More newspaper clippings about the riots—though none mention either Crowley House or anyone named Steele. The entries resume with Dwaine meeting the redheaded woman from Crowley House.

...We sat in a pub engaged in that most popular Irish pastime, debating the so-called Troubles, as they're known here. By now I'm VERY motivated, and say so. She puts me in touch with a guy named Dermott, a.k.a. "Captain Midnight", a hospital orderly by day, by night Commander in Chief of the INLA, that's Irish National Liberation Army to you innocents on the far side of the pond, another violent spin-off of the IRA, specializing in acts of mass destruction after midnight, as in KABOOM!—hence Dermott's comic-book character nom de plume.

A week later these two guys come to the flat where I'm staying. We sit down to tea and they riddle me with questions, you know, personality profile shit, wanting to make sure my Claddagh is in the right place ('tis Ireland, my Ireland). Once they decide that I can be trusted they give me my first basic assignment, namely to spy on a certain hotel lounge called the Egalitine [sic], where British officers swill away their guilt nightly. The lounge is owned by a cat lick (that's slang for Catholic) named Bruce who's been told repeatedly not to serve the Brits. My assignment: sit at a table with my notebook looking like a bored stupid tourist ("That should present no problem for you, eh, Yank?"), gathering as much reconnaissance as possible—how tables and chairs are arranged, where officers stand or sit, when they come in, when they leave, and so on. "Give us everything you can, lad," they tell me quietly, and then they leave.

So, what does you're[sic] newly minted lower-rank terrorist do? He goes to the "Egg," as it's called, orders up a pint, and sits there at a strategic table with his notebook open, trying to look nonchalant as he makes his notes. Two days into my spying mission, I'm sitting there and who should walk in but the very two Brit officers who sat me down and slapped me silly at the Crowley House? No shit, they sidle up to the bar. I'm thinking, man, this is too much for me. But I'm being tested, remember? And have a mission. So I start sketching them, little thumbnails of their faces. I'm sketching away, jotting notes, transcribing snatches of conversation, trying to be the soul of discretion when one of them turns and sees me and, sure enough, hops off his stool and comes over. And I'm thinking, now you've done it, boy now you've stepped in it big time, now you're gonna DIE. Then the guys he was talking to slide off their stools and follow him.

Oh fuck, I'm thinking, oh fuck, oh fuck.

The first goon says, "Let's see the notebook, lad," and I hand it over to him. He flips through it, with me sitting there dripping sweat, knowing if they recognize me, or decipher my handwriting, that's it, I'm cooked, I may as well sing Amhán na bhFiann *or spit in the fucker's eye. The goon nods his head and says, "Good hand you've got. But tell us, lad, what's the idea, hey? Why draw us?" He doesn't recognize me!*

"I'm an art student," I tell him. "Visiting from New York."

"A Yank, is it?"

"New York, New York," sings one of his pals. "My kind of town."

"Leonardo's got you dead to rights, eh, Ben?"

"You gonna do us in color?" the sergeant says, handing my notebook back.

"Yeah, sure, why not?" I say. (Does he not know flop-sweat when he sees it, lads? Or does he assume we Yanks always perspire like that?)

"Just don't make me ugly like you made him!" says the other goon.

They all laugh as they shuffle back to their table.

Three days later, at exactly two minutes to midnight, a yellow Morris Minor [my papa's car!] *stuffed with a mixture of C-4, gasoline and Grade-A horseshit pulls up in front of The Eglantine Lounge. Two minutes later a timing device made using an old electric clock engages a trigger mechanism, discharging 12 volts from the car's twin six-volt batteries through a set of jumper cables into the smelly mixture. The blast blows out windows two miles away. In all seven people are killed, including the lounge's Fenian owner, Bruce, three Brit officers, and two soldiers. Cheers arose when, at a cell meeting three days later, Captain Midnight proclaimed, "The Egg, ladies and gentlemen, is now officially an omelet."—a tactless observation, I*

agree, but one that met with howls of approbation and—
        The next page is torn out.
        So is the next. The rest of the notebook yawns empty.

5

It's past midnight. My parents went upstairs and to bed hours ago. Aside from the growl of the furnace and the hum of the dehumidifier, the house is silent. I switch off my desk lamp.

Through the narrow high basement window moonlight creeps, watery and gray as dishwater. I feel mildly poisoned by Dwaine's past, as if it were some rare toxin or radioactive isotope that has entered into my bloodstream through the fingers that have touched his black book. Why does he insist on dosing me with his life?—with his history? with his impossibly cinematic past? A soldier, a would-be priest, a Peace Corps volunteer, a filmmaker, a terrorist. What next? A lion tamer? An astronaut? A Secret Service agent? A stamp collector? A prizefighter? A pimp? What isn't Dwaine Fitzgibbon capable of doing?

Once I'd have given anything to know. Now I don't *want* to know. Anything.

Go away, Dwaine. *Please.* Leave me to my dull Connecticut aspiring bourgeoisie life.

6

Days later he writes me again:

I just had the most amazing dream. I'm riding in the back seat of a limo with Dustin Hoffman. Me and Dustin, man, we're having a helluva time, really paling it up, when suddenly Dusty leans over and kisses me on the mouth, tongue and all. At first I'm shocked, but then, not wanting to offend the star of such classics as The Graduate *and* Midnight Cowboy, *I play along, but after a while I start laughing.*

Dusty says, "What's so funny?" I say, "I'm not gay!" He says, "Me, neither!" And then we both crack up. Then the chauffeur turns around and takes off his cap, only he turns out to be her, and she turns out to be Venus, who's lying here next to me as I write this letter to you, babe. The bottom line being that a month from now Ms. Wiggins and I are tying the knot, so get those red overalls dry cleaned and pressed and stick a white carnation in the button hole, 'cuz like it or not you are and always will be my best man.

7

Montage, night:

    A canvas-tented barge docked on the Brooklyn side of the East River. Summer drizzle softens the night air as the fabled bridge sizzles with traffic overhead. Ice mermaids cradle silver caviar buckets; oysters in cracked shells drift on foaming seas of chipped ice; jumbo shrimp cling to the caldera rims of lurid cocktail sauce volcanoes; a swing band in vanilla jackets and gold cardboard derbies swishes and whumps rhythms into the drizzly dark. The river wears three diamond bracelet bridges on its black sleeve. Across the oily dark waters Manhattan wastes as much electricity as possible.

    Maybe it's because my mother makes bridal headpieces for a living, but I never cared for wedding receptions. Champagne makes me dizzy, so do hothouse flowers and a choice of prime rib *au jus* or poached salmon in dill sauce. This barge's steady swaying doesn't help matters.

    I lean against the railing, watching the pattern of lights stitched in gold across the water, sipping champagne despite my queasiness. Across the dance floor the newlywed groom spins his bride. Dwaine wears a white tuxedo, its lapel bloodied by a carnation. Venus floats on a cloud of taffeta and silk. Her white arms pour out of her sleeves like cold milk from a twin-spouted pitcher. They've been dancing for an hour, at least.

A dozen yards from me, standing side by side against the same railing, Mr. and Mrs. Fitzgibbon watch their newlywed son dance. Mr. Fitzgibbon wears a slate blue serge suit, smokes a fat cigar and looks like a bald paunchy Kirk Douglas. Tufts of white hair sprout from his nostrils and earlobes. Dwaine called him "black Irish," but he's not dark at all, not dark enough, anyway, to hide the gin roses that blossom on his cheeks. Nor does his wife look the least bit like she's descended from Moorish slaves. A small woman with a pinched nervous bird face, she waves her husband's cigar fumes theatrically away from her nose but makes no effort to remove herself from them.

What are Dwaine's parents doing here, anyway? I wonder. Didn't he disown them, or vice-versa? I had put the very same question to Dwaine earlier.

"Two things the Irish can't resist," he replied, his breath reeking with cigars and gin, "weddings and wakes. Any excuse to get tanked."

A waiter floats by. I toss back my champagne dregs and nip myself a fresh flute. The waiters and I are dressed exactly alike. How was I supposed to know that only butlers and waiters wear *black* ties with tails?

The dance ends. Dwaine breaks away to maneuver among guests, shaking hands, slapping backs, yelling out orders to photographers and caterers, presiding over his own wedding like Joseph L. Mankiewicz directing *Cleopatra*. Is this the gritty filmmaker I once knew and loved? Can Dwaine possibly be the force behind this gaudy, overproduced tripe? Where are the dope needles? Where are the lobotomy victims, the spurting amputees? Where are the bullet holes and the buckets of (fake) blood?

8

A wedding cake shaped like an old-fashioned movie camera is wheeled onto the barge deck. As best man it's up to me to give

a toast. The band drummer taps a perfunctory roll. My tongue
lubricated by five flutes of bubbly, I stammer out something to
the effect that life with Dwaine, however likely to be fraught
and unpredictable, is just as bound not to be dull.

"To Mr. and Mrs. Dwaine Sean Fitzgibbon," I slur. "May
theirs be a colorfully fucked-up future!"

My specious speech earns a smattering of applause, but not
from Mr. and Mrs. Fitzgibbon, who glare at me as bride feeds
cake to groom. Just as Venus turns to feed me a slice a tugboat blunders by, churning up a swell that rocks the barge on
its moorings, causing those less seaworthy among us—a popula-
tion including yours truly—to lose their balance. Venus and I
grab hold of each other, only to tumble as one into the cart that
holds the cake. And down everything goes.

"I always thought you were sweet," she says to me afterwards, wiping frosting from my tuxedo lapel with a wet napkin.
Under the colored lights strung over the barge Venus' cheeks
glow tutti-frutti.

"That was a nice little speech you gave there," she tells me
while wiping.

"Spare me, Venus. I spoke crap."

The smell of vanilla rises and flares. It takes me all my self-
control not to pull her into my frosted chest and kiss her—not a
brotherly, best-man kiss, either, but one designed to complicate
things infinitely.

The Blue Danube starts playing. Dwaine snatches his bride
back onto the portable dance floor. I watch them waltz. For a
moment I forget I'm on a barge. I'm deep in space, alone among
planets and stars, watching them waltz across the Milky Way.
The heavens close in, engulfing water, buildings and bridges.
I'm about to skip out of the universe altogether when suddenly
the brightest planet in the sky swings by, grabs me by the arm
and drags me out onto the dance floor.

"Come on now," Venus says, seeing my reluctance. "The
best man is supposed to dance with the bride. It's tradition!"

As in Van Gogh's most famous painting the blazing skyline swirls. Bodies drift, vessels and buildings bob, skyscrapers sway. Suddenly the barge starts pitching violently, hawsers snapping, breaking free from the dock to drift away on swollen seas. Having grabbed the video camera from the photographer the groom records our careening dance.

"Take one!" he shouts. "Treachery on the high seas as best man woos fickle bride! Laughter, tears, curtain!"

The dark waters rise and I lurch.

Groom keeps shooting as best man pukes over barge rail.

9

A month and a week after the wedding Venus phoned. I was asleep in the basement when the telephone rang. It was after midnight. Guessing that the call was for me and wanting to spare my parents a rude awakening, I hurried up the stairs in the dark. On the way I knocked over a bottle of calamine lotion I'd been applying to the mosquito bites I got at my job, emptying those barrels of parts cleaner solvent at dusk. The bottle shattered with a wet thwack on the cement basement floor. I turned to see the pink puddle spread like a lugubrious dream of summers past, then darted the rest of the way up the stairs to grab the phone on the fourth ring.

"Nigel? You sound out of breath."

"I just ran up a set of stairs," I said, my heart thudding against my chest. Compared to the always cool basement the upstairs air felt soupy. A thin bright slice of moonlight shone under the kitchen door. Since the wedding, except for a postcard from Spain where Venus and Dwaine honeymooned, I hadn't heard a thing from them. I sat in the dark hallway.

"How are you?" I said, my voice fuzzy with sleep.

"Oh, I could be worse." She didn't sound right.

We waded through a river of small talk. Her voice sounded

fragile as if spun from glass. Finally she got to the point.

"Dwaine's missing," she said. "He's been gone for a week. He just disappeared." They hadn't fought, she said. "You don't have any idea where he is, do you, Nigel?"

I almost mentioned his hideaway under Times Square, then thought better of it.

"He used to go visit his brother's grave."

"Dwaine has a *brother?*"

"Jack. He's buried in Calvary Cemetery."

"He never said anything about a brother. When did he die? *How* did he die?"

"In the war."

"Which war?"

"Vietnam."

"Dwaine had a brother in *Vietnam?*"

I said nothing.

She asked, "Older or younger?"

"Older. Look, don't you think it would be better if Dwaine told you these things himself?"

"It would be," she replied bitterly, "except Dwaine didn't tell me, and besides, he's not here, remember? Sorry, Nigel. I don't mean to jump down your throat. I'm upset, that's all."

"I'm sure he'll turn up," I said. "Dwaine's like that. He does things on impulse. He'll be all right. He's like a cat; he always lands on his feet." I scratched a mosquito bite on my neck:

"There's something else I need to ask you, Nigel."

"Shoot."

"Is Dwaine an alcoholic?"

The tip of a laugh almost snorted its way through my nostrils, but I managed to convert it into a cough. How could Venus not know that Dwaine drank? His drinking was as much a part of Dwaine as that whale of a forehead, as that fake front tooth.

"He drinks," I said.

"That's not what I'm asking. I'm asking is he an alcoholic?"

"I'm no expert on these things, Venus."

"Just say what you *think!*"

A pause. "Yeah. I guess so."

She thanked me and hung up.

10

Three weeks later Venus phoned again. She said she was leaving Dwaine. She'd been offered a job with a theater down in North Carolina and was taking it.

"At least it'll give me some time to decide whether or not I want to stay married to a lunatic," she said.

It was a Thursday morning. The house was empty. My mother was at the bridal boutique and my father had just left for Waterbury to buy some electronic parts. I sat in the breakfast nook. The cold September sun leaked in through the gaps in the yellow kitchen curtains to bounce off the chrome top of my mother's stove.

"To think of all the crazy things I could've done with my life," Venus said, sniffing. "I could have gotten a full body tattoo. I could have dined on Japanese blowfish livers. I could have bungee-jumped off the top of the Empire State Building. But no, I had to go and do the craziest thing of all and marry Dwaine Fitzgibbon."

"Why *did* you marry him?" I couldn't help asking.

"Because he was exciting. Because I felt sorry for him. Because he asked me to. I don't know. Why does anyone do anything? Why did you *let me* marry him?"

" ... "

"You could have stopped me, you know. But you didn't. Why didn't you, Nigel? Why did you leave New York? Why didn't you stay and fight for me, if you liked me so much? If you were in love with me, instead of running off like a coward? What were you afraid of? The city? Dwaine? Me? Life? *Everything?*" I heard her blow her nose. "I'm sorry, Nigel; I don't know what

I'm saying. I'm blaming you, like it's your fault that I did something so totally stupid. You had nothing to do with it. And anyway Dwaine's my problem. I shouldn't take it out on you." She sniffles. "It's just been hard. We never do normal things together, dull, ordinary, boring things. You know, like watching the six o'clock news on TV, eating a quiet meal, playing Scrabble. Every moment has to be fraught with passion or fury or comedy or conflict, there can't be any non-dramatic moments, like every frame has to be filled, like—like it's all one big—"

"Movie?" I guessed.

"That's right, like a big movie. That's just how it is with Dwaine, isn't it? I used to believe him when he said he wanted movies to live up to reality. But it's not true. He wants reality to live up to the movies. He insists on it. My God, how can he *stand* it? I know *I* can't." She sniffled. "God, I'm such a wreck. I haven't slept in three days. I've got these great dark circles under my eyes. My cheeks are turning yellow. I look like the Pillsbury Doughboy with a progressive liver disease."

I offered up a few lame excuses on Dwaine's behalf, but whatever I said only pointed up his deficits and made things that much worse. Anyway it was too late; she'd already made up her mind.

"Unless he quits drinking and starts going to A.A. meetings—" she said.

And then we were interrupted.

11

The odd mewling sound came from somewhere outdoors. I parted the yellow curtains. Through the garage door window I saw the rounded top of my father's car. I told Venus that I was sorry, but something had come up; "I think my father may be in trouble. I'll call you back," I said and I hung up.

Barefoot, I hurried out into the garage. My father sat in the back seat of his Morris Minor, tears in his eyes. His face was ashen. "Ah, there you are, Nigel, old boy. Perhaps you'll enlighten me: Where the devil is the bloody steering wheel?"

I drove him to the emergency room. As my mother and I waited they tested his brain. The results indicated a minor stroke brought on either by late-onset diabetes or a sky-high cholesterol count, or both.

Too much coarse-cut Chiver's orange marmalade on buttered Thomas' protein toast. Too many soft-boiled eggs.

12

My father recovered, or seemed to. But then it happened again. We'd gone for a little hike. It was one of those mild Indian summer days, with a wet, mossy smell in the air. A rainstorm the night before had rinsed all the colors of the world, leaving them so clear and crisp they looked as though they could shatter like glass.

The hike was my father's idea. We drove to Newtown, five miles away, to an abandoned railroad bed we had explored when I was five or six years old, and where a pair of tunnels carved into the limestone passed over and under each other. I remembered how, back then, as we walked through one of the two tunnels, I saw a hornet's nest looming, big as a barrel, fat white hornets buzzing all around it. I refused to go on. "I'll get stung!" I said. "Rubbish!" my father replied, urging me forward as I buried my face in his ratty cardigan. Sure enough, as we passed by the nest a hornet stung me with a blinding white flash. The pain swelled like a dissonant symphony in my cheek. I wailed all the way back to my father's car. "There, there, old boy," he said, holding me. "There, there."

This time we didn't enter either of the tunnels. Instead we walked the opposite way down the gravelly railroad bed to where it cut past a stand of willow trees. There, at the base of the embankment, lay a pond, a small one, its surface covered with small yellow leaves shed by the willow trees. The sun felt warm on my arms and neck. I couldn't resist. I sat on a rock and untied my shoelaces. My father said, "What are you doing?"

"Going for a dip, what does it look like?"

"Are you daft? It's much too cold!"

"Rubbish!"

In fact the water turned out to be surprisingly warm. I had already entered when, to my surprise and delight, my father followed suit, going in slowly, his way, massaging handfuls of water over his sunken sagging gray chest, his ancient uncircumcised penis casting a drooping shadow as I treaded water nearby, floating via the faintest butterfly-like movements of my fingers. Together we swam across the pond, me freestyle, my father doing his sidestroke-scissorkick, our bodies cutting black trails through the carpet of golden leaves.

We were headed back to the car when suddenly my father couldn't remember the word for *forest*. He said "wood", "arms," "alberi" (Italian for "trees")…As he kept trying to speak simple words gave way like those flimsy rope bridges in old Tarzan movies, leaving him stranded at the edge of a chasm. He kept struggling, his whole face turning a series of increasingly deep shades of red until I made him stop. By the time we got to the hospital, my poor father couldn't remember his own name.

13

Papa was still in the hospital when, as if protesting his absence, The Building burned down. I was sleeping in my basement bedroom when the pounding on the kitchen door woke me. I opened it to the silhouette of a fireman, his helmet haloed in flickering orange light.

"You folks own that building down there?"

"Yeah."

"Well—it's on fire."

Minutes later my mother and I stood with winter coats over pajamas watching as firemen smashed windows and aimed their languid hoses at flames that licked telephone wires. My mother raised a handful of trembling fingers to her Sophia Loren lips.

"*O dio*," she said.

That same morning, after sunrise, I sifted through the sour ashes and muck. Boxes of drowned transistors, lenses and tubes, a waterlogged oscilloscope, a typewriter, its keys splayed and already rusted. I salvaged a few of my father's old notebooks, some relays and transformers and a big box of lenses. Except for a light coating of soot, miraculously, my father's painting-in-progress, the one of the monastery built on top of the Palisades overlooking the Hudson River, survived. Otherwise the loss was total.

I was just about to leave when I noticed something gleaming in a mound of ashes and vermiculite, a copper turning from my father's lathe.

With it in my shirt pocket I climbed back up the hill.

X

*Figure
In
Orange
(Message Movie)*

Soon after earning my bachelor's degree, in the fall of 1983, I was hired by a small local advertising agency specializing in periodical inserts, those pesky little promotional cards stamped BUSINESS REPLY MAIL that clutter everyone's favorite magazines. The firm was housed in a converted brass wire and screw factory in Waterbury, twenty miles north of Barnum. My office faced out onto a concrete lot presided over by a tall brick smokestack with a red blinking light on top of it to ward off small aircraft. The railroad ran close by. Every hour endlessly long freight trains jounced the implements I kept in a distributor cap by my drafting table. I was in charge of design and layout. I wrote some ad copy, too.

Meanwhile I sent my C.V. off to the big Manhattan agencies, one of which hired me.

2

The advertising agency I work at takes up the top four floors of the Danforth Building, an art deco skyscraper on Lexington Avenue in the high forties. According to local myth its architect and builder, Raymond Charles Danforth III, dreamed of building the world's tallest skyscraper, only to see his dream shattered when, late one night within days of his building's completion, a shimmering 197-foot-tall ziggurat of stainless steel was hoisted by derrick out of the rival Chrysler Building's unfinished crown, flipping Danforth the equivalent of an architectural middle finger. Danforth lived out his remaining years in seclusion, seldom venturing forth from the penthouse he built for himself on the top floor—and which the president of my agency now occupies. The suite's southern-facing windows, the ones that would have gazed upon the Chrysler Building, Danforth had painted over with a *trump l'oeil* skyline, one wherein that *other* skyscraper didn't exist.

My office has one slim window, a slit of glass where a partition has lopped off a once imposing view of the harbor, with ferries, freighters and other vessels scratching chalk marks in the pea-green water. If I crane my neck slightly I can even see the Statue of Liberty, as small as the tip of my mechanical pencil, her torch restored recently back to gilded glory courtesy of President Ronald Reagan, Lee Iococca, and the freshly bailed-out Chrysler Corporation.

I am of the city, one with its plan and purpose. I remember those days back in art school, after Dwaine left, scudding along anonymous streets like yesterday's *Post* kicked by a dirty breeze. Now I'm as integral to the city as its subterranean steam pipes and vertiginous towers, as its yellow taxis and black headlines. Entering my building's polished lobby each morning, standing before its rows of filigreed brass elevators, I feel a solid rush of pride, as if I, not Mr. Danforth, built the skyscraper named for him, girder by girder.

I'm not just living the American Dream, I'm driving it, engineering it —like those streamlined locomotives that thunder across the screen in old movies—throttling it toward that elusive vanishing point on the horizon known as Success.

3

The advertising business has long thrived on its system of mentors. Mine was a broad-shouldered, barrel-chested, Yonkers

born-and-raised goombah named Donald "Donny" Colosimo.
A foaming pompadour surfed over his Neanderthal forehead.
He wore fat rings on all seven of his fingers (the other three
lost to a Viet Cong bayonet), and psychedelic paisley neckties
with clashing rainbow suspenders. Stubble shadowed his jowls
by noon. He had a solid reputation for goosing female cowork-
ers as they bent to slurp from the water fountain.

Bad taste was Donny's creed. He practiced it like a funda-
mentalist zealot, he preached it like an apostle. According to
Donny, good taste was elitist, fragile, feminine, transitory, devi-
ous and doomed. Bad taste—on the other hand—was pluralis-
tic, patriotic, honest and rugged. Bad taste had staying power. It
was the future.

"Good taste is dead," Donny proclaimed. "I killed it sixteen
years ago. I drove a stake through its refined heart."

4

Our first lunch together isn't a Smith & Wolensky steak and
martini job, but sushi and cold soda at the Golden Cucumber,
around the corner from the United Nations.

In keeping with the global theme the Golden Cucumber's
ceiling is festooned with flags from around the world, with the
stars and stripes taking center stage. "You see that," says Donny,
pointing a wasabi-laden chopstick at it. "That's the flag of the
United States of America. It's a pretty flag, a very pretty flag. I
lost three fingers for that flag. But it's not the flag we salute."
He peels the label off his cola bottle. "*This* is the flag we salute,
our biggest account, or it will be soon. Up there is the flag of
America. This is the flag of the flag of America. And this," he
takes out his wallet, takes a twenty from it, "is the flag of the flag
of the flag of America." He lifts a brown slab of raw eel to his
mouth. "*Capeesh?*

"Now. What do you want to know about me? Never mind:

I'll tell you what you need to know. At fourteen I weighed three hundred and twenty-seven pounds. At fifteen my mom and pop died in a car accident on the Deegan on the way home from a Yanks-Red Sox game (the Yankees lost seven to nothing). At sixteen I moved in with Skip D'Angelo, the famous fighter trainer, he trained Patterson, Torres, Sugar Ray, you name it, up in Catskill. Skip taught me to respect myself and stop being a fuck-off wise-ass, which I was. I lost a hundred pounds, learned to box, got drafted, went to 'Nam, got my fingers sliced off, served my country, survived. I'm here. I've said enough. Short and sweet: I don't put up with any bullshit. Now tell me your story. And make it snappy 'cause time is money and I'm a man of costly means. You dig that California roll?"

"It's not a hamburger," I said, "but it'll do."

"Kid, I like your brass."

5

Donny invites me to his home: a six thousand square foot northern Westchester ice-cream headache compounded of a half-dozen architectural styles, as if as many drunken builders had engaged in a game of exquisite corpse. His "estate," as Donny refers to it, is arrived at by way of a twisting driveway of white gravel winding its way through a dappled tunnel of sycamore trees, past banks of tulips and rosebushes, and up a stretch of lawn impervious to dandelions and so resolutely green it might have been painted on with a roller. As Donny's convertible Jaguar pulls closer I see the artificial babbling brook spanned by a red pagoda bridge, and the red clay tennis court. Sharing the lawn with a lavender gazing ball and the lantern-bearing ceramic coachman is a trampoline-sized satellite dish ringed with purple and pink azaleas.

As for the house itself, along with its hodgepodge of gables and rooflines it features gargoyle downspouts and gutter sprites, a veneer stone facade, and an attached garage with efficiency apartment inhabited by Donny's mother, who sits sunning herself in a folding lawn chair in the yard alongside it. As we roll into the garage Donny blows her a kiss.

The gallon-jug zinfandel aesthetic persists indoors, where my mentor shows off his passive magnetic field burglar alarm system, his brass-plated touchpad doorknobs, his Côte D'Azur hanging tapestries, his pianoforte, his functionless ceiling beams, and his aquarium coffee table populated by scarred Siamese fighting fish. Downstairs, in the finished basement, Donny leads me from walk-in humidor to mini-bar to wine cellar to paneled rumpus room with convertible gaming console. One by one, from a golden oak gun cabinet, he extracts the crown jewels of his arsenal, floating them on the emerald sea of his billiards table, their polished parts redolent of gun cream and stock oil.

Donny hands me his prize possession, an Israeli-made AK-47 that he invites me to fondle while offering to let me give "her" a try. "I got a pile of cinderblocks out back we can shoot the shit out of," he informs me.

Firearms frighten me. It has long been my understanding that they are used to kill people. At my lack of enthusiasm Donny pulls a long face. To make amends I say, "But it really is a most beautiful gun. Truly."

"Gun?" Donny snatches the AK-47 from me. "Kid, this ain't no gun. This is a *weapon*." He grabs his crotch. "*This* is a gun."

With me holding my own crotch he makes me repeat after him, *This is my weapon, this is my gun; this is for fighting, this is for fun.*

Within a year I've made Junior Creative Director.

6

My apartment was a brownstone one-bedroom in the upper seventies, in a neighborhood of shabby low buildings that let in lots of air and sunlight. My neighbors were mostly Puerto

Ricans. On sweltering summer days they would sit on their stoops shirtless or in bathing suits, watching their children play in the puddle of an opened fire hydrant, the whoosh of passing traffic a poor substitute for the crashing of surf.

Though no larger than my Barnum basement, I liked my new home. It had high molded ceilings and a fireplace (with enameled tiles and a beveled mirror over the mantle piece). There was a set of bowed mullioned bay windows with built-in box seats and other items that the *New York Times* real estate ad referred to collectively as "nice details." The window faced the three brownstones across the street: brown, pink, and white—like a freshly-opened carton of Neapolitan ice cream, a view snared by the branches of a ginkgo tree flaunting its demure, fan-shaped leaves.

The tree was a female. In summer its rotting fruit exuded an odor reminiscent of vomit. But even that I learned to like.

I furnished the place with a brown leather sofa, an antique Kadmus & Kimble rocker, two kilims, and—my one pure extravagance—a 1930's English maple bar unit whose inged top opened to a display of bright lights and mirrors etched with floating cocktail shakers and droll martini glasses. At two hundred and fifty dollars it was by far the most expensive thing I owned, its ostentation compounded by the fact that I rarely drank hard liquor. Still, its mere presence brightened that already bright apartment up. To open its top was to throw an instant, Prohibition-era cocktail party.

7

I'm sitting on the built-in window bench, sipping my morning coffee, when a voice climbs up from below. I lean out of the window and see a man dressed from head to toe in orange—orange wool beanie, pumpkin windbreaker, tangerine gloves, nasturtium sneakers…He wears a Howdie Doodie mask. On the sidewalk next to him sits a familiar-looking, brass-fixtured aluminum trunk.

He yells up at my window:

"Stellla! Hey, *Steeelllllllaaaa!*"

"Dwaine?" I shout down. "Is that you?"

"No, it's the ghost of Stanley Kowalski wearing a Howdie Doodie mask."

"How did you find me?" Except for my parents and some people at work I haven't given anyone my new address.

"Help me up with this trunk, will you, babe, and then I promise to answer all of your pointless and impertinent questions."

I help him lug the trunk up to my apartment. The thing weighs a ton. "What the hell's in it, anyway?" I ask, lugging.

"A dead body. No, the uncut *Citizen Kane.*"

We lug it up my three flights. While we do I ask about Venus, trying to sound as casual as possible. I've gotten over her, of course. Completely. Still, I don't want Dwaine to think I'm too interested.

"Better without me, apparently," he says. We stop and rest on a landing. Dwaine braces himself, hands on knees, coughing. He's still wearing the Howdy Doodie mask. "So," he says when the coughing fit ends, "do I rate a hug from my best pal, or what?"

"Not with that thing on, you don't."

He takes the mask off. He's shaven not just the beard but his entire head, Marine-style. *Semper Fi.* He looks pale, thin, and more than a little dangerous. I give him a hug.

We pull the trunk into my apartment. He falls into my Kadmus & Kimble rocking chair. "Walk-ups, man. There ought to be a law."

"Seriously, Dwaine, what's in the trunk?"

"Seriously? My whole life. Notebooks, screenplay drafts, all the short films we made in college. And a power of attorney, signed and notarized. I'm feeding myself to the authorities. It's why I'm wearing these duds. I figure if I'm going to be a Federal prisoner I might as well dress the part. By the way, did you know orange is Frank Sinatra's favorite color?"

"You're going to *prison?*"

"Close. I'm signing myself into the V.A. hospital."

"Are you serious?"

"Oh, yeah. As serious as a judge having a heart attack."

"Does Venus know about this?"

"It was her idea, practically. She seems to think I need a gaggle of shrinks to keep me from going deep. Calls me a suicidal dipso, imagine that? Speaking of which: got anything decent to drink in this yuppie palace of yours?" His eyes zero in on my English bar unit, the one with the hinged top. "What's this?" he says, going to and opening it. The lights and mirrors dazzle. "Holy shit, there's a whole Busby Berkley musical going on in here! Man, look at this shit! He's got a sterling silver ice bucket, with *penguins* on it, for Christ's sake!"

"It's stainless steel. Two dollars at the flea market."

"I've got a sudden craving for a martini, extra dry and dirty. Just have the vermouth blow a kiss to the gin."

"How about a glass of water?"

"'Water is for those who have sinned.' Remember that waiter in Florida telling us that?"

"It was the sommelier."

"Huh?"

"It was the sommelier, not the waiter."

"You really do worry me at times, you know that, now, don't you, babe?"

I grab a bottle of seltzer from my refrigerator. Except for some olives and a half-finished bottle of Riesling left over from a date two nights before there's not much in there. Like most bachelors I rarely cook. The stereotype pleases me. It pleases me to fit into any largely accepted social pattern, including this one that Dwaine, now, with his surprise visit, threatens to dash like a rock hurled into a reflection on still water. When I come back with the water Dwaine is holding one of my pipes, the ones I keep in a rack next to the Kadmus rocker. I keep them for decorative purposes, though occasionally I give one a puff or two.

"You'll die of jaw cancer," he says, twirling it. "Like Dr. Freud."

I take the pipe from him, put it away.

"Speaking of geniuses: how's Professor Whip 'n' Chill?"

"My father? He's fine." In fact my father isn't. He's had two more mini-strokes. With each he becomes more forgetful. "He forgets things," I say.

"Man, I'd like to forget a few things myself, like the last fifteen years. My dogs are killing me. Got any Epson salts, by any chance?"

I fill a big pot with steaming water and salt. With his feet immersed Dwaine sits back sighing and moaning, making soft, low, faintly orgasmic sounds. The aluminum trunk sits on my kilim. I tap it with my toe.

"What am I supposed to do with this?"

"Up to you, babe. Have it auctioned at Sotheby's. Bury it. Send it over Niagara Falls in a barrel. Better yet send it to Charles Scribner's Sons and have them publish it before I perish. Write a killer cover letter."

"I'm serious, Dwaine."

"I'm serious, too, dead serious. Oh, speaking of which: now that you're the executor in charge of my estate, you have to promise me one thing: that you won't kill yourself, at least not any time soon, not while my life is in your hands. Promise?"

"I promise."

"Honest Injun?"

"Yes." (My head is spinning.)

"Good, 'cause when you kill yourself you're killing the wrong person. You've heard that one before, I bet." He eyes the glass of seltzer I've given him with tremendous distaste. "This stuff stinks." He puts the soda down, stands up, hugs me. "Gotta run. See you at the funny farm.

"Oh, one last thing," he says on his way out. "Look out for Venus for me, huh, will you? The brightest natural object in the night sky. I'm counting on you to look out for her. You're the only one I trust to look out for her. Okay?"

He runs down the stairs, shouting "Stella!" as he goes.

8

Five thirty a.m. My phone rings.

"Scared." Dwaine breathes heavily, obscenely. "I got scared."

"Where are you?"

With little or no traffic it takes me only twenty minutes to get downtown. I find him sitting in a pay phone booth at the corner of 14th and Avenue C, in the shadow of a Con Ed smokestack belching gloom into the dawn sky. A drizzle falls. He clutches a dead Smirnoff pint. His teeth chatter. Yards away the East River rolls, dark and greasy.

"I chickened out," he says. "I'm a coward."

"No you're not."

"I am, babe. I'm as yellow as a New York City taxi."

Cars and trucks buzz down the avenue, taillights bleeding into puddles. In the proper gloom and from a certain distance all vehicles look poetic. I'm carrying a briefcase full of ad concept boards and my umbrella. I hold the umbrella over our heads. Between Avenues B and A the rain drenches. We duck into Our Lady of the Immaculate Conception. Dwaine kneels at the altar, holding the railing with one hand, the arm of my Burberry raincoat with the other. He sniffs. His nose runs. I let him wipe his snot on my raincoat sleeve. He drops to all fours, crawls up to the Virgin Mary statue, kisses her marble toes. I pull his arm over my shoulder. His fingernails are wedged with dirt. He stinks. He smells like the men's room at Grand Central Station, like a bum. Two old Hispanic ladies who've come to count their rosary beads gape from the pews. One crosses herself.

"*I want a military funeral, and I'm entitled to one, free of charge!*"

"It's not a movie, Dwaine."

"Sure it is, *Dog Day Afternoon*."

The old ladies shuffle nervously out of the church. On our way out, as we pass the votive stands, Dwaine digs into his pea coat pockets, dredges up some coins and hurls them. They clatter down through the banked rows of candles.

"Have you got the papers?"

"Papers?"

"The hospital admission papers?"

"Papers … papers …"

I frisk him. From the depths of his coat lining I withdraw a tattered document.

Name: Fitzgibbon, Sean Dwaine

Department Component and Branch / Class: Army RA UN

Occupation: filmmaker

Date of Birth: 10-31-52

Race (check one): White: Black: Hispanic: Other: Irish

Social Security Number: 074-63-2254

DD214: yes

Occupational Specialties: 91 Alpha 10 (medical corpsman)

Grade, Rate or Rank: PFC

Awards/Citations: Vietnam Campaign Ribbon, National Defense Service Ribbon, Combat Infantry Badge, Expert (rifle), Sharp-shooter Medal

DEROS: May 5, 1973

Reason and Authority: Conscientious Objection

Character of Discharge: Honorable

Name of Spouse: Veronica (nee Wiggins)

In case of emergency contact: Nigel DePoli.

9

At the revolving door entrance of the Veteran's Affairs Medical Center at First Avenue and 23rd Street he pulls me into a fierce hug, his three-day stubble scratching my cheek.

"Will you always be my friend? A-a-always, you stinking yuppie greaseball?" He gives my earlobe a lick, then pushes through the revolving doors.

It's for his own good, I tell myself, standing there with my briefcase, forgetting to hold the umbrella over my head. His own good.

He faces me, grinning through glaring layers of plate glass, mouthing something.

Steve McQueen, I mouth back. *Papillon.*

XI

*In
Cloud-Cuckoo
Land
(Gritty Grim
Documentary)*

High-angle crane shot: the illicit lovers holding hands as they climb up the steep driveway toward a cluster of red brick buildings perched on a grassy acropolis overlooking the wide, silent Hudson River.

Burn in: April, 1984.

At first they don't notice the walls, then they're everywhere: walls of stone, brick, metal and cinderblock, some crowned with razor wire, others spangled with institutional ivy. Surrounding them.

"Are they to keep crazy folk in or sane people out?" Venus wonders.

"Both, I suppose."

They pass a miniature wooden lighthouse ringed with tulips in full bloom. Planted among the tulips, a varnished wooden sign says:

DWIGHT DAVID EISENHOWER
VETERAN'S ADMINISTRATION MEDICAL CENTER

A lovely day, the sky a blue bowl dolloped with whipped clouds. It's spring, but with a wintry nip to the air. A chilled breeze stirs the buds of a copper beech tree. The beech trees are everywhere, with asphalt sidewalks winding around them and benches parked in their shade, one bench per tree. The grounds are pristine, no bottle caps, gum wrappers or cigarette butts anywhere to be seen. Except for the walls and fences, they could easily be the grounds of a typical second-tier northeastern college campus.

Halfway up the driveway a trim memorial garden bristles with budding rosebushes and bronze busts of dead generals.

Nigel shivers. He hasn't had anything for breakfast, hadn't been feeling hungry. Now he feels lightheaded. He stops walking.

"You okay?" Venus asks him. She wears dark sunglasses and a canary scarf over her head.

"Fine." He shivers again, deeply.

"Nervous?"

"Nah, just a bit cold."

Through Venus's sunglasses he can't see her ice-blue eyes, with their pink coronas. Under the yellow scarf her parchment-colored hair is shaven down to pale fuzz. Martyred to Dwaine's cause.

"Dwaine will be so glad to see you. You know he asks about you every time we talk. Sometimes I swear he should have married you instead of me."

Nigel laughs.

"I'm not kidding. He loves you, Nigel. He really does."

It's a steep climb. They pause again to catch their breaths.

"He told me to tell you you're his best friend."

"Did he?"

"He did."

Nigel nods. With friends like me, he thinks.

2

They stop walking, hold each other. Venus wears her red plaid L.L. Beam blazer with the collar up. Nigel closes his eyes and pulls her closer, bringing her fingers to his nostrils, smelling the residue of that morning's sex. Her fingernails (he sees when he opens his eyes again) are gnawed to the quick; her fingers look like tomato grubs. With his free hand he reaches under her coat to feel the swelling there. "Someone might see us," she says.

"Let them." He kisses her.

"No. Not here." She pulls away. "Not like this."

A resident escorted by two attendants ("angels," Dwaine calls them in his letters) passes by: goggle-eyed, making baboon chatter, drooling, his stubbled chin glossy with spittle. Nigel wonders out loud, "Why *do* crazy people drool?"

"It's the drugs that they put them on. They affect the salivary glands."

"Huh. That explains it, then."

Clouds drift over the Palisades. A cardinal sings on a beech tree branch, a butterfly embroiders the air. Birds, benches, beeches, butterflies: all seem to take madness in stride.

The main building's echoing marble vestibule reminds Nigel of the lobby of the skyscraper where he works. A security guard has them sign a register and points the way. A dim passageway leads to a sliding door that opens automatically into a bright realm of fluorescent light, where a second guard has them sign another register. Another passageway, another sliding door. Footsteps echo off bright disinfected walls. With each step Nigel's apprehensions grow. What if he lets something slip? What if she does? He's never been much of a good liar, has never been good at all at keeping secrets. Should he even be trying? Why not just have everything out in the open?

Venus stops, faces him.

"You won't say anything, Nigel, will you? About us, or the baby? Please promise me you won't."

He shakes his head.

3

Was just interviewed by the psychiatrist in charge of my "case," a Filipino whose accent was so thick I could barely make out every third syllable. He wrote out my "meds": sincquion(sp?) trilathon(??) and chloral hydrate PRN, with which I've been duly and doubly dosed and which make me feel like a very soft car whose motor keeps idling. The Filipino watched the drugs take effect, made note of my psychic "adjustment," then led me down a hallway smelling of Spic 'n' Span, Clorox, coffee, piss, cigarette smoke, vomit, cum, and carbolic-acid to my new home, where a dozen haggard residents danced the Thorazine shuffle, all giving off the sour wine-and-cheese smell of neglected flesh (why is it, I wonder, that the insane and the dying give off the same cheesy odor?). The first words spoken to me were, "You want me to give you a blow job?" whispered in my ear by a beady-eyed, dandruff-ridden, skeletal chronic…

At the entrance to the Level III Psychiatric Ward (a.k.a. The Bubble), they're greeted by the duty nurse, one Margaret O'Shan, according to the plastic name tag clinging to her bosom. True to Dwaine's description, the living article's face does indeed resemble "a soft pink toilet seat, wide and flat." She wears dark red lipstick, smells of drugstore perfume, and bears an uncanny resemblance to Nurse Rachet in *One Flew Over the Cuckoo's Nest*.

"Wait here please," Ms. O'Shan says, pointing to a pair of steel chairs, then goes off to summon the resident. Nigel's eyes follow her professional white nursing sneakers as they recede down the corridor, kicking up plumes of brightness that echo the fluorescent bulbs slithering along the ceiling. Minutes later she returns with a man who, though not yet middle-aged, is clearly past the glow of youth and whose features, sunken under the faintly strobing lights, bear a sickly caramel hue. He wears a backwards Yankee's baseball cap, dark blue with the initials NY stitched in white, forming an ersatz ideogram. He smiles a gap-toothed smile, the hole where his false tooth used to be. He twitches his lips and shoulders like Bogie. "Of all the gin joints in all the towns in the world, they walk into mine."

The gap in Dwaine's smile grows bigger, the corridor gets smaller. The bright walls close in until there's nothing but a black hole into which Nigel falls, tumbles, swallowed up by a wave of dizziness that starts in his eyes and moves down to his knees, which buckle.

4

All of my personal belongings have been tagged and bagged and stored away in various institutional hiding places, to wit:

1 shoulder bag and portable typewriter: room KG (bldg 12)

1 notebook, 1 gold Claddagh ring, 1 black book & 3 pens (Patient Effects).

1 travel bag containing electric razor & other small valuables (?)

1 patch jacket, Navy pea coat, 2 vests, three shirts & four pairs pants (Patient Effects);

1 knife & scissors: Montrose Police Department…

Close-up: Nigel sipping water from a Dixie cup. Dwaine stands there smiling. He wears a brown pinstriped robe and soft black slippers. He looks dusty and soft, like a charcoal sketch smudged by a kneaded eraser.

It's been three months since Nigel last saw him, three months since the day the police led him off in handcuffs. They had put out an APB a week before, ten days after Dwaine's escape—his third—from the V.A. center in Manhattan, two days after Venus received a letter postmarked Coney Island and containing a small, dense object that Venus for some reason assumed was her husband's false tooth that a dentist had replaced. But when she tore the envelope open a shiny, .44-caliber bullet clattered onto her linoleum kitchen floor. The letter (if you could call it that) was a single sheet of lined paper covered with names in capital letters, with no punctuation or spaces in between. Among those named were two former U.S. Presidents, one former Secretary of State, six former Joint Chiefs of Staff, one Armed Forces Recruiting Station Staff Sergeant Rubin Joseph Fisher, a Dr. Maurice Shattnuck, Dwaine's parents, Venus Wiggins and Nigel DePoli. The letter was pocked with cigarette burns and smudged with what at first looked like chocolate syrup. Then Nigel realized it wasn't chocolate, it was dried blood.

"It's a hit list," Venus explained as they stood side by side examining the instrument by the dull lavender light through her Canal Street window. Venus had painted the brick living room wall a richly lurid shade and hung matching translucent drapes over the sooty windows and gone to town with Chinese paper lanterns, yet still the place felt as tentative and dreary as shirt cardboard. There were pretty things in the apartment but no one seemed to live there, really.

"He's got it all planned. He wants to kill us all, Nigel."

"Dwaine's not going to kill anyone."

"How can you be sure?"

"Because—he's never killed anyone." Though as a matter of fact Nigel wasn't—couldn't be—sure. What about the tales in Dwaine's black books? What about that Belfast pub, or hotel lounge, or whatever it was? The Egg-something? Of all people Dwaine was not the least capable of murder.

Venus shook her head. "I don't know what thought scares me more, him not coming back home or him coming home."

That same morning Nigel phoned Dwaine's V.A. hospital psychiatrist, the Dr. Shattnuck whose name appeared in the letter. He drew up the commitment papers. That same afternoon the papers were signed by a judge Terrance Morrell. The police were informed, the APB put out.

The next few nights Nigel stayed at Venus's Chinatown apartment. She wanted him there if and when Dwaine came home. Nigel was asleep on the couch when the sound of the door opening quietly woke him. He saw Dwaine's creeping shadow, and smelled the sour smell that came with it, wrapped like a piece of strong cheese in a draft of cold air. As Dwaine draped his coat over the back of a kitchen chair he said, "Dwaine?"

"Babe, what are you doing here?"

"Venus asked me to stay."

"Where is she?"

Nigel sat up and watched as Dwaine opened the door to their bedroom and slipped silently inside. He heard their voices whispering. As they went on whispering Nigel rifled the pockets of Dwaine's pea coat, which reeked of vomit. Nothing, no gun or pistol, just the empty silver flask. He heard the shower go on. When it stopped he lay perfectly still on the sofa, listening for other sounds, hearing only murmurs. He lay there that way until dawn. Then he phoned the local precinct.

"Give us an hour," he said.

When the police came Dwaine was already up and dressed. Two uniformed officers stood at the door. Dwaine held his arms out for the handcuffs.

"All right, Mr. DeMille, I'm ready for my close-up now."

5

That night there was supposed to be a full lunar eclipse. Venus and Nigel stayed up late watching *Rear Window*. During the scene where Jimmy Stewart watches Raymond Burr walking out of his apartment with a big suitcase, Nigel fell asleep. When he woke Venus stood there in a kimono. She bent forward and kissed him deeply, her tongue taking the measure of his mouth like a blind person groping inside a cave. Like a pair of sleepwalkers they walked into the bedroom. As Venus let the kimono fall it seemed to dissolve into bare flesh. Moonlight through her fire-escape window painted thick slabs of light, bright as burning magnesium, across her skin.

To what at first sounded like a distant foghorn Nigel awoke.

Somewhere down in the street below a car alarm whooped. The room was filled with an oddly non-discriminating darkness. He woke Venus and pointed out the window and through the fire escape just as the last red-rimmed wedge of moon slipped behind earth's shadow, like the lid of an eye closing.

6

It's not quite defined yet, but there appear to be those on this gone-ward who've been here forever, tied to beds, strapped to chairs, pumped full of enough psychotropic drugs to make a whole herd of elephant drool...Mind you, this place has its advantages. Where else can you watch Channel 5 all day long to a pall of people's chain smoking, the volume drowned out by stream-of-consciousness bellowing along the lines of Christohchristmakeitgoawayit'sworsethan mywifeafterIstuckthesteakknifeinherear and stuff like that that makes me laugh so hard I fart out loud...

Dwaine puts an arm around Nigel and hugs him. The short hairs poking out from under his backwards Yankees cap have turned gray. The visible skin above the gown's neckline is stamped with a grid-like pattern, like he's been sleeping on a waffle iron. "It's been a long time since anyone has swooned for me," he says, kissing Nigel under his ear, then turning and giving Venus an almost identical kiss.

"You look good. Both of you. Really good."

He kisses Venus again, a real kiss, giving her hind parts a squeeze. She yelps. Then he grabs Nigel and pulls him into a fierce sudden bear hug that takes Nigel's breath away. Instantly Nurse O'Shan is there, a bleached white wall of authority erected spontaneously between them.

"Will you behave yourself, Mr. Fitzgibbon, or do I have to send you back into the Bubble?" she says in her central casting brogue. Dwaine does a burlesque of cowardly obedience, toes touching, shoulders scrunched, hands folded over his belly.

When she turns her back he shoots an anemic tongue out at her. Nigel snickers; he can't help it.

"So." Dwaine fakes a jab at Nigel's shoulder. "Have you heard the one about the mental patient? He's lying in his hospital bed with a peanut balanced on the tip of his dick. The nurse walks in, sees him and says, 'And just what do you think you're doing, Mr. Bradshaw?' 'Me?' says the guy. *I'm fucking nuts!*'"

Under the banks of fluorescent lights Nurse O'Shan escorts them to the Conference Room, passing a series of opened doors along the way. Standing in one doorway a resident makes a sacrificial offering of a small turd, cupped in his palms like a jewel on a velvet pillow. Nurse O'Shan guides him gently back into his room and closes the door behind him.

"So—how are you, babe?" says Dwaine, putting an arm around Nigel as they follow the nurse down the carbolic acid scented corridor. "Still working at—?" He butchers the name of the ad agency where Nigel works, and where he has just been promoted to Junior Executive in charge of the Purina account. "Saving up for that Bimmer? Moon roof, leather seats?"

"I hate to disappoint you, but I still ride the subway with the rest of the hoi polloi."

"I *am* disappointed indeed. What sort of ad man are you, babe? Don't you want to be gripped by the smell of Corinthian leather as you sit stuck in traffic at the approach to the Midtown Tunnel?" He cuffs Nigel's chin. Nigel looks down at the floor, at the scuffed tiles gliding by under his shiny shoes, moving in tandem with Dwaine's squishy blue hospital slippers.

"What about you?" Nigel asks. "How are you?"

"Me? I'm *fucking nuts!*"

7

In the hallway outside the Conference Room the attendant rises from a table where he's been sitting reading the current issue of *People,* with a grinning photo of Steven Spielberg on the cover. The attendant checks them for contraband, including food (other than soft drinks or tea), newspapers (for some reason books and magazines are okay), and weapons—a category embracing everything from toenail clippers to a surface-to-air missile. Nigel is told to turn out his sports jacket pockets; Venus empties her purse. Margaret O'Shan consults her wristwatch. She tells them they have fifteen minutes, then leaves, her sneakers kicking up fresh white plumes.

"I bet in a week I can plant a bug so far up her ass she won't know whether to shit or wind her wristwatch."

"Be nice," says Venus, who keeps on her plaid jacket though the Conference Room is as warm as a solarium. There's a single barred window through which daylight enters tentatively, and a long folding table surrounded by cheap white plastic chairs. The furniture smells of some form of disinfectant. A framed glassless Van Gogh print, a view of the garden through the epileptic artist's asylum window, is the room's chief adornment, its irony (presumably) inadvertent. Dwaine doffs the Yankees' cap, unveiling a shaven skull, its stubble as ashen as Venus's. Side by side their heads are as smooth and pale as Brancusi marbles.

"You like my new haircut?" Dwaine says, seeing Nigel eye his flesh and bone moon. "The V.A. barber here is a fucking Nazi. I tell him to give me a pair of whitewalls, with a Ricky Nelson flip, so what does Herr Himmler do? He spins me around in his damn barber chair so I can't see the mirror and zzzzzzzzzz—drives a pair of dog-clippers down my skull like it's a '62 Corvette and my head is Route 66." Dwaine's voice, Nigel observes, is low and slurred, like his batteries need charging. "It's the drugs," Dwaine explains. "They've got me on enough lithium to float the Hindenburg." Like a dog he rests his chin on Nigel's shoulder.

"We brought you some tea," Venus says, pulling out the Hellenic to-go cup in its crumpled brown bag and stepping forward with it. "We'd have brought you a bagel, too, but they said it's against the rules."

"Yeah, I might choke myself with the damn thing, or pummel an orderly or two, and then where would I be? They don't call them blunt instruments for nothing." Dwaine turns to Nigel, smiles. "So, what are you out hawking these days? Cheez Whiz? Marshmallow Fluff? S.O.S pads?"

"Don't tease him, Dwaine."

"I'm not teasing, I'm just asking, wondering what's bubbling on the Madison Avenue Wunderkind's front burner? Huh? Pop Tarts? Tang? Strawberry Quick?"

"Meaty Dog," says Nigel reluctantly.

"*Meaty Dog?* They've got you selling *dog* food?"

"Dwaine, come on—"

"Wait, wait. You mean the one where they brand the name into the hamburger patty? That one?"

"They're called Ranch Patties. Meaty Dog Ranch Patties. And the branding iron says '100% Beef.' "

"The branding iron—that wasn't *your* idea? Was it?"

"I had some input on it," Nigel has to admit.

"By God, I'm standing next to a *genius!* Don't tell me to hush-up, Venus, I'm *serious!* I *love* that TV commercial, I do. It's made an indelible impression on me, if you'll pardon the pun. I'll bet half the people in America have seen that commercial, at least half. That makes you more influential than Picasso and Martin Scorsese put together! Hey, do they really brand every ranch patty like that? I mean, if I should go out and buy a box of Meaty Dog Ranch Patties, will I see the name burned in there like they show it on TV?"

"For God's sake it's a commercial, Dwaine," Venus says.

"I *know* it's a commercial; I'm asking the babe, here."

"No. No, you won't."

"In other words it's *fake?*"

"Yes, yes, it's fake."

"I *knew* it!"

"Dwaine, *stop!* That's *enough!*"

Venus has spoken loudly enough to make the attendant put down his *People* and poke his nose into the Conference Room.

"Is there, uh, some problem in here?" he asks.

"No problem at all," says Nigel. "Everything's fine."

8

"They say I'm hearing voices."

"Who says you're hearing voices?"

"They, they. The people in charge of this place, doctors, nurses, shrinks."

"What makes them say that?"

"I don't know: could it be that I'm hearing voices?"

"Are you hearing voices?"

"*They* say I'm hearing them."

"But *are* you?"

"I don't say it."

"So you're not hearing voices?"

"I didn't say that, either."

"Well what are you saying, Dwaine?"

"I'm saying people are talking to me."

"People?"

"Yes, people."

"What people?"

"Different people. People from the past. People who are long dead and gone, or should be. People who aren't in the room when I hear them."

"So in other words the voices are in your head?"

"No, Venus, the voices aren't in my head, the people just aren't in the room."

"Great," says Venus.

"What?"

"If you say you're hearing voices then they'll never let you out of here."

"I didn't *say* I heard voices, I said people are *talking* to me. If the people happen to be invisible that's not *my* fault, now, is it?"

"Who are these people?"

"I *told* you: ghosts."

"Ghosts?"

"Yes, ghosts. Spiritus mundi. Restless souls. They wander into my room when the lights are off and I'm lying in bed. If they have bodies then I don't see them. One of them sounds like Mister Magoo. And one sounds like Henry Kissinger or like Peter Sellers playing Henry Kissinger."

"It's no joke, Dwaine."

"No kidding it's no joke. Who said it was? Do you think I *like* having Henry Kissinger sneak up on me while I'm lying in bed in the dark? You think it *amuses* me? You think I'm *amusing* myself? Is that what you think? Huh? Is it?"

9

Dwaine's forehead burns. His eyes glow bright. He licks his lips, hangs his head, says, "Sorry, sorry." He starts crying. Venus holds him. Over his quaking shoulders she looks at Nigel, who steps over to the window and looks out past its white bars at a beech tree growing there, a big old grandfather of a tree, its trunk six feet wide at the base at least, its bark gray and smooth like an elephant's hide. He thinks of the ginkgo tree outside his apartment window. He wishes he were sitting there, in his window bench in his pajamas. Home.

Somewhere out in the corridor a grown man's voice cries, *Hey mom, mom, mooooommmy!* A second voice, as if in response, yells, *The banks! The banks! The banks!*

Nurse O'Shan knocks, enters.

"Time's up," she says.

10

Out in the hallway the attendant frisks Dwaine again. The nurse escorts him back to the Bubble. Venus and Nigel follow. At the ward entrance Dwaine kisses and hugs them both goodbye. While hugging Dwaine, Nigel slips him the pen he's been hiding up his sleeve all this time, a Pentel Rolling Writer, black.

"Use it in good health," he whispers.

Outside Venus and Nigel hold hands again. Like lovers who've just watched a sad movie they move through the daylight as through fog, their thoughts still wrapped around the plot and characters, not willing to break the mood with small talk. Instead they stop to admire the tulips growing at the base of the miniature lighthouse, then look out across the river at the Palisades, a turquoise wall stretching all the way down to New York City. At the top of the cliff Nigel notices a white structure jutting out from some trees, with a cross on its roof and a peculiar, star-shaped window under the cross. Spanish mission. A monastery. It puts him in mind of something.

They turn and keep walking down the hill.

XII

*The River
of Mixed
Feelings
(Tearjerker)*

We put the brass cage holding Venus's parakeets, Abbot and Costello, in front of the bay window. We'd bought it down at the Sixth Avenue flea market, where we spent most of our Sundays hunting for items with which to adorn our home. We spent hours one day debating which of our latest flea market paintings—the reverse one of the *Titanic* about to hit the iceberg, or the painting-by-numbers of a grizzly bear pouncing on a salmon in a rushing stream—to hang over the English bar unit, and devoted a whole weekend to restoring a beaded Victorian room divider, replacing beads of amber, hornblende, and tourmaline, staining white cotton fibers with tea bags to make them look genuinely aged.

As far as Dwaine was concerned, Venus's moving in with me was strictly a matter of convenience. Venus alone couldn't swing the rent on their Chinatown apartment, so she moved into mine. She slept in my bedroom, while I slept in the living room, on my leather couch, alone.

That's what we told Dwaine, anyway.

Venus's belly grew. With my ear pressed to it I heard the throbbing of more than one human heart. I put my lips to that bleached round softness and simultaneously kissed my lover and my child. If a boy we'd name him Bill or Greg, if a girl Jane or Sarah with an 'h'. Good, solid American names.

By wearing loose clothes and keeping her visits with him to a minimum and brief Venus was able to hide her pregnancy from Dwaine. Until they divorced—and she fully intended to divorce him—she didn't want him to know that a child that might be his grew inside her.

I'd planned our whole future. We'd move to a larger apartment, and from there to a house in the suburbs of Long Island or Westchester. Money wouldn't be a problem. I had feathered our nest with junk bonds. My stockbroker recommended them to me. He told me they were a sure thing.

Coming home from a long day's work at the ad agency I'd hear the whirs of Venus' sewing machine blended with the parakeets' vehement shrieks, and my heart would do a brief fluttery dance in the stairwell.

2

Four months into his confinement the hospital authorities gave Dwaine his first day pass. We met him at Grand Central, and spent the day in town. Dwaine still spoke in a slow, syrupy drawl. Otherwise he looked healthy. He wore street clothes: jeans, a plaid shirt, a windbreaker.

A lovely day, cool and sunny, a blue sky feathered with wispy clouds. We walk down Lexington Avenue, headed for Chinatown to have lunch there. On the way we pass a sidewalk vendor dusting off his display of sunglasses with a feather duster. Dwaine tries on a pair of Ray Charles wraparounds.

"How do I look?" he asks us.

"Like a sign that says don't fuck with me," says Venus.

"Good. That's just how I feel."

Near the seaport we stop at the new Vietnam War Memorial, a sculpture of glass bricks etched with soldier's letters to home, dwarfed by financial towers so tall they blot out most of the sky.

"Those are the real war monuments," Dwaine concludes, looking up.

We take turns photographing each other with Venus's Kodak Instammatic. I take one of Dwaine and Venus, Venus takes one of Dwaine and me, Dwaine takes one of me with Venus. A stranger takes one of all three of us together. (I still have that photo, the only one of us all, sunny and smiling, members emeritus of the Proto Realist Society, looking like we don't have a care in the world.)

In Chinatown over bowls of slippery noodle soup Dwaine tells us his latest movie idea. The plot revolves around a controversial Polaroid snapshot in which Marilyn Monroe's lips feature prominently, along with a very private and sensitive part of our 35th President's anatomy.

"I'm going to call it *Jack's Balls*," says Dwaine.

"Charming," Venus says.

"A family picture," I say.

"I've got the cast all figured out," Dwaine goes on. "Warren Beatty as JFK, Karen Black as Marilyn Monroe, Pacino as Bobby Kennedy, Walter Matthau as J. Edgar Hoover, Dustin Hoffman as Fidel Castro, and Peter Lawford as, uh, Peter Lawford. Pretty neat, huh?"

He inhales an endlessly long noodle.

Then Dwaine fills us in on the latest apocalyptic doomsday scenarios; he collects them the way some people collect comic books or cobalt blue bottles. He's got quite a collection. Are we aware that Muslim extremists are plotting to poison New York City's drinking water supply? That paramilitary groups are stockpiling ammonium nitrate to blow up Yankee Stadium during the next World Series? That the CIA is bulk-producing the AIDS virus in a Guantanamo Bay facility and shipping it to third world countries in boxes of Carnation powdered milk?

"Oh, come, now, really," Venus can't resist saying.

"What," says Dwaine. "You don't *believe* me?"

"AIDS in powdered milk? Isn't that stretching things just a wee bit?"

"That's the whole point! They know it's unbelievable, which is why they'll get away with it!" His forehead achieves that red,

feverish glow that might as well be a sign saying Beware of Dog:
KEEP OUT.

"I've got an idea," I say, "Why don't we change the subject."

"Good one," says Venus. "Let's talk about pleasant things.
Any guess who'll clinch the series this fall? Looks like Detroit's
got a lock on things, huh?"

"Sure," says Dwaine. "Let's look at the bright side! Accentuate
the positive, E-liminate the negative? Don't mess with mister
in-between?"

"Could you, like, lower your voice just a little bit, please?"
Venus asks.

"Why, is someone actually *listening?*" Dwaine scans the
crowd of mostly Asian faces looking up from their rice bowls.
"That's right, folks," he addresses them all. "I am a mental patient. Just your run-of-the-mill garden variety borderline paranoid schizophrenic with transistorized tooth fillings and a vast
repertoire of conspiracy theories." He tears off his skullcap, revealing a bullseye tattoo printed on the back of his shaven skull.
Venus blanches. No mean feat for an albino.

"Oh, God," she says and covers her face as our waiter deposits a plate of fortune cookies and sliced oranges.

"Correct me if I'm wrong, but what I think you're saying is
that I should shut up, right? Isn't that what you're both trying
to tell me?"

"No," I say. "That's not what—"

"Wait, wait!" He cups a hand to his ear. "I'm getting a
broadcast. It's coming in loud and clear on my lower left molar.
Ffff…ffff…fuh…kuh…kyoo…FUCK YOU. That's the mes-
sage. Right? *Right?*"

Venus pushes her chair back, gets up and hurries through the
crowded restaurant. I start after her. With a rigid arm Dwaine
stops me.

"Let her go, babe."

"Fuck you. Why did you do that?"

"Honestly, babe? I don't know. I guess I felt like it."

With his free arm he reaches for a fortune cookie. As he bites into it I push past his arm and go after Venus, who's in the ladies' room downstairs.

"Venus?" I say knocking. "Are you in there?"

Water sings through pipes. A voice says: *Go away.*

"Venus, come on."

"I hate him. I hate him."

"You don't."

"I do. He's the devil."

"He's sick. He needs our help."

"He's sick all right. I wish I'd never met him. I wish that I'd never met either of you."

A lady needs to use the bathroom. I let her by. As she goes in Venus steps out, her face a Pollock painted with tears.

"May I strike that last remark Your Honor?"

"Come back to the table, okay?"

"Give me a minute."

3

All of the fortune cookies are all gone, the fortunes, too. Dwaine has eaten them all. "And I regret to inform you," he says, still chewing, "that the future tastes as bland and stale as it looks."

"I want you to lay off Venus," I say, sitting.

"Really? Why?"

"Even if the world is coming to an end it's not her fault."

"Is that so? What are your sources?"

"Just lay off, Dwaine. I mean it."

"Have you been fucking her, babe?"

"Jesus, Dwaine—"

"I'm asking, have you?"

"What is this, more *Raging Bull?*"

"It's not a movie quote. I'm asking: have you?"

Dwaine smiles, a different smile than the one that I'm used

to. His lower lip catches the surface of the new false tooth the V.A. dentist has made for him. I can't say I haven't been expecting the question. I have; I've been dreading it. And I have prepared an answer, but now that I've got my cue suddenly I forget all my lines. The only words that reach my tongue are Joe Pesci's from that movie Dwaine and I sat through a dozen times at least, lines that we both committed to memory and used to laugh over, and which I don't dare repeat now, under the circumstances. Instead I sit there, matching Dwaine's smile with my own, trying to, until finally he reaches an arm out and pinches my cheek, hard, saying, "No need to answer. You know I trust you, babe. To the end of the world, or as far as I can throw you, whichever comes first." He pinches me again, harder.

Venus returns, raw from crying. She smoothes the front of her baggy sweater, revealing for an instant (and to my eyes only, I hope) the faint global contour beneath. She sniffs back a tear.

"So—is the mongoose back in his cage?"

"Hey, I'm behaving," says Dwaine. "See? I'm buttoning my lips, look. Hm? Mmmm, mmm, mmm. *Mmmmm?*"

4

At Grand Central we say our goodbyes. As the train slides down the platform and we wave goodbye Dwaine presses his lips to the window and lets a thin stream of drool roll down the glass. We watch the train's taillights grow smaller, dissolving into the tunnel's darkness.

"Thank God," says Venus.

5

A barge piled high with assorted colorful trash lumbers downstream, pulled by a pair of red tugboats. We watch its progress,

Venus and I, standing by the promenade railing, bundled in mutual scarves and silence. She is showing, the life inside her twenty-one weeks old. A cloud of gulls follows the barge as as it pushes through drab waves.

"Know what the Indians used to call this river?" I ask mainly to shatter the silence. "The Mohicanituck. It means River of Mixed Feelings, because it flows both ways. The current flows south, the estuary tide flows north." It's been three weeks since Venus and I last made love. We blame her pregnancy and our demanding jobs, Venus designing costumes for two downtown theaters, me concocting an ad campaign for a new brand of colorless mouthwash built around the slogan, "The Clear Choice for Bad Breath"—my brainchild. Nightly we lie face to face in bed, breathing each other's dreams, content and safe but void of anything resembling lust. Sometimes by day I cannot remember her face. I see her features distinctly one by one, but can't assemble them into a whole, and this bothers me. It bothers me a lot. And I'm aware, too, of an unspoken distress that keeps us from looking each other in the eyes.

"We should tell him," Venus announces suddenly, looking out over the river as the barge drifts by with its cargo of garbage and corona of gulls. She waits for me to say something, and when I don't she turns with a sudden fury in her eyes that even her dark sunglasses can't hide. "I want him to know we're living together as lovers, Nigel, that you're in love with me. And I want *you* to tell him. You do love me, don't you, Nigel?"

A cardboard coffee to-go container bobs among waterlogged crates and other jetsam sloshing down below.

"That was a question."

"I heard it. And you know the answer."

"Please say it, if it's not too much trouble."

"Of course I do."

"You *love* me?"

"I love you."

"Then you'll do this for me. I want Dwaine out of the equation, out of our lives, out of both our lives. Is that straightforward enough for you? I want you to choose between us: me or Dwaine. Which will it be?"

"Dwaine's not part of the equation. He's locked up inside a mental hospital, Venus."

"Wrong, he's right here, Nigel, holding us together and tearing us apart. We're both tied to him, just like those tugboats are tied to that barge. Only he's the one pulling us. One of us has got to cut the rope or he'll tug us straight out to sea. Will it be you, Nigel, or does it have to be me?"

She looks into my eyes, searching for something—I'm not sure what, maybe the answer that she refuses to accept in the form of words. She takes my hand then and presses it flat to her belly, delicately curved and hard. "Feel," she says. "Can you feel? Know what's in there, Nigel? Everything worth living for, that's what. Do you agree?"

Then she leans close and kisses me softly, so softly I barely feel her lips. So softly I should realize it's a kiss goodbye.

6

She left a note:

Nigel,

This is the best plan. Don't ask me where I am, and please don't try to find out, because I plan to keep it a secret for as long as possible. I'll be divorced by the time the baby comes. As for the baby, it will be mine: not yours, not Dwaine's, not ours. I'll send a photograph. I don't mean to be cold. You know I love you, Nigel. But I also know that this is the right thing to do. You and Dwaine love each other, and no one is ever going to change that. Even if I could, I don't think I'd really want to. You're salt and pepper. You need each other. More than you know.

V.

7

The photographs arrived in January. Boys, two of them, five and three-quarter pounds each. The identical bundles of flesh were swarthy, but then so are most newborns. No return address. The postmark said Albuquerque. Albuquerque? What kind of place is that for an albino, I asked myself. By southwestern standards a sunny northeastern day qualifies as rain. She'd have to baste herself daily in sunscreen. She'd have to carry a beach umbrella everywhere. She'd be like one of those bubble people, a prisoner of her own pigmentless skin.

The same morning that the letter arrived with the photos I booked a flight to Albuquerque. I'd track Venus down. How many albino costume designers could there be in the state of New Mexico? I'd marry her. We'd live in an adobe house in the desert. I'd turn to pottery making, or turquoise jewelry. I'd be a devoted husband and father. Whether mine by blood or by marriage, I'd love those children as if they were my own. Under the dry desert sun our very mixed memories of Dwaine would slowly fade. Life would be, if not exactly sweet, good. Anyway it would be real and not someone else's bloody movie.

The taxicab roared across the Triboro Bridge, bound for LaGuardia Airport. As it did I was seized by that dizzy weightless feeling people get when they realize they've started something they can't possibly finish. I wasn't going to make pottery. I wasn't going to be a father. I wasn't going to live in New Mexico. I wasn't going to give up everything I'd worked hard for over the past four years. I wouldn't find Venus. And even if I did find her, and even if she did agree to marry me, she would not want to come back to New York City, nor was I about to drag her and her infant children back here against their will.

The whole exercise, I realized, was pointless.

I watched the smoke clouds billow from the three candy-striped Con Edison smokestacks rising surreally from a dense growth of trees on the bridge's lee side, gray smoke clouds. I felt an overwhelming sense of defeat and exhaustion just then, a feeling that was accompanied by my father's voice repeating *It's not worth it, it's not worth it*—over and over again, like the tolling of a cracked, doomed bell.

I tapped on the Plexiglas partition. The driver, who wore a checkered burnoose, caught my eye in his rearview mirror.

I said, "Turn around."

XIII

The
Pure Truth II:
The Sequel
(War Movie)

"A man fights for what he believes, Fernando."
—Gary Cooper, *For Whom the Bell Tolls*
THE PERTINENT MOVIE QUOTE WALL

That November I got a call from Dr. Shattnuck, Dwaine's veteran hospital psychiatrist. He asked me if by any chance I'd heard from Dwaine lately.

"No. Why, isn't he supposed to be up there with you?"

A week earlier, Dwaine's doctor informed me, Dwaine had gouged open his wrists with one of the pens he used to fill his black books. He had escaped from the surgical recovery room where he had been taken after his wrists were stitched and had not been seen or heard from since.

"You have no idea where he might be, by any chance?" Dr. Shattnuck asked.

2

I found him in his hellhole of a hideaway underneath Times Square. From what I could discern by candlelight, his short-cropped hair jutted in flattened hunks from his skull, and his skin was as waxy as the candles that spluttered and dripped in the darkness. Both his wrists were still bandaged. He lay curled up on the filthy mattress, so cold his teeth chattered when he spoke. Under his voice I heard the faint deep OM.

"Know what's f-f-funny?" he said, laughing through shivers. "It wasn't losing all that b-b-blood that almost d-d-did me, it was blood p-p-poisoning from the ink. The pen truly is m-m-mightier than the sword."

"Why did you do it?"

He shrugged. "What can I say, b-babe. It seemed like a g-good idea at the time."

We spoke for a while. He wanted to know about Venus. I told him only that she had gone to New Mexico. I didn't say a word about the circumstances of our parting, or about the babies. "Come on," I said to him after we'd spoken for a while, "let's get out of here," and tried to move him, but he wouldn't budge. He started rambling, saying how the city was an apocalypse waiting to happen, how any day now the gutters would run with blood, so on and so forth. I let him ramble on for a few minutes, his voice weak as water, letting the words drizzle like warm rain all over me. He rambled on until his voice broke into ragged coughs. "You okay?" I said.

"No," he said. "No, I'm n-not okay. The w-war's over, babe. We've l-lost. The B-B-Balkanization is c-c-complete, the Orwellian state has taken control. I thought movies might b-b-be the answer, that they might offer a w-way to combat the killer clichés. How wrong I was. Now there's n-nothing left, n-nothing but d-demons and h-h-husks..."

"Come on." I coaxed him off the mattress and onto his knees, so we could crawl the hell out of there. As we did I heard him sniffling behind me, saying, "*I k-killed them, I k-killed them all.*"

"Who? What?"

"*All of 'em, babe; I killed all of 'em...*"

"All of *who?*"

"All of 'em ... all of 'em ..."

He's just rambling, I thought. Being cinematically, melodramatically cryptic. Being Dwaine.

"H-have you g-got any a-a-aspirin?" he said. "My head's s-splitting."

"Hell, I'm in advertising. If it's an analgesic I've got it. Come on."

He slept on my sofa that night. I was glad to have him there, glad to have anyone to fill the space vacated by Venus. I sat in my rocking chair watching him sleep, remembering the last time I'd done so, when he asked me to film him bleeding.

3

Almost a year passed before I saw him again. Just after Christmas the agency lost two of its biggest accounts, and everyone was scrambling to stanch the wound, leaving me with little time to think about, much less visit, Dwaine. Meanwhile his letters to me grew more and more sporadic, until finally they stopped coming completely. I started to wonder if something was wrong. When I called the hospital to see how he was doing, I always got the same answer:

"He's doing fine."

Then a letter came, written on both sides of sheets of construction paper, the kind they give you to draw on in first grade. Dwaine's handwriting, more jagged and hurried than ever, was especially hard to read. What follows is my deciphering.

4

For the record, babe, after enlisting in the U.S. Army on August 2, 1971, I was assigned to the medical corps, where I worked mostly on helicopters, doing what they called mop-ups, picking up wounded soldiers from the field. Along with my waterproof canvas M5 medical bag I carried an M1911A1 pistol, but I never fired a shot in anger. Still, I served my country, or tried to, anyway, until two days after Christmas, 1973, when

I gave the first of two lethal injections to soldiers wounded in the field.

The first was a Marine Lance Corporal named Pennington who'd stepped on a Claymore mine. Both his legs were blown off at the hip. His stomach looked like a freshly plowed field. But that didn't concern him as much as his manhood. "Is my manhood still there," he kept saying. "Tell me, doc, is it? Cause if isn't I'd just as soon die here and now."

Normally I'd have said anything to calm him down. I'd have fed him some line of bullshit, "don't worry, everything's going to be fine," some crap like that. But something about this guy, the way he looked at me, made it hard for me to lie to him. Instead I looked down at the bloody shredded mess that used to be his fruit basket and shook my head.

"Then please, please kill me," he said, grabbing my arm and shaking it. "No one will ever know. It'll be our little secret, yours and mine."

I hadn't slept all that week. None of us in my unit slept very much. We put in forty-hour days, fueled mostly by pot and adrenaline and sick jokes about wounds and body parts ... oh, yeah, and baseball metaphors, we loved baseball metaphors, first base being a lost limb, second base two lost limbs, third base an arm and two legs, a home run all four limbs, and a Grand Slam gone to that big baseball stadium in the sky. I was dead tired. Meanwhile the lance corporal, he keeps smiling this yellow-toothed smile up at me, like he knows that I'm his salvation, his personal Angel of Death. Next thing I know, without even having to think that much about it, I'm reaching into my rucksack and giving him three, four, five syrettes of Mother M—that's morphine, in case you don't know, about twenty cc's worth, more than enough to grant him his wish.

The second soldier was an army sergeant who'd taken a sniper's bullet to the jaw. His name was Sergeant Ed Myers, of Yankton, South Dakota. Half his face from his nostrils down was gone, with the rest of his head a mask of iodine stained gauze. He didn't beg me to kill him. He couldn't, having no mouth to beg with. Whenever he tried to talk this wet sucking sound came out, along with a fine spray of blood and spit, and tears would roll down his one solid cheek. When I OD'd him, it was as much to end my own suffering as his.

The next day I refused to report for duty. I was put under house arrest pending a court martial and confined to my barracks. After a day or two they transferred me under guard to a detox ward where twelve addicted soldiers went cold turkey without so much as an aspirin tablet to get them over the hump. Twenty-four hours a day, three weeks straight I listened to their screams, moans, howls and whimpers. Meanwhile I applied for a conscientious objector discharge. If the C.O. papers came through in time, I'd get an honorable discharge. If not, I'd be court-martialed.

I had been under house arrest for a month when the war ended, supposedly. Over Armed Forces radio a sexy-voiced lady announcer described the lowering of the stars and stripes over headquarters in Saigon. As she did I wandered onto the tarmac and watched a squad of camouflaged B-52's take off roaring into the sky. I sat on an oil drum and started laughing. The war was over, but the killing went on and on. I laughed until an MP drove by in his Jeep, saw me and said, "Get a grip on yourself, soldier!"

The next day my C.O. papers came through.

They loaded me on a transport and shipped me home.

Fragged, tagged, and bagged, as we used to say.

That's how the war ended for me, so I thought. I didn't know it would follow me home, that it was inside me, like some radioactive isotope. Being a good little Catholic, I still felt that I needed to save the world, that or die for its sins. So I tried out for the priesthood, and when that blew apart I joined the Peace Corps. But it wasn't until I got to Belfast and helped blow that hotel lounge to smithereens that I saw just how alive the murderer in me still was.

When I returned from Belfast to New York my parents had downsized to a one-bedroom, their closets crammed with jugs of Ernest and Julio Gallo. Peggy and Jack Sr. seemed shocked to see me. It had only been two years. My mother looked like a ghost. It seems Jack had come home, too. By then the Feds were on his tail. They'd already seized his hacienda, his planes, everything.

"Where is he?" I said.

"Your father and I don't know," she said, "and we don't care. Your brother is a filthy drug addict! We want nothing to do with

him!" Spoken with booze on her breath.

A few days later I saw him. I was coming out of the Russian baths down on Fulton Street when I heard my name being called. I turn and see this skeleton looking at me. "It's me," the skeleton says. "Jack! Your brother!"

Without a how-de-doo Jack tells me he needs a favor. I'm thinking he's going to hit me up for some cash, but no, he wants me to score for him. He's too sick to go uptown, he says. He tells me where to go. He writes it on a piece of paper.

So I go. He's my big brother, after all, it's the least I can do, right? I take the subway to Dyckman Street, where Jack's supplier threatens me at gunpoint. It took some doing, but I managed to come back with both Jack's fix and my life.

I met him at the squat house where he was living, if you can call it that, a gutted brownstone on East Fourth. A band of addicts lived there with him, all of them copping and fixing together. Jack's room had ugly sky-blue wallpaper with brown water stains all over it. He had a mattress with a filthy blanket, a hot plate, some paperbacks, an alcohol lamp, an eyedropper, a box of cotton, and a spoon—like in the first movie we made together, remember?

Have you ever watched someone fix? It's like watching them mas-turbate, that's how private, personal and pleasurable an act it is. So fixing for someone else—what's that like? And how about fixing for your brother? *Day after day for the next two weeks I copped and fixed for Jack, cooking his heroine in a spoon over the alcohol lamp, sucking it up into a syringe, finding an undamaged vein somewhere on him, injecting him. I was his private nurse, his personal medic, his brother in chemical masturbation.*

I told you Jack died of an overdose. True. But I didn't tell you he died in my arms. Street heroin is usually sold cut with quinine, codeine, sometimes even sugar. The difference between cut smack and pure horse is like the difference between heaven and a heart attack. The last time I cooked up for him, when I lit the alcohol lamp and put the spoon over the flame and melted the powder and drew it through a cotton ball into the eyedropper, it was the same amount of shit, but ten times more potent, potent enough to kill him twice over.

Jack had tied up and held the rubber tourniquet while I drove the needle into the one good vein he had left, two inches from his balls. "Here you go, Jack," I said.

I watched Jack's blood drift up in a brownish-pink cloud in the eye-dropper, then injected again. I did it a few times to make sure it hit hard. It hit hard, all right. Jack turned blue and died in my arms.

As I walked out of that building into the bright sunshine I swear I didn't feel a thing, no remorse, no guilt, nothing. I was Death's Angel, doing God's work, or something like it. I'd sent Jack to heaven—or hell. Either way, it was someplace a lot better than where he'd been.

As I left the East Village, headed nowhere in particular, it struck me that I still wasn't through doing the Lord's work, I still had one more person left to kill, myself. Why hadn't I thought of it sooner, you ask? Well, as they say, better late than never. By the time I got to Union Square I had everything all figured out. I'd go to the movies, catch a matinee, then walk to the East River, smoke a last cigarette and jump in. That was my plan.

Taxi Driver *was playing at the Coronet, at Third Avenue at 59th Street, just a few blocks from the river. Perfect, I thought. How was I supposed to know that movie would change my life?* Taxi Driver *blew me away. It was like the sky opened up and light poured down on me. From the opening shot of that taxi moving through red steam clouds like some glazed yellow apocalyptic beast slinking its way through the inferno, I was hooked. And Travis Bickel, the loneliest, least heroic hero ever, talking to himself, holding his fist over a gas flame, piloting his Stygian taxi across the River Styx. I never dreamed anything so beautiful could be made from loneliness, violence, alienation, despair, murder, perversity, boredom—all the things I had been experiencing. I identified with Travis, sure, but I identified even more with the direc-tor, Martin Scorsese, the guy who turned all that blood-soaked rage and loneliness into a thing of beauty. An hour and thirteen minutes later when I staggered out of that theater, I felt like Moses must have felt when he staggered down Mt. Sinai with the Ten Commandments tucked under his arm. I knew then that I was going to make movies; I was going to be a filmmaker. I'd still be playing God, true, but without having to kill anyone, including myself.*

A few days later I enrolled at Pratt Institute, which is where we met and which is where you come into the picture. What happened from then on I won't bother going into here, since you've already seen that *movie.*

Now I'm here, in another kind of 'institute,' in this place where all my emotions are guarded and weighed like the gold in Fort Knox, for which I happen to be very *glad. And you should be glad, too, dammit.*

That's it, babe, that's my whole story, the Pure Truth. If all of the above makes me a coward, so be it. But I'm also pretty damned tired, and as General Macarthur said, "Fatigue makes cowards of us all."

Yours in Everloving Madness,
Rainer Werner Fassbinder

5

I saw him the day before Halloween, his birthday. I left work early and took the 12:35 train to Montrose. I didn't announce my visit. I assumed if I called ahead I would be given the bum's rush from him or from his institiutional keepers, and so I just went. When I got there, as expected, the authorities put me off, or tried to. I sat in a chair and refused to leave until they gave me an audience with their charge.

An hour or so later Dwaine appeared. Seeing me sitting there he drew back in shock and pointed at my hair.

"Babe—what happened to your Dukes and Earls?"

"My what?"

"Your curls. What did you do to them?"

"Oh." My cheeks prickled with warmth. "I had them relaxed."

"You did *what?* Nigel DePoli without his curls! Man, what *is* this world coming to?"

Though Dwaine still wore the brown pinstriped robe and a plastic ID tag with his social security number on his wrist, everything else about him looked changed. His shaven hair had grown back. It was almost completely gray now. The gray curls looped over his ears. In place of the soft blue slippers he wore a pair of sparkling white athletic sneakers. The formerly pocketless hospital robe now featured a pocket from which a quintet of writing implements protruded. His aluminum gray eyes gleamed. He looked suntanned, muscular, fit, like he'd just wound-up a two-week stint at Club Med. He shook my hand, his grip that of a university dean greeting freshmen on Orientation Day. "So—to what do I owe this unexpected honor?"

6

His voice has changed, too. The syrupy quality is gone. He smiles. I'm carrying a briefcase stuffed with comps for my latest advertising campaign. He stoops to smooth a palm over its leather surface. "Italian? Nice, *very* nice."

I give him a box of pens, a notebook, three packs of cigarettes. He needs none of these things. As for cigarettes, he has quit smoking. "It raises hell with my lap swimming. I'm down to a twenty-two minute mile. Not bad, huh?" With an arm around my shoulder he leads me down the hallway to a small kitchen where there's a coffee machine. He asks me how I take mine. I say milk and sugar. He wags a finger at me. "Sugar in suspension, worst thing for your system. Let's step into my office, shall we?"

Dwaine's "office" is the same conference room where Venus and I met with him on our last visit, with the same view through the same barred window of the same beech tree. The walls are adorned with crayon drawings mostly of combat scenes, of exploding tanks, plummeting paratroopers, and soldiers brandishing spouting flamethrowers. Dwaine explains that he has been conducting workshops there in drawing, journal keeping, and screenwriting.

"The screenwriting workshop is by far the most popular," Dwaine says. "People are going nuts to get in." He mimics a rim shot. "Seriously, next month we're going on a field trip to the new Vietnam war memorial they just built down in D.C.

You know—the Wall?" From a cardboard box in the conference room closet he unfolds one of the T-shirts he designed and had silk screened for the occasion. It shows a line of soldiers in formation, silhouetted in white on a black background. WE'VE BEEN TO THE WALL.

"Looks like you've been keeping pretty busy," I note.

"Yeah, my dance card's pretty full, all right."

I explain that I've been busy myself following a major shake-up at the agency. Donny pulled what in the advertising industry is called a "palace coup," raiding a rival agency's reject drawer to win over their biggest client with a campaign its officers had snubbed a mere six months earlier. Thanks to this act of not-so-petty larceny my mentor and I have escaped dog food purgatory to enter Coca-Cola Heaven.

"Cola wars!" Dwaine says, shaking his head. "Man, I love it! When not sponsoring genocide in Third World countries they're going at each other's throats at home! So tell me, babe, what's the latest advertising campaign in the works? Displacing red wine at French dinner tables? Brainwashing voodoo priest-esses into substituting cola for their witch's brew? Down with coffee, tea, mother's milk?"

"Those were last year's crusades," I submit dryly.

"The Liquid Messiah," says Dwaine. "*Come unto me all ye that travail and I will refresh you.* Face it, babe, your clients won't rest until their dark tonic has conquered the stars."

"Maybe, but I suspect they'd settle for a three percent market share increase."

7

We make small talk. When I ask him when the heck he plans to get out of there, Dwaine gives me a funny look. "Now why would I want to do a crazy thing like that?"

"But you seem healthy. You look great."

"Oh, I'm doing just fine," he says. "In fact I feel eighteen years old. Best of all I'm not killing anyone, including yours truly."

"So what's the problem, then," I say as casually as possible. "I mean, sooner or later they've got to discharge you, right?"

"Oh, really? Says who?"

"I mean—isn't that the whole point?"

Dwaine throws me the indulgent smile, the kind grammar school teachers routinely apply to earnest yet dim-witted pupils. "No, babe, that is not the whole point. It's not even half the point. The point isn't even for me to get better. It's for me *not* to get worse, which means staying right here."

"You *want* to stay here? You can't be serious!"

"You always say that, babe. You always say I'm not serious. What do I have to do to convince you? I'm as serious as a maladaptive pancreas. Please believe me, for once."

"So you're just going to stay here forever, is that the plan?"

"That's sort of the idea, as of now."

I shake my head. "But you can't, Dwaine."

"Why not?"

"For a start they won't let you."

"You don't think so? Listen, babe. I can stay here as long as I want. See, it all depends on whether or not I continue to pose a quote potential threat to myself and others unquote. Meaning the minute I feel the lid starting to come off I just need to act out a wee bit and down it comes again, shutting me in nice and tight. I'm manning the controls here. It's my baseball; I'm on the pitcher's mound. Yanks lead, four nothing."

A warm wetness spreads itself like wintergreen oil across my shoulders and back. The conference room walls close in on me. Sunlight screams through the barred window, slicing the opposite walls into a dozen glowing white bars. The air in the room turns as dry as vacuum cleaner dust. "Dwaine, this isn't funny," I say. "This is your *life* we're talking about. Tell me you don't ever want to get out of this goddamn place!"

"I don't want to get out of this place."

"But you don't *mean* that!"

"But I do."

"*Why?*"

"Because it's a bloodbath out there, that's why. How many times do I need to tell you that? Don't you understand, babe? Of course I'm getting better; that's not the point. The point is the world is getting worse! Hegal said, 'History repeats itself the first time as tragedy, the second time as farce.' We're up to about the twentieth time here. We're way past farce! We're living in a George Grotz etching! Excuse me; *you're* living in a George Grotz etching! *You're* the one who's in the nuthouse, not me. They call this place a mental hospital, and true, there happen to be some crazy people in here. But here at least there's some *supervision*. All you've got *out there* is a bunch of soldiers and cops and other armed maniacs as bad or worse than the people they're supposed to be protecting. I should know, babe; I used to be one of the so-called protectors. The first sane thing I ever did in my life was to come here. Believe it."

"The world's not as bad as you make it out to be, Dwaine."

"So *you* say, babe. And you're entitled to your opinion. But look where that opinion is coming from: from *out there*, from deep inside the George Grotz etching, which is to say that you have *no* perspective, none. Remember what Kerouac said?"

"No," I answer wearily. "What did Kerouac say?"

"Kerouac said 'life will be over when there is that blue-gray glow of television coming from every living room window in every home, and with everyone in them watching the same channel.' What channel are you watching, babe? Me, I've tuned into Looney Tunes, as you see. When this thing completes itself, which will be soon, hopefully, when the last shoe drops, will you just leave, like those bourgeoisie Jews in Berlin, leaving their less fortunate brethren behind to their gristly fates? Will you always play it safe? Will you stay 'above the fray,' the unsullied advertising executive launching his pristine TV campaigns from up in the clouds? They didn't just gas the poor Jews, you know; these monsters took out a lot of socialists and writers and painters, too, for the record. When they come for you, where will you be, huh? Having a *party?* Aboard your yacht docked in Portofino? It may have escaped your notice, babe, but there's a class component to all of this, a hard-wiring, a kind of cultural DNA rooted in history. There's also a highly regarded German social psychiatrist—his name escapes me—who postulated that in times of tremendous stress organisms seek like organisms. Which is to say, dear Ralph Waldo, that the question is not what I am doing in here, but what are you doing *out there?*"

As always in times like this Dwaine has me totally confused. On the one hand, it's clear to me that he's stark raving mad; on the other, it seems to me, despite my inability to understand this latest onslaught of paranoid gibberish, that he's entirely right. "And what about all the things you hoped to accomplish in your life?"

"Such as what, babe?"

"Such as being an artist. Such as making great movies. Such as waking up the world. Have you given up on all of that?"

"You don't get it, do you, babe? You really don't get it." He taps his skull. "I'm not giving up anything. I'm still making movies. In here, where the budgets are unlimited and where I can cast all the stars in the universe, living and dead. Marlon Brando? He's mine for the asking. Bogart, Bacall, Fatty Arbuckle—name your favorites; I've got 'em—right in here. Here, where I don't need a camera or lights or film or a distribution deal or a theater or an audience or that disgusting popcorn smell. *Here*," he keeps on tapping, "where *I'm* in charge. *I'm* the mogul; *I'm* the director; *I'm* the producer, *I'm* the art director, the key grip, the best boy, the caterer. My life, *that's* the movie. *Le cinema, c'est moi!*"

"You really are crazy," I put in softly.

"So I'm told, babe; so I'm told…"

There's no point arguing things any further. Is there?

No, there isn't.

I pick up my briefcase and go.

8

Cut to Donny Colosimo's backyard. A crisp November morning just days before Thanksgiving. The lawn, cut fairway-short and flanked by clouds of brittle brown hydrangeas, slopes down to a reflecting pool, its black waters prowled by plump orange fish, passing, en route, a mauve reflecting ball, a birdbath in the shape of a giant mollusk, and a flagpole. Behind us, Donny's kidney-shaped pool squats under a blue tarpaulin.

We take turns shooting clay ducks. Donny wears his Ralph Lauren moleskin hunting jacket with leather shoulder pads, and his Abercrombie & Fitch knickers with genuine horse bone fly buttons. Except for the clanking of the halyard against the pole, the wind sighing through trees ablaze with autumn colors, the skeet launcher's cartoony boing and the earsplitting report of a Mossberg P-835 Ulti-Mag, there's not a sound to be heard. I ask, "Don't your neighbors complain?"

"Kid," Donny answers while reloading, "I got eighteen watershed acres here. I can shoot what the fuck I want."

Skeets burst into puffs of ruddy dust. Donny lowers the rifle to gaze wistfully at the patch of blue sky where a clay duck has known brief flight. We're here not mainly to shoot skeet, however, but to brainstorm a television advertising campaign for our soft drink client, who is sponsoring this years' Winter Olympics. Their rival, having snared the even more greatly coveted Superbowl sponsorship, has launched its own ad campaign wherein—via digitized special effects— gridiron legends of yore in vintage black-and-white footage guzzle from dewy, full-color cans and bottles of its flagship product. It's up to us to come up with something different and better.

We have the weekend.

Donny hands me the Mossberg. Per his instructions I aim thirty degrees ahead of my target, await the *boing* and dispatch three of four skeets. The recoils vibrate my molars. With each blast the hydrangeas surrender a snowstorm of petals.

We break for lunch. Donny eats only cold foods. Chilled gazpacho, assorted cool deli meats, cheeses and pickles, tepid German potato salad. Afterwards, clutching ice-cold bottles of Coca-Cola, we stretch out on his tan Naugahyde sofa and watch videotaped footage of the space shuttle *Challenger* exploding over and over again, in fast and slow-motion, the snowy plumes parting from the doomed spacecraft like peels from a heavenly banana. With each explosion Donny nods his snowy pompadour and gives the thumbs-up, like a Roman senator at the *ludi gladiatori*.

But I'm not really paying attention to Donny or his VCR. I'm thinking about Dwaine, of him locked up in that loony bin. It's not Vietnam or booze that put him there, not Claymore mines or booby traps or Post Traumatic Whatever, not Bob McNamara or Henry Kissinger or General Westmoreland or the staff sergeant on duty at the Armed Forces Recruiting Station at Times Square, not his mother or his black Irish father or his dead drug kingpin brother or the Catholic Church or the Pope or Ireland or the IRA or the British Army or the Peace Corps.

It's movies. Movies put him in there.

And only movies can get him out.

9

Using his prize AK-47 Donny machine-guns a half dozen more skeets. With every clay duck launched and obliterated an ad campaign concept is likewise discharged and dispatched.

By sundown we've blown our last skeet.

We're about to call it quits when a flock of Canada geese flies overhead. Grabbing the Mossberg, Donny gets off three shots; as many geese fold and fall. One lands with a wet slap on the blue pool tarp. The second touches down with a stagnant splash in the concrete birdbath. The third comes to rest with a heavy dull slap in Donny's satellite dish.

A breeze flutters the flag. I watched it flutter, snap and furl, thinking: *America, the Something of America, the Cola ... the Soda ... the Soft Drink ... the Soft Drink: The Soft Drink of America ... The Soft Drink of America ...*

XIV
Cola
Wars
(TV Commercial)

Gentlemen, let's be honest with each other: what in the world can we tell the citizens of America about our flagship product that they don't already know? That it's brown? That it's fizzy? That it tastes good? That it comes in ten-ounce bottles and twelve-ounce cans?"

Facing me across the teak and granite inlay conference room table: a battlement of graying heads and padded shoulders beyond which the spires of midtown Manhattan float dreamily a silent quarter mile above the prosaic earth. The heads gape at me, eyes blinking, brows beetled, minds drifting onto fairways and putting greens, dreaming of sweet spots, birdie-birdies and scotch foursomes.

"We can't say it's cheaper, since it isn't; we can't even claim that it's any better, since that's a matter of taste, for which, as we all know, there can be no accounting (witness our rival's recent market share increase)…"

Cue polite laughter. Though I've rehearsed this pitch a dozen times with Donny as audience, he warned me that nothing would prepare me for the real thing, that I would find myself operating on sheer gall, or not at all. "You're Philippe Petite walking a tightrope," he explained. "The trick is don't look down or forget to breathe." I take a deep breath; I don't look down.

Prior to the pitch, in the men's room, as I dimpled the knot in my tie, straightened the part in my straightened hair, and popped a spearmint Lifesaver to mask the odor of gin, Donny pulled a crisp twenty from his wallet and told me to do the same. I said, "What for?"

"Just do it, kid."

I took out a twenty.

"Now crumple it up and shine your shoes with it."

"You're kidding me."

"Kid, I never kid at a time like this."

I crumpled the twenty and shined my shoes with it. Then, per Donny's instructions, I flushed the ruined bill down the toilet.

Donny put out his hand. As I reached to shake it he withdrew it and faked a jab at me instead. "Just try not to make an ass of yourself, okay?"

2

"You're aware, gentlemen, of course, that Coca-Cola was the invention of a Civil War vet seeking a cure not only for his chronic pain, but for his addiction to the bitter crystalline alkaloid of opium better known to us as heroin? That's right, gentlemen: Coca-Cola was a gift to our great nation from a drug addicted war veteran. And I say to you now, gentlemen, now at last the time has come for us to return the favor."

From there I launch into the specifics. The first time I say "Vietnam" jaws drop. No sooner do I allude to hospitalized veterans than an invisible Novocain cloud drifts into the conference room, numbing critical faculties on either side of the teak and granite table. I take advantage of this sublime moment of corporate stupefaction to unveil our campaign's most daring aspect, the singular stroke that will either propel it up into cloudy heights or weigh it like an anchor in diatomaceous muck.

To the theme from *Rocky* booming from a ghetto blaster I fling aside the royal blue chintz cloth covering the easel, revealing the campaign's logo: an eagle in silhouette, its dark wings spread across a stars and stripes backdrop, talons clutching our client's flagship product in 10-ounce bottles and 12-ounce cans. Indeed, the eagle bears a more than passing resemblance to the Eagle Electric Company mascot. But what are the odds of anyone in this room knowing that?

Under the logo Yankee Doodle style block letters spell out:

THE SOFT DRINK OF AMERICA

With palms sweeping over the screen of an imaginary TV set, I read the disclaimer:

**The Preceding Advertisement Has Been
Produced, Written, Directed and Filmed by
Disabled Veterans of the War in Vietnam**

3

Slow dissolve to a convoy of trailer and box trucks passing by a miniature lighthouse, winding up the long, steep driveway toward the Dwight D. Eisenhower Veterans Administration Medical Center. The trucks haul lights, cables, reflector shields, generators, cameras, sound equipment, cases of film and recording stock, brutes, dollies, folding tables and chairs, coffee and tea samovars, boxes of doughnuts and pizza and dozens of cases of Coca-Cola in bottles and cans (to serve as both props and refreshments).

Yawning, I watch the trucks roll by, a scene highly reminiscent of the opening title sequence in *The Great Escape*, when the truck convoy carries its cargo of fresh POWs to Stalag Luft III.

I haven't slept much, having spent most of the night before in a cemetery. At three o'clock in the morning, with a line from one of Dwaine's letters echoing in my head, I switched on my bedside lamp, got up and found the letter still folded and tucked in my jacket pocket. I re-read it, searching for the phrase. There it was. "… both Peggy and Jack Sr."

Peggy and Jack Sr.

An hour later I had boarded a subway headed for Hunter's Point, Queens. From there a gloomy walk took me to Calvary Cemetery, where I located the caretaker's stone shed just as he, the caretaker—a gruff-faced ringer for Jack Warden in *Donovan's Reef*—arrived. With a pen on a map of the cemetery he circled grave number 837, Section 4-B.

As I followed the map dawn broke, sneaking up behind low buildings. Overhead the Long Island Expressway roared with traffic rushing toward Manhattan. I cut through a field of tombstones as crooked as a bum's teeth. It didn't take long for me to find what I was looking for. The bronze flower was still there. So was the inscription:

John Daniel Fitzgibbon
b: October 15, 1946
d: February 14, 1975
Beloved Son of Sean and Irene

Beloved Son of Sean and Irene. I checked the letter again, to be sure. As the shadows lightened around me (revealing a sea of jagged tombstones) I sat on John Daniel Fitzgibbon's stone wondering if everything Dwaine had ever told me about himself is a lie, if I had been nothing more for him than a repository for his cinematic fictions, the Peoria where the grim feature of his life had played so very, very well.

Then I wondered: does it matter? So what if Dwaine's past is nothing more than a series of hyper-gritty movie scenes?

Does that make it any less frightening, or real? One thing was for sure: Dwaine's darkness was no lie. His passion was real and so was his pain. And those were the things that I'd loved him for. And even if they weren't real, even if they were products of one of our overheated imaginations, so what; what *difference* did it make? Movies, too, are made up: that doesn't make them any less loveable or moving. Whether Dwaine's past was the stuff of myth, madness, or movies, didn't matter. What mattered was that I'd believed in it. I checked my watch. Six a.m.

I hurried to catch the subway.

I had a commercial to shoot.

4

Dwaine wears a waist-cut slate Eisenhower jacket over camouflage fatigue pants. He has handpicked his crew of twelve: five black, five Hispanic, one Irish, ten Purple Hearts, five Bronze Stars, one Congressional Medal of Honor. In all, his crewmembers lack seventeen body parts: three legs, one arm, two eyes, two kneecaps, one testicle, six fingers, and two thumbs. Miguel, Dwaine's cameraman, has twenty-six confirmed Viet Cong kills to his record. Earl, his key grip, keeps a box of desiccated V.C. ears next to his inpatient bed. He sleeps better with them there, presumably.

I stand on the grassy hilltop watching Dwaine direct his scruffy platoon of defunct soldiers, his orders followed by sharp cries of "Yes, sir!" accompanied by crisp, stiff salutes. An equally stiff breeze scuffs whitecaps into the Hudson River below. Hands in pockets I stand there, wedged like a toadstool into my uselessness (question: what do we think about when we think about nothing?), aware, somewhere way back in the recesses of my fungoid brain, that however many miles of footage Dwaine and his crew shoot, the result is destined to be whittled down to sixty pithy seconds, riddled with product logos, and sweetened with a cloying choral soundtrack scored by a team of rapidly aging British pop composers, an awareness designed to enhance my already monumental obsolescence.

Still, I try to make myself useful in little ways. But the few times I try to give Dwaine any kind of advice he brushes it off like dog hairs from his Eisenhower jacket, saying to me, "Not now, babe." *Not now, babe.*

So I stand there, hands deep in the pockets of my Coke-bottle green linen Bill Blass blazer, inert as a spore-bearing fruiting fungus. Until the sailboat passes by.

5

She's an old-fashioned, square-rigged schooner, sailing upstream, her sails blown stiff as eggshells by the breeze, backlit by the sunlight that streams—or seems to—like a golden waterfall over the Palisades. I'm reminded of the Cutty Sark ads I'd cut out with scissors as a kid. I run to tell Dwaine, who is setting up a shot with his cinematographer. A temporary volleyball court has been rigged up for a staged tournament, outpatients versus orderlies. I tap his shoulder.

"Not now, babe," Dwaine says. I remind him that he's working for me and for my client. "Yeah, well these are *my* clients," he says and points to a line of residents in wheelchairs, their missing legs hidden under scratchy blankets. "It's them I'm working for, not some dippy-ass goddamn soft drink. Now if you don't mind, babe, I'm making a movie here."

I grab his sleeve. "I do mind," I say. "And don't call me 'babe.' I hate it when you call me that. I've always hated it. The name is Nigel, Nigel DePoli. And in case you've forgotten, I happen to be in charge here."

"In charge? That's a laugh." Dwaine snorts and does his best Brando. *"You're an errand boy sent by a grocery clerk to collect a bill."* The line is from *Apocalypse Now*, and it has what I assume is the intended effect. I lunge.

6

We're all over each other, grabbing, grunting, hitting, clutching, rolling. Grass, sky, river, buildings and beech trees swirl like kaleidoscope chips, as voices shout, snarling, "*Get him, Fitz! Kick his ass! Whup his butt!*" We roll down the grassy slope to the memorial garden, where oxidized bronze generals watch me pin Dwaine to the lawn and straddle him, his forehead reddening as he twitches with laughter. Stop it! I say. Cut it out! But he won't. I draw back and hit him with my open hand. Still he won't stop. So I do it again, and again, trying to force some feeling other than sarcasm out of him, but he just keeps on laughing, like my blows tickle him, the snorts bursting through blood bubbles in his nostrils. We're still rolling down the lawn. We roll halfway to the Hudson River.

Then a flurry of arms—including Miguel's singular but very strong arm—pulls me through a crowd of stupefied faces, sits me down in a patch of grass. My throat, my arms, my ears burn. Voices ask if I'm all right.

You all right, there, Mr. DePoli?

Yeah, Mr. D, you okay?

I see Dwaine being helped to his feet by his crew, his face a striped mask of blood (like Marlon Brando's at the end of *On the Waterfront*). As they hold him I stand up and yell—the words tearing out of me like a magician's colored rags, "*You son of a bitch—you bastard. You had me mugged!*" Miguel grips me harder. "*You thought I forgot, did you? You think I don't remember? Well I remember, you bastard; I didn't forget, you son of a bitch!*" Everyone stares, including Dwaine, who wipes the blood off his face.

"You slept with my wife," he says.

"*Because you decided to go crazy! You never loved her anyway! You only married her to fuck with me, like you've always fucked with me, from the very beginning! I bet you never had a brother! I bet you were never in Vietnam! Black Irish my ass!*"

They keep staring as I take off my jacket, tuck in my shirt, and start walking. As I pass by Dwaine he says something, I'm not sure what, I'm too dazed to hear much of anything beyond a buzzing in my ears that may be the blood rushing through my skull, or it may be the aural version of vertigo. With my jacket slung over my shoulder I walk back up the hill for my briefcase, then walk back down again and keep walking, all the way to the Montrose train station where, as I sit on the platform, a sudden sun-shower falls. With its falling a rainbow vaults across the river, beautiful. I sit with the back of my head resting against a movie poster for *Wall Street*, starring Michael Douglas and Charlie Sheen.

7

Splice by splice, we murdered Dwaine's movie, a death of a thousand cuts. Grim scenes of chronically institutionalized vets cursing, moping, spitting, yawning, shuffling, pissing into corners and banging their heads into walls were replaced with uplifting footage of veterans in and out of wheelchairs shooting hoop after hoop *(swish, swish)* on the basketball court, to converge afterwards around a gleaming Coca-Cola machine like truth seekers around an oracle. Of Dwaine's gritty documentary not one single grim frame remained.

By the time I leave the editing bay it's already dark out. A harvest moon—or what substitutes for a harvest moon in the city—shines through a raggedy blanket of clouds. Not ready to go home, I wander around, down streets and avenues haunted by moonlight. My wanderings take me to Beekman Place, where I stand looking across the East River, at the Pepsi-Cola sign on its far shore, remembering how, ten years ago, Dwaine and I stood in this very spot looking across the very same river at night. I remember the smoke rings Dwaine was constantly blowing, gray doughnut ghosts wavering into the air. I have a sudden craving for a cigarette. I put a finger to my lips and taste something sticky, salty, and sweet.

Blood from a film cut.

8

I schedule an emergency editing session. For four and a half hours I sit behind the console of a Steenbeck flatbed, reinserting many of the trims and outs Donny and I had extricated two days before. Done with the footage, I turn to the soundtrack, and am hard pressed to choose between the theme from Peter Gunn and Gershwin's *Lullaby for Strings.* In the end, though, I opt for silence. What could be grittier?

Done, I drop the result off at the lab for transfer to video.

I order two copies. Make it three.

Back at my apartment, I pack Dwaine's aluminum trunk with his belongings—letters, black books, screenplays, 8– and 16-millimeter short films, rubber bullet, Academy Award (the Oscar is damaged; the statuette tilts twenty degrees from its base and is sticky with duct tape residue), then pack some clothes and toilet articles into a duffel bag for myself. I phone a car service. While waiting for the livery I empty and unplug the refrigerator, leave its door yawning, and give a good soaking to my snake plants and spider ferns.

The driver helps me with the trunk. From the processing lab he takes me to Grand Central, where I seal one of the tapes in a jiffy envelope addressed to Dwaine S. Fitzgibbon care of the Veteran's Administration Hospital in Montrose. I drop it in a mailbox. With the other tape in my briefcase I rush to the Danforth Building.

9

When I step out of the elevator Donny's there, scowling at me, thumbs hooked under fat rainbow suspenders, an unlit cigarette bobbing between his lips.

"Kid, where the Christ have you been? We got a presentation to make here, or did you forget, you were so busy jerking off?"

I hand Donny the videotape. "Last minute touches," I say.

Donny eyes the cassette dubiously, then looks at me and shakes his head. "You've got some pair on you, you know that, kid?" He turns and starts toward the screening theater where our clients await the presentation. Seeing me not following him he stops, turns. "Now what?"

"I don't feel so hot. No shit, Donny, I—*I think I'm gonna puke.*"

I dash to the men's room and bury myself in a stall. I let a few minutes pass before poking my head into the hallway to see Donny gone and the coast clear. Then I sprint to the elevator and—just as the brass doors are about to close—jump in.

XV
*Hudson
Priory,
1987*

By the time the train pulled into Barnum it was pouring. Lightning cracked the silver dome of the sky. My father wore his tattered Inverness cape with drooping deerstalker cap. Over his head he held an umbrella that had seen better days. He looked like a soggy, down-on-his-luck Sherlock Holmes. He smiled, or half of his face smiled, the muscles of the other half having been paralyzed by his latest stroke. The whole left side of his face drooped like a pair of wet drawers on a clothesline.

Since the fire he'd put aside inventing things to focus on his painting, doing landscapes of the flower garden behind our house. Seeing me watching him through the smutty green window, he waved in that funny way of his, his right hand miming a chatterbox over his head, the smile holding up the right side of his face. The same stroke that sundered his smile also impaired his speech, making him sound like an English Elmer Fudd.

"Wewh wewh wewh, Niyel, mabwah. Ow gowzit? Zow guddah zee yhew," he said, helping me wrestle Dwaine's trunk into the back of his car, the yellow 1960 Morris Minor, its paint faded to clotted cream, its rocker panels mostly rusted through. For a change I got the feeling that he actually meant it, that he was genuinely happy to see me. I admit I was happy to see him, too. "Are you sure you should be lifting things?" I asked.

"Zhur, why nod? Ze hew wi zhe bwuddy dogdurz."

The Morris' engine turned over and over and finally caught and sputtered, filling the rainy station parking lot with blue fumes. By mistake my father put the transmission in the wrong gear and nearly drove us into a telephone booth in which a horrified commuter stood making a call. With the Morris sagging under the trunk's weight and my father gripping the wheel (his face evenly divided between concern and pleasure), we rode to town. My father had been told by his doctor not to drive, but drove he did, in full Magoo fashion, beeping his horn, cutting curbs, splashing pedestrians who stood unwittingly by puddles.

At the local diner my father and I ate breakfast, with him foregoing his two customary soft-boiled eggs in favor of a cholesterol-free bowl of oatmeal. We sat in a booth next to the window through which we had a clear view of Barnum's Florentine clock tower (with its ever-inaccurate clock), a slice of the flood-prone river, and the Chamber of Commerce building, on the lee stucco wall of which the town's mascot had been recreated in paint: a white circus elephant rearing up on its hind legs. The elephant is, of course, in honor of the town's namesake, Phineas Taylor Barnum, the famous showman born there in 1810, and whose patinated bronze likeness—seated in a throne-like armchair—lorded over the village green. It suddenly struck me that Mr. Barnum and Dwaine had more than a little in common, that they were both hucksters, selling hoaxes to a gullible public, as I, too, had been a huckster; as all Americans worthy of the name were and are and always will be hucksters. Through the rain-pocked window I noted the generous pile of dung painted under the elephant's legs by local delinquents of artistic bent. However often the town fathers ordered it painted over, that dung-heap always endured, adding tribute to tribute.

"Za elephan nevah stobs zhitting, duzzy?" my father, as if having read my mind, observed while slurping away at what he called "porridge."

"He is prolific," I had to agree.

After breakfast we stopped at the bridal boutique, where I found my mother secreted behind a curtain in the back workroom, wedged among boxes of sequins and rhinestones and mostly fake pearls, rolls of white taffeta, crinoline and frilly lace. She failed to look up at me from her worktable.

"*Finalemente!*" she said. "De probable son!"

"Prodigal," I corrected her, and bent to kiss her wrinkled, soft cheek. The high intensity lamp under which she labored hardened the lines in her face, making her look every one of her fifty-four years. That I'd just quit my job didn't soften her looks any, though by then she must have been used to these sudden curves, slaloms, and dips in her only son's reprobate life: anyway, she was resigned to them. She licked the end of a white thread and, while passing it through the eye of a needle, asked me—with the usual strong whiff of irony and disdain—how was my friend, what his name, Dwaine?

"Frankly, mom," I answered, "I really have no idea. And I don't give a damn."

"*Pffff,*" she replied.

I then did the one thing guaranteed to win an Italian boy back into his mother's good graces, bent and kissed her again. saying I loved her very much, which was true, and that she was the very best mother a son could possibly ask for, which may not have been true, exactly, but it was true enough, and to which she reiterated her "*Pffff,*" but could not hide a smile.

2

After leaving mom's store we got on the interstate. I'd promised my mother that, before we got on the highway, I'd take over the driving, but when the time came my father insisted on remaining behind the wheel. I was just as glad; I needed to get some sleep. Within a dozen miles, with raindrops sliding down the passenger window like children on toboggans and sleds, I let my head drop and drifted off. When I woke my father was humming to *On the Beautiful Blue Danube* on public radio. The sun had

broken through the clouds. We crossed over the Newburgh—
or was it the Bear Mountain?—Bridge. My neck felt loose as if
stretched by the miles. I hummed along with my father.

When *The Blue Danube* ended the news came on. The Dow
Jones industrial average had fallen 508 points, the largest sin-
gle-day point drop since the Great Depression, a record 22.6
percent decline. Analysts pointed to rising interest rates, com-
puter-driven selling, and the threat of war in the Persian Gulf.
In the blink of an eye my life savings were gone, evaporated. I
could picture Dwaine laughing at the news, throwing his shaven
tattooed skull back and howling up at the falling sky.

I fell asleep again, a deep sleep crowded with vivid, stupid
dreams in kitschy Technicolor. While I slept, with Dwaine's belongings rattling away in the battered aluminum trunk behind
me, my father drove me here.

3

Sat., October 31 (Halloween). I write this in a room perched high
above the eastern edge of a lava sheet thrust five hundred feet
straight up from below sea level at the close of the Triassic
period, after the dinosaurs bit the dust and the first mammals
started crawling out of their caves. They call this line of steep,
lonely cliffs the Palisades, a word derived from the French
word for a fence of pales forming a defensive structure usually
around a stronghold.

Which I guess makes this monastery a stronghold of sorts.

A fog has rolled in, wrapping everything in a gray blanket. I
can't see the sky, the trees, the river, or the barge that's doubt-
lessly passing by at this very moment, being pushed or pulled
up or downstream by an equally invisible tugboat. Nor do I see
the cluster of red brick buildings clinging to the opposite shore,
though I know they are there.

All I see is fog: gray, dull, silvery fog, the same color as the aluminum trunk squatting on the floor here next to me.

My room holds a small bed, a child's wooden desk, a stiff-backed cane chair, a lamp, floorboards of thick, knotted pine, and a window shaped like a star. Not a patriotic five-pointed star, or the Star of David, but an enigmatic polygon with four sharp extrusions pointing North, South, East, and West—like a compass rose. The room is right under the bell tower. When the bell tolls the walls quiver and shake. It tolls thirty-six times at six-thirty every morning. Why thirty-six I have no idea, but it's the only dramatic thing that happens here all day long.

There it goes now. *Dwaine, Dwaine, Dwaine....* (that's D for Death, W for War, A for Anarchy, I for Insane, N for Nightmare, and E for the End of the World.)

Finally, the tolling stops. The last iron waves fade, leaving a silence so severe the flushing of a toilet somewhere down the hall seems like an act of insurrection. I can hear my brain cells humming, whispering to each other.

The silence gives way to chanting. A dozen voices, all male, waft up through the thick floorboards.

I burn a stick of incense, gaze out my star-shaped window. As voices chant below me, with the befogged view as bright and pale and colorless as an empty screen, I pretend that I'm in a movie theater. The room darkens around me, the fog brightens and starts to sparkle and flicker. The smell of incense morphs into that of hot buttered popcorn. Soon I'm watching a movie, one starring Dwaine and me. And all I've had to do to tell our story is sit here and keep watching and write down what I see. It's been that simple.

Now, at this hour, that's when I do my best writing. When the fog clears the spell breaks. With a fluttering sound the film trips out of the projector gate. The sprocket holes swing into view; the celluloid shrivels and combusts, the vermilion bloom gives way to the brightness of a limpid, sunny day.

4

Tuesday, November 3. That's what I remember, Brother Joseph. How much is real and how much I've invented—as my father invented machines for measuring the consistency of Whip 'n' Chill and peanut butter—I can't say for sure. But then don't we all invent, or re-invent, the things we love?

Which makes me Dwaine's father, in a way, doesn't it?

And a father's greatest fear is that he can't live up to father-hood, that he won't be able to protect his child. In the end nei-ther Venus nor I could protect Dwaine from himself, any more than we could protect ourselves from him. A Holy Trinity, we were: me, Dwaine, and Venus: The Father, the Son, and Casper the Friendly Ghost.

5

Sat., Nov. 7th, 8 a.m. The fall colors have peaked here. I'd forgot-ten how much I love the seasons, especially autumn's last blazing hurrah, with every maple tree a clipper ship in flames, heralding winter's smoke and ash (wheras the city has only three seasons: too hot, too cold, and neither too hot nor too cold).

A gang of brothers performs chores below, repairing a bro-ken drain spout on the tool shed on the far side of the driveway, alongside a small pumpkin patch. Under the sun's glare the river looks like a valley of broken bottles. Beyond the dazzle I see the buildings on the opposite shore, their red bricks burnished with sunlight. If I look long enough I see—or I imagine that I can see—patients being escorted across the grounds by angelic fig-ures in white.

Strange, isn't it, how Dwaine and I wound up with almost identical views, me here among monks, him there with his fel-low lunatics. Mirror images, we reflect and reverse each other.

How to distinguish between the reflection and the mirror?
The face that looks in the mirror is real, the one that looks out isn't.
If that doesn't clear things up, try scratching both.
When all else fails, smash the mirror.

6

Thursday, November 12th. For the past three days you've been teaching me, or trying to teach me, the peaceful and practical art of meditation. Evenings, just before vespers, I find you sitting lotus-style in front of a burning candle in the otherwise dark, deserted meditation hall, a rope of incense smoke curling up to the spackled ceiling. No one else is there; no one else meditates. Of the twelve brothers here, you are apparently alone in your enthusiasm for passive self-annihilation.

"Just sit," are your two gentle words of instruction. "Just sit." And so, hands folded in my lap, gazing into the candle flame, I sit, just sit.

Meditating is a lot like going to the movies. You sit in the dark doing nothing, letting the movie of your thoughts wash over you. The meditation hall is the theater, the flickering candle flame the projector bulb. Eyes closed, you sit and watch as the heavy velvet curtain parts. The barrage of coming attraction trailers (as inane and frenetic as a pillow fight) finally ends, and the feature begins, a movie with a simple yet surprisingly gripping plot in which nothing, absolutely nothing, happens.

The trick is to realize that the movie isn't about you. It's not *about* anything but a single point in time called here and now.

Two nights ago in the meditation hall as I sat watching the movie of my life unwind, it struck me that it wasn't my life at all that I had been living, it was Dwaine's. He was the star, the hero, the villain. He stole every scene. I was just a sidekick—not even, just an audience member, a spectator among spectators slouched in padded seats. I sat there watching the candle flame flicker, wondering: what happened to me, to *my* life? Where was it? Where had it gone? Plummeting back to earth, wings singed off, crashed into the ocean: that's what happens when you fly too close to the sun. Whether the sun is a black dwarf or white giant makes no difference. It'll still melt wax off your wings.

I started crying then, gasping, body-jerking sobs. I couldn't stop. The tears rose up from somewhere so deep down inside of me I thought they would tear my intestines out.

And though you obviously saw and heard me crying, you didn't do anything. You sat there—just sat—until the meditation hour ended. Then, with a gentle hand upon my shoulder, you said,

"I think we're done here."

7

Saturday, November 14. That same night, following dinner and Compline, when the Great Silence descended on the monastery, I stayed up late packing all of Dwaine's things, sealing them in layers of plastic bags, the squawk of packing tape stretching off the dispenser echoing off of my room's stucco walls. I packed away black books, screenplays, rubber bullet, all of the movies Dwaine and I had made. With everything packed I sealed the trunk with duct tape from the tool shed, and went to bed.

The mountains were still black against a star-pocked sky when your knocking woke me. Grasping one of the trunk's handles each we made our way up the trail to the clearing. The river lay huddled in fog. For a man of seventy-four you're in excellent shape. Still we both had to stop every fifty feet or so to catch our breaths. For some strange reason, as we walked I pictured my father, not you, carrying Dwaine's trunk behind me.

By the time we reached the clearing the fog had lifted. Patches of blue broke through the cloud cover. The hole that

I'd dug days before in the stiff earth was still there, a shovel
sticking out of the mound of dirt piled beside it. We put down
the trunk and sat on it, facing in opposite directions, catching
our breaths. After a few minutes, responding wordlessly to some
silent prompt, we stood up again, picked the trunk up, and lowered it slowly down into the hole.

You said a prayer:

> *Oh God, whose blessed son was laid in a sepulcher in the
> garden: Bless, we pray, this grave, and grant that he whose
> trunk is to be buried here may dwell with Christ in para-
> dise, and may come to thy heavenly kingdom, through thy
> son Jesus Christ our Lord. Amen.*

I draped Dwaine's pea coat over the trunk and sprinkled in
a handful of dirt. As it fell the dirt made a chuckling sound, like
the muffled laughter of children. We shoveled the rest of the
dirt in and tamped it down.

I dug a small hole at the head of the grave and buried the
Oscar, our bent tarnished grail, to its hilt. You remarked that
it was a shame, that the golden statuette was sure to be stolen,
eventually. I said it didn't matter, that in fact it was fitting, that
the Oscar was already stolen.

8

Noon. Tires crunching on gravel, my father's Morris Minor rolls
up the monastery driveway. Through my star-shaped window I
see him step out. He wears his tattered Inverness cape. Loose
threads dangle from its hem. Seeing me watching him he waves
up at me.

From the Morris trunk he pulls out a folding campstool, an
easel, a box of oil tubes, and the half-finished painting of the
monastery salvaged from the fire. He sets up the easel, lays out
his palette, and goes to work.

"Theah," he says an hour or so later, showing me the finished painting. "A fwoo stwokes, thas allut needud."

He folds the campstool, closes his paint box lid.

We've all just about said our goodbyes when my father remembers something. "Oh, zith came fuh yhew, ma bwah." He takes an envelope from his pocket and hands it to me. Inside are two other envelopes, both forwarded to my parents' address. The first holds a telegram from Northern Ireland. It's so like Dwaine to send telegrams when no one else does anymore.

**SOLD SCREENPLAY TERRIBLE BEAUTY STOP
ADVANCE 35G STOP SHOOTING BEGINS NEXT
YEAR BELFAST STOP ERIN GO BRAGH**

The second envelope contains a photocopy of a check made out to Dwaine S. Fitzgibbon in the amount of $25,750 ($35,000 minus fifteen percent) drawn from the account of Mr. William "Bull" Duncan, Literary & Film Agent.

"Bad news?" you ask.

I hand you the telegram.

The wind sighs through trees as you read it and smile.

"He is risen," you say, handing it back.

EPILOGUE:

Summer,
2007

Twenty years later.

I'm back in New York, where I make a living as an illustrator and teacher. During those twenty years I have heard from Dwaine sporadically, mainly by way of dispatches sent from disaster zones, from the West Bank, from Somalia, from Belgrade, from Gujarat, from Afghanistan...His second-to-last letter included an attached diagram of his Harlem flat, showing the exact locations of all his stored notebooks, screenplays, synopses, novels-in-progress, etc. The one after that, the last one, arrived by email on June 25, 2004, from Bagdad, Iraq:

> *Babe, I'm short-circuited enough to not remember if I told you that I'm headed home. I am. Iraq is a slaughterhouse. So is Harlem. So is every other place I've lived in. That is my solidarity. I HATE the slaughterers and would kill every one of them if I could, right now. But I'm not sure which is worse, the slaughterhouse or the INDIFFERENCE—especially the brand that's purposeful. I see it all around me among the tsk-tskers too paralyzed—CHOKED—by fear and guilt and just fat and HAPPY enough to stay inside the system that's killing them, too, an inch at a time. But enough about THEM...*
>
> *I'm not sure if I ever told you this, but just before coming here I was tossed in the hoosegow for spray-painting 500 SUVs with blood-colored paint, after which King George II's mignons [sic] raided my Harlem digs, confiscated a dozen notebooks, and tapped my phone. For seven nights*

*running, about an hour after I went to bed, the phone
would ring and a male voice would shout, "Four More
Years! Four More Years!" Every night for three hours
it kept ringing, and every time the same voice shouted,
"Four More Years!" before hanging up.*

Such are the hallucinations generated by reality.

*Early this a.m., just after dawn, I filmed my final se-
quence here, in the killing pen behind an abattoir in
Fallujah—the Muslim ritual slaughter of the sheep,
whose blood splashed all over my lens (and face and pants
and shoes), who took way too long, for my money, to go
to heaven, whose tongue lolled, whose legs twitched, whose
executioner giggled, whose imam shouted, right on cue as
the blade fell, "Allahu akbar!"—which, in case you didn't
know, means "Four more years!"*

*I don't know about THAT, but I do know the only thing
left for me to film now is the ritualistic slaughter of certain heads of state(s).*

Talk about activist cinema verité!

*So—what's it gonna be, babe? There's always an extra buck-
et of vermillion [sic] paint around, and a THOUSAND
more SUVs.*

I'll see you in HELL!

D. F.

I haven't heard from him since.

ACKNOWLEDGEMENTS

The author gratefully acknowledges the following publications wherein portions of this novel first appeared in earlier form: "Greetings From Hollywood," *The Literary Review*, Winter 2007; "A Pre-Victorian Bathtub," *Indiana Review*, Summer 2007; "Eagle Electric," *The Florida Review*, Spring 2007; "It's So Good Don't Even Try it Once," *Inkwell*, Spring 2007; "Playing it Out," *Alaska Quarterly Review*, Fall 2007; "The Bubble,"*Bellevue Literary Review*, Fall 2003; "Blacken the Space," *The Madison Review*, Fall 2002.

For their help, encouragement, good advice, and general laying on of artistic and friendly hands in connection with this effort, I thank Mark Borax, Claudia Carlson, Walter Cummins and other members of Two Bridges Writing Group, Cortney Davis, Jonathan Dee, Patrick Dillon, Jennie Dunham, Michael Nethercott, Katinka Neuhof, Donald Newlove, Roxanna Robinson, Christopher Rowland, Oliver Sacks, George Selgin, Pinuccia Selgin, Elizabeth Socolow, Vincent Stanley, Robert Stone, Joanna Torrey, and Gerald Warfield.

To my brave publishers—Steve Gillis, Dan Wickett, and Steven Seighman—a special thanks for every possible consideration. No author could ask for more.